To Judith, my darling wife, who would have loved to be part of this happy band of women until…

Tony Andras

THE GIRLS IN THE HALL

Julie & John,

The story so far has been called "immersive, full of unexpected surprises". I hope that spells "enjoyment!"

Tony Andras

AUSTIN MACAULEY PUBLISHERS™
LONDON * CAMBRIDGE * NEW YORK * SHARJAH

Copyright © Tony Andras 2024

The right of Tony Andras to be identified as author of this work has been asserted by the author in accordance with sections 77 and 78 of the Copyright, Designs and Patents Act 1988.

All rights reserved. No part of this publication may be reproduced, stored in a retrieval system, or transmitted in any form or by any means, electronic, mechanical, photocopying, recording, or otherwise, without the prior permission of the publishers.

Any person who commits any unauthorised act in relation to this publication may be liable to criminal prosecution and civil claims for damages.

This is a work of fiction. Names, characters, businesses, places, events, locales, and incidents are either the products of the author's imagination or used in a fictitious manner. Any resemblance to actual persons, living or dead, or actual events is purely coincidental.

A CIP catalogue record for this title is available from the British Library.

ISBN 9781398493995 (Paperback)
ISBN 9781398497153 (ePub e-book)

www.austinmacauley.com

First Published 2024
Austin Macauley Publishers Ltd®
1 Canada Square
Canary Wharf
London
E14 5AA

Moving In 1

It was not the best start.

She grabbed the towel from the counter.

"Who the *shit* are you? Get the hell out! Now!"

"Sorry, sorry. Wrong door. I'm your new neighbour…"

"Hey! Hey! I don't want to know! Get out!"

Brian Upjohn closed the door gingerly. He was moving his furniture into one of those older, low-rise apartment buildings. Few of such places remain – roomy old fossils demolished in record numbers for the shiny towers and condos that today's buyers seek for that shiny, Ikea-stark lifestyle.

Jake came up, carrying a box. "What was that?"

"Wrong door. Caught her starkers. Jeez, don't they lock their doors around here?"

"You lucky bastard. What's she like? How old?"

"It was so quick. I'm not sure."

"What a waste. You're here, Number 1. Oh hey, that's why you went to the wrong door. She's got no number. So, she's 2. Ooo, right beside Miss Nudie."

KELLY. Girl in the Hall. Apartment 2. A cynical and witty striver. Everything is geared to improving her lot from her mobile park past. This apartment is a first step up and out. Right address, right car, right job, right man – that's the ticket. She hated anything that smacked of her past – bad manners, bad language, bad choices. These past failings would seep into the present causing her grief mostly with questionable men.

"Don't joke. I've got to make it right. She's my new neighbour."

"Standard fix: roses and *bonbon mots*."

"Which – bonbons or bon mots? She'd take either from a boyfriend, maybe. Not me. I'm a stranger and I just violated her."

"Violated? C'mon. For a peep? Whatcha gonna do?"

"I'd ask my girlfriend … if I had one. I've got to do something. Oh, wait, Stella said she'd check in later to see how I'm making out. She'll know what to do."

"Who's Stella?"

"My mother."

"Your *mother?*"

"Ye-ah! Look, I'm not as old as I look, I'm only thirty-eight and single, so we still keep in touch. She was great in my teens…"

"Your mother."

"Give it a rest, Jake. She really helped me get through. She'd say, 'Put yourself in her place, Sammy'. She'd always call me Sammy when she was telling me something. 'Put yourself in her place, and try and feel how she'd feel. What do you think she'd want you to do to make up?' I'd always draw a blank. Then she'd take me through it step-by-step. It always worked, so I trust her completely."

"Sammy *loves* his *mummy*," sang Jake.

"Ha-ha. Yeah, I do, Jake. I love her very much. Deal with it."

"Okay."

"So, this is my new cave. What'd you think?"

"Big. Open concept. Some reno here. These places used to be so cut up. So, the pillars've replaced the load-bearing wall. They kept the cornice and wainscoting. Okay. Get better rents if you upgrade. Need to modernise."

JOANNA. Girl in the Hall. Apartment 3. The most educated of the Girls. She went to the University of Toronto as an undergraduate, then Stanford for her Masters in Psychology. Born in the West, she inherited a literal-minded point of view from her immigrant parents. She fits in as one of the Girls despite being smarter and better educated. Her training enabled her to see something very disturbing in their midst.

"Going to. I've got the big suite here, two bedrooms …"

"In case your mummy comes to stay …"

"Nah, not her style."

"Where'd the stairs go – outside loft?"

"Yuh, that's the plus with this unit. I've got access to the roof garden."

"No one else has?"

"No, the fire escape's unusable. So, I've got it to myself, unless …"

"Unless Number 2 wants to tan herself *a Capello*."

"You joke, but letting her have it may be a way to make it up to her."

"It sure will, and let her have it a lot. Didn't some English guy say, 'I can resist everything but *repetition*'?"

"Don't think so. Sounds pretty dull to me."

"Only access to the roof, life won't be dull. Great possibilities, Brian."

"I think so. And you'll like this: all the other tenants are girls."

"Ooo, I do likey. How many *June fillies* are we talking about?"

"Well, four at the moment. Six units in the building."

"Great number. How's about I move in, take your last suite?"

"No way. The roach checks in, I check out."

"Why? We could have a real *Bucchaladian* sexfest here, bend a wishbone or two."

"Bucchaladian? Oh, Bacchanalian. No sexfest, Jake. Alone, I can make this work. With you, I'd spend my whole time hosing down a sex fiend. Vacant in a week."

"Yeah, but what a week!"

"I need full rents to carry the place and the renos. You know that."

SHAKIRA. Girl in the Hall. Apartment 4. Though independent, she loves to belong. Her sense of humour is a singular trait. She is also somewhat boastfully confident but deservedly. The Girls treat her carefully because a live-in boyfriend had died of sickle cell anaemia months earlier. She's a scratch golfer who coaches at a golf course she grew up on. Her often astute, culturally exclusive colloquialisms couch a tender heart.

Jake checked out the bedrooms and the bathroom between them. Brian piled some cartons up on the kitchen counter. Then they went up the stairs to the roof. It was a large space with a stout wall around, capped with a tin cover. An old barbeque tilted in one corner, and some derelict wooden lawn chairs were strewn here and there. A few large flower pots littered the space with last year's desiccated flowers. It badly needed a broom.

"Needs some love," said Brian.

"Not a problem. The building's full of it."

"As yet, unavailable. Ready to bring in the heavy stuff?"

"Sure."

"Let's do the beds first. They'll need the most attention."

"In all seriousness, this is a good set-up. You can make a life here."

"Thanks, Jake, glad to hear you say that."

They left the roof and down the long, curved flight of stairs.

"We'll bring in the big furniture and table and chairs, Jake. I'll see if I can get that barbeque working, throw on a coupla' burgers and we'll snap a few…"

"Perfect. We can ask …"

"No, Jake. We'll give *The Girls in the Hall* the first night off."

"Girls in the Hall. I like that."

"Who'd have guessed?"

"How's about I come in as a paying roommate? Take your other bedroom. You're so outnumbered here. It's rotten good."

"Same problem. One whiff of you, I'd have a permanent vacancy sign out front."

MELISSA. Girl in the Hall. Apartment 5. She is the toff of the group. She tries to be egalitarian as something of a life experiment. In truth, she is a little naive, yet socially polished and crumbly to acts of kindness. So, the Girls genuinely like and accept her. What they hate is she owes them all money despite being the wealthiest among them. Will. Then she does something rather wonderful that wipes that slate clean.

When they brought in the last load, arranging the furnishings in some man-strange order, they sat down on the roof and guzzled. By about the third beer, Brian's cell rang. He looked at the screen.

"Ah, there she is. Hi, Stella, it's me."

Brian put it on speaker mode. She wanted the men in the family to use her name. His sisters couldn't. He never asked why.

"Hello, dear. How are you making out?"

"Great. Just got it all moved in. Jake's being a big help. He's a new friend from the office. Say 'Hi', Jake."

"Hi … Stella. Can I call you Stella?"

"Sure can, Jake. Thanks for being there for Brian. Glad to meet you."

"You must be somethin'. Brian's been goin' on like you're the *cat's mouse*."

"*Meow*, I hope. He's my best man, Jake … had to look out for him with two sisters."

"Then he'll fit in real well here. He's the only guy in a building full of girls."

"Really? Tell me about it, Brian."

"That's actually why I'm glad you called."

"Oh-oh. Trouble already? What have you done, bad boy?"

"How do you know it's *trouble*? How'd you know? You're 200 miles away!"

"It's not very complicated, my love, knowing you."

Jake guffawed. "Music to my ears. He's been putting the gears to me all day about *les gals*. You just got busted, boy. Love it."

"You've got the wrong end of the stick, Jake," said Brian.

MARLA. Girl in the Hall. Apartment 6. The new arrival quickly becomes one of the Girls because she works at being what she thinks the others expect. Yet she carries an air of disaffection like a constant companion. There is a mystery here; an impression nags of something concealed. What's behind the mask? She is very fit, a real barbell, who can handle herself in a scrap. That iron might will manifest in unexpected ways.

"Yes, you have, Jake. He's very respectful of women. But he had to learn. It looks like I'm going to have put you through some training too."

"Any time, Stella. I promise to be your worst student."

"Not for long you won't. So, what's the problem, dear?"

"I got the wrong door and opened it on a girl who just got out of the shower. She's pretty upset, I think. I've got to fix this."

"Okay, that's all right. Understandable mistake. You didn't do it on purpose. I hope you didn't. No. So, here's what you do, Sammy …"

"You've got a solution already?" asked Jake.

"Of course. I'm a mother. Here's what you do: have a housewarming to get to know your tenants. The girl you walked in on will probably say 'no' because she's still embarrassed. So, during the party, go to her door with two glasses of champagne. Knock and ask her to join the party. Leave her with a glass and say, 'It's all right if you don't want to come, I understand. I just wanted to make it all right'. That's the last time you ever even mention the incident unless she brings it up. Chances are she'll spruce up and join the group."

"You're the best, Stella, thanks," said Brian.

"Wow. You give great advice, Stella. When are you coming to visit? I gotta meet you."

"You will, Jake. And you'll be a better man when I'm finished with you."

They all laughed.

"Oooo, bring it on, Stella!"

"Jake, this is my *mother*, remember? Jake's a little girl crazy, Stella. No, a *lot* girl crazy."

"I'm flattered. Call me when you've truly settled, dear, and we'll all come to visit. *And* be sure to ask your lippy new friend."

Jake leaned forward in his seat with his mouth ajar.

"Jake's lurching with his mouth open. Your magic is already working. I'll call you soon. Say 'hi' to Dad and the harpies when you're talking to them. I miss you."

"We miss you too, sweetie. You're a daily reminder. Bye, dear. As for you, Jake …"

"Yes, me, Stella. I want you to be my mother too. I need your advice on girls."

"Mother no, advice yes, Jake."

"Bye, Stella," said Brian chuckling.

He switched off the phone and gave Jake a hard stare.
"What?"

Getting to Know You   2

Brian bought the one-storey six-plex with a roof garden at 255 Covington Place as an investment. It was to help him survive his up-and-running phase as a new agent at *Telvan Realty*. He had sold his big house 100 miles to the north, making a handsome, accumulated profit from a six-year practice of buying and selling bigger and bigger houses for reno and resale. The sale of his last mansion more than covered the cost of the apartment building.

    Covington Place was built in the late 1940s. The apartments had high ceilings and distinctive millwork that a succession of tenants had painted over. Telvan had a property management arm, so Brian was able to ask one of his real estate associates, Joyce, to handle new rentals and collect rents. This meant he could be just another tenant with the others renters who had been grateful not to be forced to vacate because of the sale. Brian saw his cover as a tenant a major plus. He didn't mind doing small repairs around the place, but wanted to avoid being a glorified janitor pestered at every turn. Tenants might wait to call a big company to get something done. He could then rely on Telvan's team of contractors to stickhandle upgrades and repair jobs at a discount.

    Brian always made profitable improvements to his properties though, this time, not too many; he foresaw a developer buying it for the land to put up condos. But he saw the value of having an active, outdoor gathering space on the roof to complement the bustling female interactions that went on among the suites.

    It was trying to be spring, so now was the time to get started. He got rid of the tilting wonder of a BBQ from yesteryear and replaced it with a gleaming Napoleon Grill. They had to haul it up with tackle. He designed a plein air living area of treated lumber, featuring a pergola with a canopy that retracted in folds and under it, a well-lit outdoor kitchen and dining area; a round, decked recreation area jutted out from this pavilion, with lounge chairs under umbrellas for controlled sunbathing. To enjoy full shade, chairs could be rolled under the closed canopy and streaming curtains.

Brian felt an urgency to host that 'roof warming' as a way to work himself into that easy comfort he guessed the Girls had developed over some two years in the 'Hall'.

Brian was a good agent because he was a people person who thrived in wanting to see clients put into compatible surroundings. And what he had discerned from watching the Oprah Show a few years before was how she had created 'community' with studio audiences and viewers around the world. He wasn't sure what impressed him most – that she had accomplished such a feat or the importance he had come to realise about community in peoples' lives. Regardless, he wanted to create something of the same commonwealth in his own life and chose real estate as a means.

The remodelling costs well exceeded what he got from the rents which were largely gobbled up by the usual running expenses; but his savings covered the shortfall and sustained him during the lean period as a new agent. He had some promising leads and knew it was just a matter of time before the first of them hit. That time actually came fast.

First Patio Party

In fact, his first sale closed the same day he had set for the housewarming. So, he was a little late for his own party. But when he did arrive, it was a double celebration with three of the four girls there and Joyce who played host in his absence. She was to deliver the second hooray: filling the one vacancy in the apartment block to yet another woman named Marla.

Once at the party, Brian toasted the women.

"The owner sees the patio as a terrific asset to the building, a common area for everyone. I know access has been a problem. The fire escape's not safe. Will be this week. And when it is, you'll be welcome to use the patio through my place. My door's always open. I keep it open 'cause it's the last apartment in the Hall. Don't worry about invading my privacy; I work all hours – at this stage anyway. So, soon."

"That's great," said Joanna. "I told you the last guy in your apartment was a real jerk. Even if we went up from the outside, he'd chase us off."

"Why don't you close your door? Don't you want any privacy with a bunch of girls?" asked Melissa.

"Yeah, maybe you're hopin' to get caught in the dangle. Is your skin-show that straight fire?" asked Shakira.

"I don't wander around naked, if that's what you mean. But I'm not too fussy."

"You may not care, but we do," said Melissa. "I hope you'll be careful with us as the only man in the place."

"I will, Melissa. I'll come up with a couple of code words so you know I'm around. Say, speaking of that … uh … I see Kelly's not here. I burst into her apartment by mistake when I first arrived and caught her … unawares."

"Yeah, I sort of guessed that when you mentioned her the day we met," said Joanna. "Never heard what she said."

"The beer's in the fridge?" blurted Melissa, shocking herself. "Sorry."

"I wish. She was really put out and I guess she still is."

"That's cursed," said Shakira. "Kelly is the most … open … of us bitches."

That careful word – open – made them laugh again.

"Why don't I go and knock on her door, and ask her up? Maybe that's all it takes."

"Good idea," said Joyce. "I'll come too. It might help."

"Right. It's time to start up the new *barbie*, ladies. I haven't had a chance to break it in. But it's ready to go. The meat's in the fridge, the patio fridge (he demonstrated, opening the door) seasoned and ready when you are. Here, let me fire up the grill. Then we'll go down and see Kelly."

A few minutes later, they knocked on the door with a glass of champagne for Kelly. She opened it and gave Brian a surprised, oh-it's-you look.

"Yes?" she said matter-of-factly.

"Hello, Kelly."

"Hello, Joyce."

"Kelly, I'm Brian. I know I made a mistake when I moved in and I'm sorry for that. But we're having a patio housewarming upstairs and want you to join us. (He handed her the glass.) Will you come? I'll leave my door open. Why not come?"

She took the glass without smiling, but glinted at a possible truce.

"I'm not sure I can make it. We'll see."

"Okay. All the others are up there and I'd like you to see what's been done to the patio …"

"It's sensational, Kelly," added Joyce. "You won't recognise it."

"And it's soon going to be available to all of us in the building."

Kelly nodded but said nothing.

"And there's something else you should know. Joyce?"

"Telvan has just filled the last apartment. We're full up now with Marla in 6."

"Yeah, we're going to have five Girls in the Hall, as I call you."

Kelly nodded. "Mhmm. Anyways, thanks for this. Cheers."

"Cheers," they replied in unison.

They clinked their glasses before Kelly closed the door. They looked at each other. Brian shrugged and Joyce nodded. They re-joined the party. The GITH (as they became known for short) were crowded around the new grill and laughing above the sound of the sizzle. A little while later, Kelly came up. Brian worked at being his people-best to make Kelly feel at ease. It was going to be all right in time. Stella passed through his mind. *You were there for me again,* he thought.

In the two or so months he'd been there prior to that party, Brian had met them all with the exception of Marla who hadn't arrived and Kelly who was incommunicado. He'd seen Kelly all right, but been shy to approach her; she made no move to speak with him either. The GITH, on the other hand, were brightened by the prospect of an 'upgrade' not only to a useable patio but also to the last grumpy male in the place. And why not? Brian was tall, dark and handsome and woman-weathered from wrangling with two contentious sisters.

Melissa

It was slow at first. The Girls were so 'worked-in' with each other, even a handsome man was seen as surplus baggage. But his open door and the cooking smells that wafted out ultimately drew them in. The first was Melissa, being the most socially cultivated of the group. She found the aroma of what Brian was cooking one night alluringly familiar. She appeared and knocked.

"Hi, I'm Melissa, apartment 5."

"Melissa! Nice to meet you. Brian. Come on in."

"What're you cooking? Actually, I know. Bouillabaisse."

"You know that from the stink? That's good. D'you make it yourself?"

"Sort of. I spent almost every summer in Marseille when I was a teenager."

"That'd do it."

"Can I have a taste?"

"I dunno. You're used to the real thing. This is only my version."

"They're all versions, Brian. I don't know anyone who makes it with rockfish anymore."

"I've never even heard of rockfish. Here, here's a spoon."

She sampled it carefully. He watched her darting eyes as she moved her mouth. She gave him a hard stare.

"Oh-oh."

"No, no," she said smiling. "It's not bad. What's in your bouquet garni?"

"Fennel, saffron, salt and cayenne."

"Right. Fish? Conger, monkfish, mullet?"

"None of those. I've never eaten any of those. Some turbot and plaice."

"Turbot's right. Plaice too mild. Shellfish?"

"Mussels, crabs …"

"No octopus?"

"No, I have a fondness for them as alternative life forms. I could never eat them."

She smiled with a mocking huff. "Everything we eat is an alternative life form. I hope!" (They laughed.)

"O-kay!" he said. "But I had an experience with an octopus once and I've read a lot about them. They're just off the menu for me."

"I'd like to hear that experience."

"Stay and share my not-so-simple soup, Melissa, and I'll tell you about it."

"Great. Made the rouille yet?"

"Now you're scaring me."

"Don't be …"

"Actually, I did make one the first time. But I've forgotten what it is."

"Let me do it, then. It's just a garlic sauce. Uncle Daisy would insist on it: he'd say 'Garlic makes a man wink, drink and stink'. So, I used to make it all the time."

"In Marseille?"

"Yeh, my uncle was an avid fisherman and had a summer place down by the water. He'd make bouillabaisse once a week. I'd cut up the vegetables and make the rouille. What veggies have you got in there?"

"Leeks, onions, celery, potatoes …"

"No tomatoes?"

"One little one. Not crazy about 'em. A little goes a long way. I always rosé my sauces. I hate raw tomato sauce. My dad used to love spaghetti and meat balls. Retro even then. I'd always choke on the sauce."

"A lot of people don't like the acid."

"That's it. So, I get away from it and use tomato purée now."

"Smart. Squirt some in. Oh, I'm looking forward to this. I haven't had it for five years. Longer. It'll remind me of my uncle. And I want to hear your story."

"Well, if you like octopus, it might change your mind."

"I'll risk it."

Soon, she'd made the mayonnaise with bread crumbs because Brian didn't have anything but sandwich bread in the house to put it on. He watched her with interest as she put out double the bowls he would have because she separated the broth from the bottom. He set the table and poured out Languedoc while she did the ladling. Soon, they were raising glasses. He smiled as she gestured in a way he guessed came from her uncle – a sweep of her hand up to her nose to catch the aroma.

"You've made me a happy girl, Brian. Dear old Uncle Daisy – his real name was David – he's sitting right here with us. My father told me he made a fortune in meat processing. He sold out and retired to the south of France to fish. That was his boyhood passion. He only came back home for the winters."

"Back to the cold? That's eccentric."

"Not really. His other passion was ski-ing. Very outdoorsy. A lean and leathery old guy, but sweet as a sugar plum. I loved him to bits."

"Was he married?"

"Sure. But Aunt Bea would only stay at the villa for a couple of weeks and fly home. That's why Uncle Daisy liked us to come for the whole summer – someone to cook for. Believe it or not, she didn't like fish all that much."

"Gosh, if you didn't, then two weeks of a steady fish diet would be enough. So, it wasn't Uncle Daisy but the fish that drove her back home."

"That's about it. By the end of the summer, I was royally sick of it too. After a while, you see fish in your dreams."

"How about tonight? Is the fish dreamy?"

"This is good. I'm used to a more muscular taste. But it's a good lady's bouillabaisse."

"Is there such a thing?"

"No. But this is a lot more … refined … than I'm used to."

"Well, I think it's pretty muscular. It's got lots of mussels in it."

"You're funny," she said. "And don't get me wrong. For someone on this side of the Atlantic, you're pretty good. There can't be many home cooks who'd go to all this trouble. That's adventuresome."

"Wait 'til you try my Squid a l'Orange."

"Hey! You don't cook cephalopods. You told me."

"Octopus, never. Squid, every week."

"You're kidding."

"'Fraid so."

"What a joker. That reminds me. I want my octopus story."

"All right. But no tears in my bouillabaisse."

"Promise."

"Well, it was a few years ago. I didn't have a girlfriend. So, I travelled alone a lot and sometimes met people, sometimes didn't. It was my first time to Bermuda before it changed so much. It wasn't so crowded then, no cars just mopeds, and those terrific, old colonial department stores were still going. I'm glad I saw it back when. That's all gone now."

"I was there with my parents before I started to go to France. But I don't remember it very well. We travelled so much."

"Lucky you. Anyway, I was seeing the sites … alone … did I tell you I didn't have a girlfriend?"

"Yes," Melissa said with a suppressed laugh. "But I don't need a hanky yet."

"I was speeding around the island on my moped and decided to wheel into the sea aquarium. It's quite the attraction to see the local species. I found myself at a large tank holding an adult octopus. This was the first time I'd seen one live, so I was intrigued. Our eyes met. Or at least one of its eyes met mine. It came right up to the window pane and seemed to show interest. I've since learned that they are very curious. I flattered myself that he chose to interact with me, when hundreds must stop at the tank and get nothing. In fact, they read people very well. Must be a survival skill. Mind you, I'd be better at reading people too if I had nine brains and three hearts like your average octo."

"Nine brains? Wow. Think of the inner conflicts that must go on. They'd need three hearts to calm them down from all that static."

"If they were human, yeah. But octopuses are about as far from the evolutionary tree from us as you can get. There's a brain in every one of their arms so they can operate independently but work in unison at the same time. Fascinating, eh?"

"It makes perfect sense. If I had that many arms, I'd need more brainpower than I've got."

"That's funny, because you'd say a man who's all hands hasn't got any brains at all. (He waited for her laugh.) Back to my story."

"That'd be nice."

"Well, the octopus and I stared at each other for quite a while not moving. Then, I put my hand up against the glass. It put three or four of its arms up against the glass. I wriggled my fingers. It wriggled too. I moved my hand; it moved too. Then it got really interesting …"

"What? Did it climb out and give you a good squirt?"

"No." Brian laughed. "But they do that if they don't like someone. No, Henry – I call him Henry now – he started a really unusual motion, a moving carousel, like a dance of his tendrils around my hand. He sorts of flipped them up and down one-by-one. Maybe he could feel the energy or the heat my hand made against the glass and he reacted to that. That went on for about five minutes. Then I moved my hand off and started tapping my fingers on the glass. Henry did the same. I backed off and he did the same. We looked at each other in a silent – obviously silent – but pretty intense stare for a while before I turned to go. But I looked back and saw him floating motionless, watching me go. I was sad. I could feel sadness. Isn't that strange? But I couldn't stay there forever. So I left. Somehow, I thought this was a one-off, a moment that couldn't be repeated."

"Sort of like your first kiss …"

"This can't be good: we just met and you're already making fun of me."

"No, no, Brian," said Melissa laughing dismissively. "I'm serious. First impressions, first-time experiences always seem to have the most impact. At least, I find that."

"Right. But it's not the end of the story."

"You went back and he wasn't there anymore."

"That's it. It wasn't Henry. Another one. I asked and they told me Henry was stolen. Not the first time. They're sure people grab them right out of the tank, like lobsters, to eat them."

"How horrible!"

"Just kidding. I didn't go back."

"Brian! I can't trust you!"

"I'd have been upset if that was true, but it wasn't. No, the real end of the story happened about three years ago. I was sitting in a restaurant on Santorini with a couple of tour groups. A woman traveller told an almost identical tale with her octopus. Same sort of connection."

"Wow. What are the chances?"

"Yeh, and I was a little upset to hear it because I thought my contact had been pretty special. My only consolation was she was a little irked too. She obviously thought it only happened to her."

"I think you're both right. It's unique twice."

"It isn't though. There's some kind of amazing cooperation that can go on between species, and that's true between people and octopuses – real contact."

After several ladlings of soup and lashings of Languedoc, Melissa was feeling free-wheeling enough to expound on her favourite subject and what was most closely related to that – her family.

"I come from conservative people, the 'hard work breeds success' types. It was a life with all the trimmings: private schools, cottage summers, jaunts on yachts, big travel junkets, big houses, big life. I loved it when I was younger. Now, I've outgrown all that. I want freedom to live my life my own way."

"Does that mean you've severed all ties with them?"

"Oh no, they insist on staying in touch with me, but only in ways I want."

She spoke of her family as having many generations of notables in the military, politics and the law with that one odd duck who made good in meat packing.

Through his real estate work, Brian had some familiarity with this highfalutin subculture: many in this milieu carry an unspoken confidence of expected success; it's a swagger derived from consistent prosperity. That was less true of her generation. She and her peers seemed to favour semblance over substance, carats over character – an entitlement mentality that was long on talk, short on talent. In her case, certainly, no talent for managing money.

She consistently drove through her generous incomes with an inattention guaranteed to keep her broke. For apart from a good salary as the parachuted director of communications of a family-invested conglomerate nearby, she was also warmly cosseted with an infusion of allowances from home.

Brian read it as almost a boast that Melissa looked at leaving her well-feathered nest to venture into the hard, cold world as the move of a brave, independent spirit.

"I couldn't stay at home. I love my family, but not their stodgy old values."

"Like what?"

"Like it was drummed into me that 'victory has a thousand fathers but defeat is an orphan'. I don't know what that means to this day. I guess I find my parents a little ponderous."

He wondered if it were outworn values she was escaping or an unwavering family obligation to make a great success of something. By leaving, she may have realised she could get out from under such an obligation and still have her cake.

But, as he witnessed already, she was a good companion and a budding egalitarian, despite the efflux of entitlement that had been weaned into her since her mother's milk. Another affectation that had been deeply inborn was the spouting of aphorisms; they flowed out of her naturally, almost unconsciously; they were usually met with eye-rolling from the GITH. They found her a little 'ponderous'. But they never said as much around her. It was Melissa and they accepted it. They were tolerant of one another which is probably why they were a happy group.

Brian would become an adopted member of that group, but hardly one of the Girls. Understandably, they couldn't quite close the ring on that, at least not consciously. In reality, however, he became the ringleader who provided the much-needed community glue.

Joanna and Shakira

Melissa must have talked with the other Girls about having a spontaneous dinner with Brian. For a week or so later, he met Joanna at the bank of post boxes near the front door, and she mentioned it.

"Yeah, that was great. Say, I'm making Kung Pao tonight. Heard of it?"

She looked at him from under her brow. "No, what's that?"

"Ha. Why not drop in tonight and sample my version? Door is open. Follow the smells."

"Great. I'll bring some Tsingtao. Heard of it?"

"Touché. Let's make it a party. Bring the other Girls if you want."

"Shak's around tonight, I think. I'll find out."

"That's 'Shakira', right? (Joanna nodded.) Perfect. Then I'll know you all."

"Oh, you met Kelly too, then?"

"Yeah, in more ways than one."

Joanna nodded saucily from a real understanding of Kelly. *Say no more,* she thought.

"Okay. Tonight. Six, 6:30?" she asked.

"Six-thirty. That'll give me time."

"Time for what?"

Brian just smiled. He couldn't think of a quick riposte.

"Oh, by the way, keep off any talk of boyfriends. Shak lost hers a few months back. He died … of a disease. She's okay now, but we don't talk about it."

"Okay. Thanks for the heads up."

The thickening dinner smells in the Hall prompted the Girls to appear on the dot of 6:30. Joanna carried a promised sixer of beer, and Shakira trailed in with a ball-returning putter cup, a putter and two golf balls. Brian looked at this gear smilingly enough for them to discern he played.

"We come bearing gifts," said Joanna.

"I'm makin' no gift, bro, unless you top me. And you won't."

"If you don't, how red you'll be. I'm Brian."

"Red ain't a colour I show too easily … or need to."

Brian laughed. "No, I guess not. Hi, Joanna. You weren't kidding about the beer."

"A white guy cooking Chinese, we're gonna need something to wash it down."

"You're quite the pair … one too much confidence, the other not enough."

His responses relaxed them. Finally, a man who could bounce. They couldn't know he had spent conscious time cultivating the art of the stingless negative.

"I'm just about ready, so why not snap three cool ones, Joanna and Shakira, you set up the all-or-nothing test match."

"Glasses?"

"Cupboard right of the sink." (Shakira pointed to a spot for the gear.)

"Works for me …"

"… 'til you putt."

"Practice a couple before the match. You'll need the extra limber time."

Shakira did a small jerk at her mid-riff. She relished this sort of competitive joshing that always goes on at the golf course. Joanna volunteered to plate up while they had a few putts. Shakira knocked in three straight, Brian two. He smiled and nodded at her as they sat.

"Pretty good. You've got skills."

"Fill in the blank, bro – iconic. And those skills are gonna make you lighter."

"Lighter?"

Joanna explained. "Shak's going to ask you to play a round with her. If you do, don't put money on the game. She'll skin you. That's how you'll come back lighter."

"Well, thank you, girl! I sure loved takin' your skins! And I'd just love to take 'em again."

"No chance, champ. She's the assistant golf pro at Delhaven. Her dad's the course superintendent. She had a pretty good amateur career going …"

"Yeah, but I like to coach. I got the chance at my home course, so there I is."

"You better be scratch, Brian," continued Joanna, "or you'll owe her money too."

"Hey, I jus' wanna fair fight. You snarfs di'nt have the stuff to make it fair."

"You're stirring my blood, Shakira. I'll give you a fair fight."

"See, Jo? Ya tried but ya di'n't knock the sportin' spirit outa the man."

"You're starting to look lighter already, Brian. It must be this diet Chinese."

"Jo's just bein' salty, bro. She's always working on her stand-up."

"Stand-up? Are you a comedian?"

"No, Shak's making that up. I'm a host on the shopping channel."

"Yeah, but she's got this big college diploma in headshrinkin' and all her kin are profs …"

"My mum is, my dad's a nuclear scientist. There was always pressure to get good marks. It's not over. I'll get my PhD one of these days."

"Really? 'Head shrinking'. We're talking what, psychiatry?"

"Psychology. Head shrinking is a misnomer."

"Far cry to be hawking it on the shopping channel. Still, you've got to be pretty sharp. You need a good patter to keep it going, sometimes an hour at a time."

"She's got the mouth fer it."

Brian broke into a laugh. "You Girls are tough …"

"You'll get used to us," said Joanna. "We actually love each other."

"Yeah, we're Gucci."

"So, Brian, how did you get to be the only rat in this nest of vipers?"

"Care to re-phrase that, Miss Fer de Lance."

"Hey, what's that in yer boot – the world's most poisonous snake?" asked Shakira.

"It's up there. I'm a new agent with Telvan Realty. They operate as a property manager for the new owner, and I got here through that connection. The owner's hands-off but wants to make improvements. They're starting with a big job on the patio, repair the fire escape, put a new runner down the Hall et cetera."

"We'll give him a list too. A good, long one," said Joanna.

"I'm sure you could. But it has to be reasonable. If you want new bathrooms and kitchens, that isn't going to happen."

"Yeah, we got the usual sling from the old slum landlord. We don't do this, we don't do that, we don't do nuttin'. We change your tap, but don't expect no chandelier."

"That's the notice you got, right? It's not personal, Shakira. They can only do what's affordable. If they don't make money, they can't hold the place. Then it *will* go to a slum landlord."

"It's already better than it was. The really ratty owner who lived here before'd take our money, then treat us like a bunch of delinquents. Really impatient if we complained or needed a repair. We'd ask for a paint job; he gave us one paint chip – off white – and make us pay for the paint and do the work."

"Me and my boyfriend were shacked in 4. He was ripped. Kept tryin' to double the rent 'cause there were two of us. An' kept giving us looks, like we were gonna murder him in his bed or somethin'. We thought about it."

Joanna laughed. "We all thought about it. The shittiest of all was not being able to use the patio. He didn't want to repair the rickety fire escape and sure wasn't going-a let us go through this apartment to get to it. Can we use the patio now?"

"Not yet. But when the work's done, absolutely."

The Girls looked at each other and smiled.

"Great!" said Joanna.

"The owner and Telvan want the patio ready by late spring or so. And I want to have a party to open it up. Just for the Girls in the Hall. Oh, that's my name for you."

Joanna and Shakira looked at him seriously, taking it in. It was hard to read if they thought he was a nutcase making up a name for women he didn't know or happy their luck may have changed with someone nice with an inside track. Perhaps this was the start of being treated properly. It seemed promising. Still, the two couldn't resist relaying the apparent good news to Kelly and Melissa. It was met with cool scepticism by Kelly but Melissa was effusive about it.

Marla

The new arrival had no history of the place like the other Girls, so she remained impassive to the change in their fortunes or to the hot new guy down the Hall. That was patently obvious when she opened her door to his knock shortly after the housewarming. Marla was a (peroxided) black-haired, black-eyed beauty whose lustrous eyes looked into his with a frightening directness. She waited.

"Holy … uh, oh, sorry. You surprised me, you're so great looking …"

Marla held him in her dark gaze. "So what?"

"Yuh, I'm Brian …"

"Yup."

"I wanted to meet you. It was time we met. I've met everyone else. You're the last … to meet."

Marla withered at him for a few moments more before unlocking her fix with a slow blink.

"Okay. I know about you, Brian. What are you expecting?"

Brian found himself and smiled. "I'm expecting you to join me in my apartment for a glass of wine. It won't hurt you to be friendly for half an hour. I'm harmless."

Her eyebrows went up a little. He put it right out there, as she might. It worked.

"Lead the way."

"Right. I'm apartment …"

"One. I know."

They walked for a moment without talking. She didn't actually walk, she strode, five feet ten inches of her – a female tower of strength shaped into an hour-glass figure. Somehow, she managed to look lean and large at the same time. Lithely muscular. She gave him a look, expecting him to say something.

"You've been here for a little over a week, I think. Have you met everyone?"

"I have *now*."

"The Girls've been together for a long time, and you're new. I hope they made you feel welcome."

"Why do you care?"

"I know what it's like when they don't. I grew up with two sisters who were mean to me. It can be a real drag."

"How much fun was it to be mean to them?"

"I wasn't, not deliberately. Maybe a little thoughtless. Typical boy."

"Yup."

"Here we are. Come on in. Red or white?"

"Red."

As he poured, he watched her as she moved and surveyed his large space in silence.

"What'd you do, Marla?"

"I'm a butcher."

"Butcher? You surprise me again."

"Why? You shop at Duguid's. I see you there every week."

"Are you kidding me? Why don't I …"

"… I don't serve the counter. I'm on the block behind the counter wearing a bouffant and hycar …"

"… and wielding a cleaver."

She riveted him with a black-eyed stare. He felt a shiver run down.

"How did all that happen, you, a butcher?"

"No mystery. I grew up on a farm slaughtering cattle and pigs, worked in a slaughter house and processing plant and now a specialty meat shop where, by the way, you buy a wider variety of cuts than any other private customer."

"How do you know that?"

"I wield the cleaver."

"What a coincidence you ended up here."

"Is it?"

"Isn't it?"

"Does it matter?"

"Yow. I'm being stalked. By a beautiful woman. How exciting."

"Don't be."

"Why?"

"I wield the cleaver!"

"You wield the cleaver!"

Then she broke into a wonderful, open laugh revealing ultra-white teeth.

"Oh, you had me there for a minute."

"There's no limit to how far I can take things."

"There you go again," said Brian, laughing. "I sure hope you're joking. (Marla just smiled under her brow.) R-ight. Anyway, I wanted to meet you to tell you a couple of things. The first thing is as one of the Girls in the Hall, you've got privileges …"

"As part of your harem?"

"Oh no, not that. That's not going to happen. It means you'll soon be able to use the roof from those stairs any time, day or night. But not yet. The reno is going on now. My door's always open."

"Aren't you afraid an intruder might murder you in your bed?"

"Nope. If it happens, it happens. If it's a cleaver, I'll know who did it."

"I'll keep that in mind. What's the second thing?"

"I want us to be friends. You prepare my meat, so you know I cook. And I'd like to do it for all the Girls. Even now, I leave my door open hoping the smells'll bring you in."

"And do they?"

"Starting to. So, if you like what you're smelling, come on down."

"For a come-on line, that's one of the best … for a moose."

He laughed. "Moose or not, let's get this out of the way, Marla. I'm not on the make. Anything can happen. But I'm not out to make any conquests here."

"Okay. I like you're up front. We know where we stand."

They clicked glasses, as if to seal an agreement. Just then, a trap sounded.

"Agh, just caught another one. I've got a rat problem. They get in from the patio. (He took a knife from the block.) Sorry, I've got to look after it."

Her eyes brightened. "You don't mind killing those things?"

"No, not really. I'm not sentimental about it. It's got to be done, so why sweat it?"

"I'm the same, obviously. Killing has always been part of my life."

"Great. You can join the Extermination League."

"I'd love that. Can I start today?"

He handed her the knife, curious. "Knock yourself out."

Marla went over to where the rat was still squirming. In a swift and adroit motion, she brought the knife down. She turned to Brian, a glow in her eyes. She had spiked the carcass and carried it over, blood dripping down her hand and arm.

"R-ight. You're hired. That obviously gave you no pain. Here, I put them in baggies and drop 'em in the green bin at the back."

"I'm going to like living here."

"Yeah, well, Marla, we only kill rats, so don't get too excited."

"You gotta start somewhere," she said, as she washed off the blood.

"Like a re-fill?"

"No, but I'll see you again … at the shop."

At the door, she half-turned and looked at him. No man could fail to be beguiled by her physical appearance. But Brian decided not to let it distract him – in vain.

Settling In 3

On the edge of summer, the patio construction was completed. And after the housewarming party, the rooftop soon started to be used as the social nexus for the GITH. Brian did two others things quickly that brought an even greater cohesion to the group. His first action was to get a cat from the local pound.

He knew *Oprah* would be his cat because he fed her. But she would become like a shared moppet for them all. Not Marla, the cat was scared to death of her. But she loved the others, particularly Kelly.

Oprah was a plush Maine Coon who took chesire pleasure going from room to room, sleeping over with one or the other of them; whoever won her that night would leave the door ajar so Oprah could squeeze through to make a quick dash to Brian's for her early morning repast. Brian was always the first up and initially would rattle kibble in her bowl to rouse her to run the Hall. In short order, Oprah's ears would be tuned to the familiar long-distance rustlings from his open door, and she'd be brushing his leg before he got the food poured.

The other thing Brian did was put in new steel-reinforced front and back doors with deadbolt locks. This afforded fortress-like protection to the inhabitants who were disposed (even more than before) to leave their doors open in the evenings to sororitize. This was a free-market sharing of all that goes into the maintenance of a woman. Not just a host of new and old moisturisers, volumizers, cleansers, cocoa butters and aloe gels would change hands, but also borrowed hardware to put a wave in or out of the hair or an exfoliate, peel or scrub for the body.

That brisk traffic was dwarfed, however, by the wholesale swapping of their existing clothing, where fit permitted. It led to a few short-lived hissies – 'I thought you gave it to me' and 'I need it back, I just loaned it to you for a night' and 'That's not Mel's, that's mine'. Whenever voices were raised, the GITH would swoop in and mediate all disputes.

New clothing was also flowing in constantly thanks to Joanna via the shopping channel (with her discount). She told the Girls when to watch for their favourite designers, and they'd consult and organise their orders, according to size, number and colours. Christmas-like boxes clogged the foyer every week and clothes would be traded and tried on, a flurry of decisions made, and a majority of rejections and returns would usually result. All this activity required a great deal of 'visiting', sometimes in states of relative undress as they traded and borrowed back and forth.

Brian had quickly developed the promised warning codes to allow for the unadorned freedom the Girls were used to. Alerts became all the more imperative when he made some male friends and they'd drop in.

He would shout "Man in the Hall" for all intrusions inside or "Man on Deck" at the top of the stairs to the patio. If he went to the front door to let men in, the Call in the Hall would go out; then physical traffic and the excited buzz of their interaction would stop with doors closing until the man threat had passed. On the patio, the alert would give the GITH time to tell the interloper to hold off until they could veil their 'delicacies' – Melissa's word.

It took time before the Girls got used to having a man flitting in and out of the patio often with only a small towel covering them. A lifetime of conditioning ensured they could never trust completely and so would always check to make sure he wasn't leering. It didn't hurt his stock he never was. They warmed to that as very a-typical and respectful behaviour.

He wasn't much of a sunbather, but occasionally he'd take to a deck chair in his bathing suit. Most of the time, he was looking after them, with lemonade or treats he'd just baked. But what they needed most was getting him to apply sun lotion where they couldn't reach – their backs or backs of their thighs. And always for some unspoken reason, they all liked him to do it, rather than ask a Girl. It may have been a way of satisfying their sensual needs, without sexual compromise. There was none of the latter or the requests would have stopped fast. So, whenever there was a bather on the roof and Brian was in the Hall, he was called upon to lather it on. He obviously didn't think it an unpleasant task for he never, ever refused the call.

The Girls had been a lot more careful with the previous owner. He was older and stayed mostly in his apartment and would slip in and out the back door which was closest to him. But, with Brian, they sensed correctly – or because they knew he grew up with sisters – he had a drubbing understanding of women's needs. So, for Brian's consideration of them and for the simple changes he'd made early on, 255 Covington Place became a very cosy nook. And those changes yielded an added benefit.

The Extermination League got a third member. Oprah found her calling as a very enthusiastic ratter. It annoyed Brian to see her eviscerated carcasses around his suite, staining his rugs and furniture sometimes indelibly. But Marla was highly amused when she saw the carnage. Not that it improved her relationship with Oprah.

The cat was never seen in the same space with her for more than two scrambling seconds. One of the feline's preoccupations was sunbathing on the hot tin ledge of the patio, a chersonese she favoured of a sunny, warm afternoon. Early in her reign, Oprah was caught unawares as she dozed on the ledge when Marla approached. She jumped, lost her balance and scrabbled to stop from going over the edge. Marla smiled at her as she hunched and hissed, then tore off at speed to hide under Brian's for the entire day. Brian saw it all. So did Joanna.

"What's with you and Oprah?" she asked. "She takes to us other Girls."

"I'm an animal killer," said Marla. "On the farm and slaughter house, I put 'em away wholesale. The only time I was around a pet was on the farm – a mangy pup called Bull. When I was young, he was very aggressive with me. When I got older, I was killing animals 100 times his size. So, he didn't take any chances. He knew it'd be dangerous to be alone in the barn with me. They know. They sense it somehow."

"You wouldn't hurt Oprah, would you?" Brian frowned.

"No. She'd never let me get close enough. You just saw her reaction when I got close this once. She won't let that happen again."

By contrast, Oprah was often on the Girls' laps, particularly Kelly's, but they discouraged the practice later when they were tanning in bathing suits for fear of being scratched. Sunbathing was one of the main activities on the patio – the other was eating – but they decided they needed something more to keep them entertained.

Tell Me a Story

Joanna came up with the notion to research and read aloud short, human interest stories that would add something more meaningful to their pleasurable moments together. It was a good idea because the Girls had little intrinsically in common except for similar tastes and tendencies of women in the same age range.

Brian offered to relate the first story. He had just come up with some cut-up fruit over ice cream topped with hemp hearts in his favourite glass dishes. He distributed them around as he started to tell of this foreign adventure.

> "It's a personal incident of mine when I went on a culinary tour of Asia. You know my interest in cooking. What you don't know is my fondness for food that's serious-hot; so I was in the right place to sample the spiciest. You name it: five-pepper Szechuan in China, Indian curries – naga, phall – top on the Scoville scale of hotness, no problem. By the time I reached Malaysia, I wanted to go to Fatt Kee Roast Fish Restaurant. It's the top spot for spicy seafood in the country. It's a famous enough place that I'd read a couple of stories of people who'd gone there and chosen the hottest of seven levels of spiciness on their menu. It never ended well. One

was even hospitalised. Better to avoid. So, second to fish, I like hot noodles and decided to go to Han Woo's restaurant that serves up Special Korean Spicy Noodles. It's also in the Klang Valley, where all the spiciest places are in Malaysia.

A little cocky what with my seasoned palate, I went ahead and ordered the dish with the top spice level, number ten. Anything above four is considered dangerously hot. The waiter brought the owner over, and he asked me if I was used to really spicy food. I said I'd been breathing fire in stops all over Asia. I could handle it. The buzz went around the diners and staff that someone had ordered the hottest mess of noodles, and soon all eyes were glaring at me in disbelief. I glowed in their admiration. I'd soon be glowing even brighter! Soon, the waiter arrived, showing the whites of his eyes, and dropped a large plate of noodles in front of me. It's basically a stir fry with beef, onions, carrots buried in lots of noodles. It's the sauce that kills with a chilli paste called *gochujang*. The smell alone tried to warn me off: my nose hairs literally twitched. I took a messy forkful. The entire restaurant was still fixed on me. So, I took a second swirl.

In two seconds, the delayed incendiary bomb went off. Ears, nose and throat went up in flames! I was choking, coughing, sneezing and crying for dear life. I grabbed for the water. Drinking it did nothing. I rose up and splashed it on my face. Wet didn't matter; I was covered in sweat. I must have been red as a beet, wiping sweat, tears and surely blood from my nose and face. Then it died down. Oooo, I sat and caught my breath. The entire restaurant applauded. I felt I had to live up to their approval. Fool! That's the only word for it.

I took in a big whack of the noodles and gulped it down so it wouldn't burn my mouth. Big mistake. I was on my feet, spluttering, choking, screaming worse than before. I made a beeline for the bathroom just in time to hurl my guts out.

Howls of laughter followed me into the Men's. I soaked my head and waited for the fires to bank. I was so sick at this point, I don't remember if I paid the bill or how I got back to my hotel. But I do remember tailspinning at the toilet with diarrhoea and dry-retching on and off half the night. I finally dropped off and when I woke, my mouth felt like it was packed in cotton wool and my stomach was as tender as an open wound. I couldn't face food, so stayed numb-drunk for a full day. The words of the manager finally came back to me. "Few human people can eat Ten level. It's dish we make with fire of Korea dragon. You carry mark of *Imugi* forever."
"I went to the bathroom and looked in the mirror. I stuck out my tongue. What I saw amazed me. On my tongue was a snaky-looking dragon etched on it plain as day."

The Girls were transfixed. Kelly smirked.

"Stick it out, Bry, let's see your little snake," she said coyly to laughing agreement.

Brian opened his mouth and stuck out his tongue like a Maori. On it was a decal of Imugi, a coiled python-like serpent with a long beard.

The GITH stared at it disconcerted, then laughed and applauded.

"I believe your story, Brian," said Joanna. "It's very possible. A handful of Asian countries have the spiciest food on the planet."

"This is my second story from Brian. He told me an *un*-believable story when he was cooking bouillabaisse. I grew up on it so I dropped in on him. That's when he told me about his relationship with an octopus."

"Octopus?" Kelly blurted. "Shit, Mel ..."

"... I know, I said 'unbelievable' but I believed it. Tell them, Brian."

"I wanna hear that one, bro!" said Shakira.

Brian shrugged. "It was at the Aquarium in Bermuda. The two of us made a very fast and intimate connection. It didn't seem that strange at the time. Two strangers reaching out ... ."

"How's your love life these days, Brian?" asked Kelly.

"I'll tell you: after an octopus, there's no going back …"

Shakira's diaphragm jerked,. "Why, Bry? 'Cause they're the best squeeeeze?"

Marla laughed. "Yup, and it's got one thing going for it other relationships don't: when it doesn't work out, you can always eat 'em."

"Oh, no," protested Melissa, "no, Brian said he won't eat octopus after that experience. Right?"

"R-ight. But I warn you Girls, that only applies to octopus. Marla's right. Everything else is fair game."

"With a side order of fava beans and a nice Chianti," Kelly smirked.

"That's it, Kelly. They'll be on the menu when I have *you* for dinner."

Brian and Kelly had found a quick way to renegotiate their initial embarrassment by kibitzing with each other. It was a tailor-made way for them to be safely familiar; and it started to happen when they met accidently on the street sometime after the housewarming. Brian had emerged from Duguid's one late afternoon and almost collided with her. She had just left the pharmacy and was on her way home. He offered her a lift. When they got in his car and started off, she looked at him until she thought of something to say.

"Pretty good job on the patio, Brian. We're all pretty happy the new owner's letting us use it. We hated the *Shit* in your apartment before who kept it all to himself."

"An owner's easier to take if he's off-site. But there may be a reason he didn't want to let you up, Kelly – the fire escape. It's overhauled now. It had to come up to code to use the rooftop legally."

"Meaning he didn't want to repair it. Yeah. Cheap a-hole."

"And could you see him letting you gander through his place to get to the roof?"

Kelly guffawed. "Gaaawd, no! Probably flash an open raincoat every time. Okay with you though."

"I don't own a raincoat. Sorry."

"Hilarious. I mean it's okay you're gonna let us up."

"Maybe I should buy a raincoat."

"Too late. You're already all wet."

"Hey, not bad. But yeah, for the Girls in the Hall, the door's always open."

"Great, but what happens if you get a girl?"

"A girlfriend? Me? Ha. When? No time. But if I ever get a girl, she'll have to like people. Door stays open."

"She may have a problem with that. You can like people and not want 'em tramping through your house all day."

"Privacy's overrated."

"I found that out about you already. But you don't want to put *her* through any surprises. Get it?"

"I get it, especially from you. But one problem at a time, Kelly. Girl first."

"It can happen. Even to you. (He laughs.) I got a new guy. That may change things."

"It always does. For starters, he'll move in."

"No. I'll move out. He owns a gym. And he's workin' on opening a chain of 'em. When that happens, we'll want to move up."

"Sounds serious."

"That depends if he gets a chain goin'."

Brian laughed. "Of course. He sounds pretty cool. Entrepreneur type. Not your typical 'all chin, no forehead' type."

Kelly never really laughed, but exhorted with an exhale. "Never heard that one."

"One of my dad's old expressions."

"Don't tell Melissa. She's full of 'em."

"Yeah, she dropped a couple on me already."

"She thinks you're okay, by the way. All the Girls do."

"Likewise. But yeah, Melissa's the first Girl I met. Very outgoing."

"Trouble is: if you grow up in an ivory tower, you're no good on the ground."

"Watch it! That's getting close to an aphorism. I'll tell Melissa on you."

"Go ahead. But tell her Jo said it. She'd take it from her. Both snooty college grads."

"I'm a snooty college grad. So now there're three of us to look down our long, snooty noses at you, you poor ignorant lowbrow."

"What a shithead," said Kelly, smiling. "We're gonna get on just great."

Poker Nights

That fire escape repair proved to be the open sesame for the girls to use the roof nightly and all weekends. At the same time, weekly poker nights started for the boys in Brian's apartment. Jake and two of his bachelor friends from college along with Brian made up a foursome; they favoured five-card stud and were so evenly matched in their gambling skills, the $300 or so weekly takings also traded hands pretty evenly over the course of a month's play.

They had all been inveterate players for years and loved the routine and roustabout of it. None of them had ever got a royal or straight flush and waited for the day it would happen. Or so they wishfully imagined. The odds of getting a royal flush are 649,740 to 1, and a straight flush, 72,192 to 1. One could play a lifetime away and not draw either of them. If the boys had known the odds, it would not have seemed such a puzzlement for failing to break through with one or both hands. But to date, no joy in getting one – until the next game.

The original intent was for each player to host the game at his place in turn; but at the first session at Brian's, the Girls traipsed through, in innocently alluring outfits. Before the night was out, the boys demanded that Covington be the permanent venue. Brian didn't object. With a greater immunity perhaps to the spectacular passing parade, he saw his chances grow measurably. Conversations turned from work, sports and GQ-sanctioned gizmos and gambols to the seraphic sylphs that floated by and ascended upward.

Marla was usually the first to appear, carrying a package wrapped in butcher's paper, and set the men's nostrils flaring. She would say hello to Brian and ignore the others who would look after her with lustful longing. By contrast, Melissa would go over and speak to the men, learning their names with a word to each; they loved her polite attentions but held back; 'good' girls got the soft treatment. Shakira was used to men in groups and would usually stop to talk to them, name-dropping whichever celebrity she golfed with that day; this always intrigued them, though they could never manage to talk 'sports' with her as they did among themselves; their chat would always end with a promise to visit her golf course. But Kelly was the favourite. She'd amble over and cajole. She could handle herself and the men knew it. The zingers would fly to prove it. Brian wondered why she seemed so comfortable with men, but couldn't coax that ease into making snug choices for her love partners.

In fact, her latest, the gym owner, was already proving to have a crack or two in his porcelain.

The glad-clad female distractions as they sashayed by proved to be too much game for these inveterate gamblers. After no more than a few hands, they'd hear the sounds of laughter above and the smell of meat grilling; the prospect of girding it up with the GITH began to put the game into relative shade. It was something of a pied piper pattern that when the bulging halter tops and cut-off jeans frayed invitingly appeared, it was not the hot summer that warmed their hearts and other parts; cards would be abandoned with a stampede up the stairs.

Jake, of course, couldn't resist spreading himself over the lot of them, flirting and trying to make dates. The GITH knew he was a colleague of Brian's and so tolerated him with a soft but constant 'no'. Troyan, a mystery man of finance and gypsy-touched 'Hoppy' – so called because he used weed though college and his dorm smelt like a barn – were interested but unsure how to push out. Seeing this, the GITH worked out a defensive selection system that ensured every man was hostessed on a prix fixe grid.

At the next BBQ, Shakira pared off Troyan, Melissa sweet-talked Jake, Marla chanced Hoppy, Joanna and Kelly behaved like house monitors and Brian fussed over the lot of them like a mother hen. The Girls were all on guard to see what Marla would do. She was an unknown quantity and invoked an inkling among them of something else lurking. How would that 'something else' manifest? They had never really seen her one-on-one with a man. Sideways eyes watched her with Hoppy.

He just stared at her in disbelief, never encountering an Amazon up close before. She smiled, moving his chin up so his eyes met hers. But they went back down.

"Would it help if I took off some of these uncomfortable clothes?" she asked.

That got a boisterous affidavit from all the men who somehow heard it despite being otherwise engaged.

"Straight up with Marla, boys," Kelly piped up, "if you know what's good for you."

That seemed to snap Hoppy out of his trance. He looked at Marla's face, a little embarrassed.

"Talk, Hoppy," said Joanna. "The idea is to say something."

"Tell her she's a goddam Venus de *Filo*," shouted Jake.

"That's not conversation," said Marla, looking at Jake. "Okay, Hoppy, let me start. What do you do?"

"I own a scrap yard, well, my dad does."

"That's useful. Good place to dump bodies."

His face fell, then he broke into a loud nervous laugh.

"What do you do?"

"I'm a butcher."

"Sure. A butcher? C'mon. The way you look."

"The guys forgot how I looked in the slaughterhouse when I was the best at taking down the big ones."

"Jesus."

Almost on cue, a trap sounded. Brian and she headed for the ratter knife. She put up her hand to him. She grabbed it and went over and put the rat out of its misery. It made a little scream. The boys gaped at the sight, mouths ajar; the Girls seemed hardly to notice, one yawned. Marla spiked it and brought it wriggling to the party. Brian had a baggie ready. She dropped it in still writhing. All the boys laughed nervously but were clearly in shock.

"Jesus Christ!" repeated Hoppy. "Did you see that? You *must* be a butcher! Does that happen a lot?"

"Oh yeah," Shakira wearied. "Marla's the rats' Most Wanted."

"Many rats in your yard, Hoppy?" asked Marla, wiping off the knife.

"Yuh, plenty."

"What's the address?" she asked, viewing the blade, then him.

Hoppy had a look equal parts fear and curiosity when Marla, seeing the rat still wriggling in the bag, brought it down hard on the BBQ cover. Hoppy hopped. She threw her head back in a hearty laugh full of those teeth so menacing in their whiteness.

Brian wired his iTunes into his BOSE player and switched it on as a signal to dance. He had Marla pretty much to himself at that point because the stakes for his poker pals got a little too high. That suited her fine. She tolerated Brian because she sensed he admired her gumption and not just her obvious charms. Did this mean she could, at last, relax? He talked real talk, not slick-to-sex talk. How predictably boring that was, men always hitting on her for her ornamentation, not herself. She didn't get it. The pretty steers got slaughtered just as surely as the ugly ones: carcasses were carcasses. If you're going to make it work at all, she thought, you've got to add more than clichéd carnal cravings to the effort.

Meanwhile, Shakira and Troyan had shimmied into dancing. The GITH had done a good pairing there. It turned out he even played golf, so that was one bright beam. Kelly had a clichéd craving of her own (for the good life) that would have been more than quenched by Troyan's wealth, but she saw how well Shakira took to him; besides, she had her own fish on the hook for the moment.

A Dream that Hurts

But gym owner Keith Radowski had some rough edges which Kelly's sardonic wit did nothing to knock off. The reverse. Her candour may have been why he started to abuse her. When he stayed over, they would unsettle the cosy Covington concord with raucous arguments and fists being thrown, evidenced by the bruises she couldn't hide in a bathing suit. The GITH went to work on her about dumping Keith, but Kelly was unwilling to abandon her dream attached to this man.

During this entire disruption, Marla was not around, presumably out with other men, and had never met Keith. Fortunate. For he would have been wildly attracted to her for her strapping physique and mysterious nonchalance; no doubt there because he flirted overtly with all the other Girls to their unbridled disgust. When Marla saw the violence inflicted on Kelly's body, she looked peculiarly intrigued.

"What are you looking so happy about, Marla?" asked Kelly.

"I'm not. I'm amazed you let him keep bashing you."

"Yeah, well, when we're not fighting, he's everything I want. It'll get better."

"I don't think so. He knows what he's doing. Where he hits you is strategic. It won't stop. Count on it getting worse …"

"Hey, hey, I don't need your slaughterhouse crap, Marla. Keep out of it."

"You should listen to her, Kel," Shakira piped in. "It's time to yeet the guy. Get woke to him. He's gonna keep thrashin' away at ya. Not worth the dream, if you don' get to live it."

"You put a sock in too, Shak. No one's going to die. It's my business. Let it alone."

"It *is* our business, Kelly," Melissa tried. "We look out for each other. We're concerned for you. The Girls are right. It can only get worse. Don't play, 'Give me bread and call me a fool'."

"Oh, shit, Mel, not another f-ing aphorism. When you reach planet Earth, we'll talk. Until then, shut your hackneyed little mouth! And don't you start, Jo, I don't need a college essay on battered women."

"Don't need it, Kel. You know all you need to know. You just won't act on it."

"Right, Girls," said Brian. "You've all tried. Kelly knows what she wants. If it doesn't come easy, and she is willing to pay the heavy price, that's up to her."

"Thank you, Brian! Never thought the best advice would come from a man."

"But if it does get worse," continued Brian, "you've got to report him to the police. No, Kelly, I'm serious. We're your witnesses. We'll back you up. Right, Girls?"

They all nodded and mumbled their agreement.

"If I say okay, will you drop the f-in' subject, pleeease?"

Not too long after that contretemps, Radowski broke her arm. He played the contrite card for all it was worth. Kelly forgave him. The other Girls were outraged. Their doors slammed and didn't open whenever he was in the building. Brian pushed Kelly to call the police, as they agreed. But she wouldn't. To them, the fibreglass cast she wore was a daily reminder of Kelly's failure to see her abuser for what he really was – a misogynist and a loser. His was the most abhorrent behaviour the GITH could imagine. But then something happened that topped it.

Before the month was out, Keith Radowski was found brutally murdered in his own gym. He was killed in the evening, left naked under a running shower and discovered next morning by another trainer who puked at the surgical sight of him.

Police forensics scoured the scene and came up with not one clue. Kelly was the chief suspect for a while, what with her abusive relationship with the dead man. But the police soon realised she couldn't have managed to murder much of anything. For a woman with two arms to inflict deep injuries to this ultra-fit personal trainer would have been improbable; for a woman with one good arm, impossible. The other GITH were cleared, all having interacted at home that evening. Only Marla was absent. But Brian discovered her on the patio reading a romance novel. The Girls shook their heads at such an unlikely choice of book for her.

She had been up there for some time – Brian corroborating her story to the police – because she was nearly at the end of *Caged in Winter*, had finished a dinner from the grill and drunk half a bottle of wine.

There was one inconclusive piece of evidence from one of Radowski's employees who happened to be passing the gym in a car with her husband early that evening. She saw a 'tall, full-figured woman with blonde hair' entering the building. But the gym was on the ground floor of an office tower with two IT companies where staff came and went at all hours. The case went unsolved.

Something didn't sit right with Joanna. She had a hankering of something unsettlingly proximal about the murder, a missing piece from right under their noses. She was sure Kelly had nothing to do with it, and everyone else had alibis; but her suspicions were aroused. For the moment, she'd say nothing. Something more might turn up that would put this dread deed in a clearer light for her.

Kelly, meanwhile, was left with mixed feelings. She was extremely relieved to see the end of the abuse. She was extremely sad to see the end of her dream. There was the trauma too of having her boyfriend horrifically murdered. The Girls rallied around her as much as she'd permit, which wasn't much. She went to work at McGruder's Department Store, where she was a buyer, continuing her short buying jaunts hither and yon. But otherwise, she stuck to her apartment with the door closed. After a reasonable period, she emerged from her cocoon as crispy as ever, especially with the boys at poker – probably from the flash drought of no man in her life. She stood flipping salty ones at them before deciding to join the GITH above for another story night.

"You may want to miss going up, Kelly," said Brian. "Tonight's story might be a little close to home."

"Whatdayamean, Bry?"

"They're reading a description of The Ten Men Not To Marry."

The men all looked at her seriously, expecting Kelly to break into tears any second. Instead she exhale-exhorted:

"Shit, I'm an expert on that subject. Let's start with you four jokers…"

"That's us down the drain, boys," Brian joked, "a straight flush if ever there was one."

"I wanna hear that list," said Troyan. "I don't want Shakira to take any poppin' yang to heart."

Kelly waved them on. "Then, we better get up there. You need this more than me."

Per the usual practice, they abandoned their hands in favour of the spicier delights above, though the scamper-up was not as bouncy given the night's topic. All but Troyan gathered around Marla, typically indifferent to how she attracted men so effortlessly. Melissa was shocked to see them.

"Hey, what are you boys doing here?"

"They're on a journey of self-discovery," Kelly replied quickly.

"To discover why we don't belong on the list," added Brian.

"You hope," said Joanna. "The more we get into it, the more you'll want to go back to your game."

"Jo's right," said Melissa, "We're doing this for us, not you. Don't ruin it for us."

Kelly: "Rules are, boys: no talking, no swearing, no spitting on the floor."

"Yeah, we don' need your BDE, so dummy-up, boys," said Shakira.

"What's a BDE?" asked Hoppy.

"Big Dick Energy," said Troyan. "Shak's woke. AKA keep it zipped and zippered."

"When you is ready, Mistas?" Shakira said, eyes wide with controlled impatience.

"Ready, babe, and drivin' safely," said Troyan.

Shakira doubled at the diaphragm, the only one to understand his reference.

"Enough foreplay," said Marla. "Start the execution."

Just then, Oprah ran in from downstairs. She saw Marla and gave her a wide berth, lying on her tin perch ready to bolt if the bogey girl made any move.

Marry Me Don't

"A' right, sisters," said Shakira, "Here are *The Ten Men not to Marry*. The first one's the **no-commit.** Yer gettin' the crossroads wiffle-waffle from yer dream guy, but after a few good turns on the rack, he croaks out a 'yes'. You think the ground under you is dead-earth solid. Then you looks down and you lost yer feets to the sinkin' sand. Nothin' lasts, but fast-as-a-fox, he jumped back on his am-big-uity and betrayed your sorry ass. I say: give him no ass to sass."

The Girls give it applause. The men are smiling but unsure.

"Big one here, sisters: **the rebel**. Here's yer bad boy – dashin', darin', darlin'. That's a dreamy yeah! Trouble is: once a rebel, the spots don't come off. His ole firebrand cause is now spoilin' for a few months in jail and a life of want. Yuh went and got yerself a stingin' nettle, a backward-walkin' loser and a life a' grief. Yer boots are made for walkin' and yer gonna walk right out on him."

The Girls 'yay' it and applaud. The men wear plastic smiles.

"Girls, you'll recognise this brother: **the narcissist**. Lover boy was lost to you the first time he looked in the mirror. First love at first sight. Yer in mortal combat with the needy wants of his own private, preferred and personal toy boy inside. Time to play the Princess card: three in this marriage; it's a bit crowded. Leave this man and his mirage on Fantasy Island!"

The Girls give it thumbs up with a laugh. The men have stopped smiling.

"There's one of these in every Girl's diary: **the control freak**. He's one way-my way, and that means no-play for you. We coax, we cajole, we charm. No way do yer wily women's ways cut it 'cause you're in his army now and life's a barb-wire barracks, sistas. It's all KP and latrines with no reveille and no relief. Yer just a bucked-up private. An' you wan' to get cashiered out."

The Girls whoop it up and applaud. The men are looking glum.

"Go to your closets, Girls. One of the shrunk heads on your jewellery rack is **the know-it-all**. He'll keep you over-amped and underwhelmed every boring minute of every borin' day. Knows every useless thing about every useless thing and nuttin' about that one true jewel in his life: you. If he knows so much, why didn't he see you comin' with that cauldron and cotton thread?"

The Girls give it up with a joyful high-five. The men are restless to leave.

"Yer palms' gonna sweat and yer hearts' gonna bleed if you marry **the momma's boy**. A man's gotta love his ma. Yeah. She's his first girl-friend. Yer worry is she's gonna be his *last* girl-friend. You tango too close to this boy, Girls, you marry his momma too. That day will come when he says: 'My ma doesn't do it like that'. You hear that, you pack up and you ship out. Or as quick as SkipTheDishes knocks on yer door, you go from lovin' wife to little waif; they get steak, you get spammed."

The Girls applaud and butt shoulders. The boys look at each other, nudging a departure. Jake breaks the silence, looking at Brian.

"And Sammy loves his mother."

"No talking, Jake," Joanna said firmly. "Who's Sammy?"

"He's referring to when I moved in," said Brian. "My mother called to see how I was doing."

The Girls all said, "Awww."

"Four to go, Girls," said Shakira.

"I think we'll go down and finish our game," said Jake. "Guys?"

They all nodded. The Girls just smiled at each other. Troyan looked a little ruefully at Shakira. He wanted to stay. But they all started downstairs, venting how they're so misunderstood.

"We're not like that!"

"I don't know any guys like that, do you?"

"Next up: **the pretty boy**. He's your show-off trophy. You go make yer rival girls green, you make 'em wanton! An' it means yer kids won't be ugly little scabs. But straight fairways and flat greens stop there. 'Cause when he's not pimping hisself fer hisself, yer peeling yer sisters off of his bespoke liddle bod. If 'pretty' is as good as he's got, yah did yerself a hurt.

One morning you wakes up, you looks over at yer beautiful man and, land me a whopper, he looks like a haddock!"

The Girls give it another high-five all around with 'yeah'.

"Ah, watch yer step, Girls, don't be fooled by **the pushover**. Ya think he lets you be all the girl you can be. You can think, you can speak, you can act all free and easy-like without he don't box you up and send you home to yer momma. The storm brewin' for this bro is yer doin' all the thinkin', speakin' and actin' for the both of you. Yer doin' it all and that motha' is layin' like a lizard on the loungette!"

The Girls are up dancing to 'layin' like a lizard, layin' like a lizard'.

"Get smart, Girls, 'cause it's too easy to go hard in the centre and soft in the head for **the manly man**. You thinks he just reeks sex, takes charge like a stallion, and makes you look gooood! Look twice. He reeks beer and pretzels, eclipses your ass and is AWOL in a fishin', huntin', drinkin' camp that sure ain't makin' you feel warm by yer fire! You wanna get wrapped in his big, secure arms and believe he's God's gift. But what your manly man is doin' is *Marlboring* you!"

The Girls pause over the pun, then applaud, laughing.

"The last man not to marry, Girls, is **the fitness freak**. You okay with this, Kel?" (She nods and smiles.) "Okay. He's Gucci in the buff, but lives in Speedo. This flex-and-sweat jerk-off crunches, deadlifts, presses and curls right outa your life. If he chooses his muscles over his Missus, don't be a shero. Time to say IMOH.

"If you're not gettin' it yet, girlfriends, the thread of fool's gold runnin' through all the Ten Men Not To Marry is you comin' in a distant number two to his other hard on, animal or mineral. So, if you wanna hear weddin' bells, first lay down the blood-red carpet that boy must walk with this e-dict: keep yer eyes on me, yer hands on me and yer love on me, and never take 'em off, or that sunrise over Campobello ain't never gonna happen, no way, nowhere, no how!"

The Girls rise up and applaud with 'woo-woos'. Shakira bows. After filling their glasses and commenting on bits they liked, they sat down to discuss it. Joanna spoke first.

"That was good, Shak. But here's the thing: who's left?"

"No one, Jo. And I know," said Kelly. "I've been through 'em all, not just the flex-and-sweat jerk-offs."

All the others silently nodded, knowing the last one was still a bit raw.

"The worst is behind you, Kel," Melissa said. "The fact is, we know all these types, don't we Girls?"

"Maybe we do, Mel," said Shakira, about to swagger her head. "But why does the bad stuff come out and the good stuff we don't git? Look at Troy. That boy's goood; he's not on that list. So, we outa make another list. Damn! The Ten Most Marriage-Wise Guys."

Silence descended as this was a revolutionary idea. It was going to take Herculean brain power to produce positive grades of marriageable men.

Marla spoke up, "Let's face it. There's not enough to make a list. Give me one."

Another pregnant pause made them laugh.

"Come on, one," Marla repeated.

"You ought' know, Jo, you're the psych major," said Kelly.

"I'm thinking!" Joanna intoned. "But this is new ground. There's no research."

"Does this mean we're doomed to celibacy forever?" asked Melissa.

"Who said anything about *celibacy*?" said Kelly. "Marriage-some-ness is what we talking about here."

Shakira made a suggestion. "We outa come up with two marriageable types. Each Girl. Come up with two, and then we come back in a week and make up the list."

"Good idea," said Joanna, "the ideal guy to marry times ten."

"One problem," said Melissa, "we'll never agree on what's ideal. Shaw said, 'Never do unto others what you would have them do unto you – their tastes are different'."

"Yeah, well, I don't want to eat 'em, Mel," Kelly shot back. "I just want to marry one. How hard can it be?"

"We're the Big Five," Joanna said. "All five unmarried. That's how hard."

"If we're making a list, Girls, no wishy-washy clichés," Marla warned. "Kindness, compassion, good sense of humour, likes dogs and loves kids – they don't fly."

"What's wrong with those?" asked Melissa. "Those are great."

"No they're not," said Joanna. "Those are qualities. We want positive categories, if we're matching what we heard."

"Can't think of one. That's pathetic, not one," said Kelly.

"How about, 'Family Man'?" Joanna offered.

"Using your yardstick, Jo, family man's not a type," said Marla. "That's a man who's been created."

"Make that a man who's been *renovated*!" Joanna countered.

"Hey, next week, same time, same place, we'll see what we got," repeated Shakira.

They all agreed to do so. And they did, but rather embarrassingly came up empty. Then Marla surprised them all, and herself, by spurting out:

"I got one!"

"What? Who?" they said nearly in unison.

"Brian!"

The man himself heard their peals of laughter and bustled up to the patio in his apron, with a tray of amuse bouches.

"What's so funny, Girls?"

That sight brought another eruption of laughter.

"Cook!" screamed Joanna.

That brought howls of laughter, mostly at Brian's perplexed, daffy look. And none of the GITH could hear the word 'cook' ever after without recalling that moment with joy. It remained the only category they could imagine that would make a man absolutely marriageable.

Living the Life 4

With the embrace of the warm weather, the Girls and Brian practically lived on the patio. But they split some of that time wayfaring to the nearby beach. They lived in a neighbourhood called The Beaches because its entire southern edge was on a lake with a mile-long beach threaded by a planked boardwalk above it.

It was no more than a three-block amble to the yellow sands from Covington Place. Each of the Girls carried a folding chair and towel; Brian (with help from Marla) lugged his chair, blanket, beach towels, beach umbrella and a cooler. The cold pack usually contained something like prosciutto ham, pimento and mozzarella sandwiches and a selection of fruit popsicles he'd prepared the night before. He packed flavoured spritzers in tins too so they'd all get a buzz; it added a little brio to their continued storytelling. It was Marla's turn to come up with a funny or funky human interest story, and the GITH were curious about her choice.

The practice was to set up the umbrella and put the chairs in a shaded circle where they would eat, drink and chat. Then later, they would split off to lie on the beach, swim or stay in the shade to read or just people-watch. It was always a lazy, happy time with a story often the jewel point of focus before the drink and intense heat on the beach put them into a squandering torpor.

After it was all set up, they stripped down to their bathing suits. Brian had seen Marla in her bikini before and found he had to remind himself again not to be distracted by her striking figure. The GITH were all slim and attractive young women, but Marla radiated an animal magnetism, as if she had somehow acquired the animus of all the creatures she had killed.

They started into their lunch and talked absently until Marla pulled out her notes.

Murder Unawares

"I have two stories to tell you because the first is very short. I had to include it because it is the most intriguing I've ever come across. It's a true story too or so they say, whoever 'they' are. Here goes:

> "It's a fairly typical setting. A young family in suburbia, in a large three-bedroom bungalow, married eight years with two kids, five and seven. They were a happy couple, with the mother just doting on her children. It was as if she was born to be a mother. And they all just worshipped her. It was like one of those idealised 1950s' families that advertisers lie to convince us really existed.
>
> The couple had known each other in high school and met up again after going to separate colleges; they had coincidentally ended up at the same firm both as accredited accountants. Five years in, they married and started their own firm. Within a year, they had their first child. A couple of years later, a son came along. And they were thinking of having a third child.
>
> One night, after Gloria had put their children to bed, and they had watched their favourite television shows, they got into bed. Usually, they'd chat before sleep – the typical pillow talk of an average married couple. But this night was different. She turned to Henry and said she had a confession to make. She said she loved him so much, she couldn't find it in her heart to keep her secret hidden from him any longer.
>
> 'Oh no, you want a divorce,' he moaned.
>
> 'No, it's nothing like that.'
>
> "What else could it be? It can't be an affair. We live in each other's pockets. We're never away from each other. I know you better than I know myself."

"You don't know me. Only what you want to see. What I never told you was how I hate dogs. Really hate them. There's even a long word for it. Cyno . . . something. Even to hear a dog bark, my blood runs cold."

"You mean . . . is it bad enough you'd kill?" he asked.

"Ever wonder why there's no dogs in the neighbourhood?"

"No! That's you?"

"That's me. I threw sweet treats in their back yards as far as three blocks away from the house."

"Jesus, that's you. The authorities have been looking for the dog killer for months now."

"You never asked me how I got over my insomnia, did you, love? The answer is: no more dogs."

"Why, Gloria? Why?"

"Bitten when I was a child. It's been *war* ever since. A good weekend for me is to be left alone in a dog kennel."

"You'd . . . you'd . . ."

"It wouldn't be a kennel anymore."

"Jesus! Are we safe?"

"Sure. It's just dogs."

"That's why you wouldn't let Sally have a dog."

"Right. Now you know why I got so upset when she begged us for one. I couldn't stand to have a dog in the house. It would break Sally's heart to lose her pup the same day she got it."

"You'd do away with it?"

"I'd send you out for a day with the kids, take it down to the basement and kill it very slowly."

"I can't believe it. You're so sweet and so gentle with the kids and me."

Gloria pulled him to her and kissed his cheek. He couldn't help pulling away.

"I love my family, especially you, love," she said. "And we got Sally a pet. She loves her Schmucker."

"Yes she does. Though it's only a cat of sorts – absolutely hairless."

"Oh yeah. Fur on, it'd start looking like a you-know-what," laughed Gloria, gesturing a slit across her throat. "Might overlook that it's a cat. My hatred would blind me. Oh Henry, my darling, I hope you don't mind too much. But I just love, love, love to kill dogs. It's more thrilling than sex."

They all sat there stunned, in some grisly way expecting more but not getting it. Marla, seeing their reaction, cackled.

"Holy shit, Marla," said Kelly, "you're sick."

"Scabrous, girl, you need to go smooth," said Shakira.

"It's not a true story," said Melissa. "When would she even find the time? He said they're never away from each other. It's not possible."

"Oh, it's possible all right," said Joanna. "A 2014 British study found that 20 per cent of married couples said they were keeping a major secret in their marriage. And one in four of those said the secret was so big, they worried it would end their marriage."

"But mass murder? I don't think so," added Brian.

"We don't know what those secrets are, Brian," said Joanna. "Murder could easily be one of those so-big secrets."

"You're *all* right," said Kelly. "It could be murder, but she wouldn't have enough time, so mass murder is unlikely."

"Why you so thrilled with that tale o' woe, Marl?" asked Shakira.

"It surprised me. You never know what's in people. What made her suddenly love to kill? She didn't really know. One dog bite wouldn't do it. Make you scared of dogs, not want to kill them. But I got her somehow, maybe because I've killed so much."

"Damn, should we start locking our doors, killer?" asked Kelly.

"Only two of you need to."

They laughed.

"What's the next one like, Marla?" asked Melissa. "If it's another gruesome story, I think I'll go for a swim."

"No, it's a story about eating exotic foods."

"Exotic, how?" Brian posed.

"Weird animals."

Shakira did her diaphragm jerk when she saw Melissa look strangely at her half-eaten sandwich. But they all protested strongly they'd had enough. Marla shrugged and put her notes away.

"Anyone want anything more to eat?" suppressed Brian. "I've still got cobra, owl and donkey on light rye."

They 'yewed' and laughed.

Marla smiled at him. "Ha-ha."

"Is it time for a swim?" asked Melissa. "Let's drink up and head for the surf."

The others must have thought it a good idea because they obeyed in silence, emptying their tins and handing them to Brian who put them back in the cooler.

"Stay, Kelly," said Joanna, "I want to talk."

Kelly nodded. The other four leapt up and ran down to the lake, making happy, abandoned cries and wading in. Joanna and Kelly watched them jumping up and down in the waves that knocked against the swimmers.

"Problem, Jo?"

"Don't know yet. Need a reality check. I'm watching Marla and think I'm seeing something I don't like."

"Sure you are. She's a weirdo. You and Bry told me the little bit she said about her past. So, no wonder."

"Hear me out. Her story maybe gave me a missing piece of a puzzle I've been working on. Everything was fine with the Girls until Marla came. Soon after, you were having trouble with Keith and then he's killed. Did you get that Marla was the only one he didn't meet? She wouldn't be known to him if she went to the gym, let's say, for something other than exercise …"

"Shit, Jo, are you saying Marla killed Keith?"

"I don't know. I've been looking for signs because something doesn't sit right. Look at Oprah; she's great with all of us but has a conniption fit around Marla. Animals know instinctively if there's a predator around. And we've been hearing news stories about a serial killer on the loose in the city. I know, I'm really reaching here, but coincidence? She's been out nights a lot … on dates or what? She never brings men back. And now, this scary story about a woman who secretly kills on the side. Some murderers leave clues in a cat-and-mouse game with police; others taunt their future captors with leads in the wild excitement of secretly wanting to be caught. Is her story a clue for us to pick up on?"

"You're really out on a limb there, Jo. Just because she's a lot strange and slaughters animals for a living – once – doesn't mean she killed Keith or anybody else. She was at home with us the night he was killed. Remember?"

"Was she?"

"Yeah, up on the patio."

"Listen to this scenario, Kel, and maybe it won't seem so far out. She's had a hard life. That's obvious. Then she links up with a lot of women her own age and we all get along and support each other in a way she's never known. Finally, she's got a family of sorts …"

"No problem there."

"Okay. One of the Girls – you – starts to get abused. We all took it personally, sure, but she takes it as if it had happened to her."

"You don't know that."

"If she was the one abused, how d'you think she'd react?"

"She better not have a boning knife in her hand."

"Exactly. It's possible she took it so personally, she imagined it happened to her. She's not stupid, she'd find a safe and logical way to get rid of the abuser. Keith didn't know her. She could meet him, and he wouldn't know about her connection with us. It's possible she killed him and had time to get back to the patio and pretend she'd been there all night. She just climbed up the fire escape and had it set up to look as if she'd settled in."

"Marla's one of us but she's not. She's there and not there somehow. Even if she adopted us as a sort of family, it doesn't mean she's nuts enough to murder someone."

"You're right, Kel. But I think she could easily use protecting her family as a glib excuse, a sort of imagined ploy to take the drastic action she wants to anyway."

"That's pretty wild speculation, Jo. The cops found nothing. You're not a criminologist. What makes you think you can solve their case? Geez, I'll be scared shitless if you're right. I just think you're grabbing at straws."

"Right again. It *is* speculation. But I wanted someone else in the Hall to know how I'm feeling and what I'm seeing, so we can both watch for anything else that looks suspicious. Okay?"

"Okay, no problem. I'll watch with you, Jo. Hey, what's going on out there?"

An unusually large wave had rolled in and dumped the bathers, who were swept off their feet. When they surfaced, Brian looked down and noticed Melissa had lost her bikini bottom. He patted one of her cheeks gently and spoke to her, obviously about needing to retrieve her bikini. Melissa then spoke to him from behind. He had patted someone else's bottom! Suddenly, a stocky man started to shout at Brian, words like 'my wife' and 'pervert', and then shoved him back hard into the surf. The Girls started to shout at the man about a 'mistake'. But he went at Brian again, yelling hoarsely and bracing to swing. Marla stepped in.

She grabbed the man's arm as it was about to launch the punch; she twisted it sharply backward. He yelled in pain and hit the water. Before he could recover, she was on top of him. She flayed his face with a quick succession of well-aimed blows. His face disappeared. When it came up, she peppered him again. Brian and the Girls were yelling at her to stop. She couldn't hear. The man's wife tried to stop Marla, who rose up and pushed her a good six feet away. Brian drew up and held her. "Marla, Marla". She reacted with a quick reflex unhinging his grip.

She as quickly realised who it was and relaxed into him. The stocky man was up, face bloodied, swearing at her but retreating in fear as Marla made a move toward him.

His wife took his arm to move him away, urging, pleading with him to give it up and leave. The Girls joined Brian in surrounding Marla, escorting her back onto the beach.

"Shit, Jo, that's one for *you*. Sure looks like she came to Bry's rescue."

"I tell you it's another sign – dangerous, easily out of control, protecting her family – it's all there. If Brian didn't stop her, would she go on and on hitting that guy?"

"Looked that way. I thought she was so out of it when Bry grabbed her, he was next."

The two gave each other a sideways stare. It was as if they were both thinking the same thing: is it possible that Marla's a homicidal maniac? They didn't say anything but looked back at the approaching party. Brian was venting at Marla. They could just hear him.

"I don't need you to fight my battles for me, Marla. I don't need your protection. You made me look like a wimp back there, and I don't appreciate it!"

Marla looked unperturbed at him. "I'm sorry, Brian. I just reacted. I didn't think."

"No, you didn't. Next time, if there is one, just back off and let me deal with it."

"Yup, I will."

The stocky man could be heard from a distance along the beach, shouting a threat at Marla and waving his fist.

"I get you again, and I kill you!"

Marla shouted back, "Oh please, I want you to try!"

Joanna and Kelly shook their heads at each other. They turned back to see the man and his wife leave the beach. She had a towel around her middle.

On the way back, Marla didn't help Brian haul the umbrella, cooler and other paraphernalia so as to make him feel more like a man; he divined as much and knew he had to bear the load however painfully.

They liked their excursions to the beach but only when they were all together which became less frequent. Occasionally, one of the GITH would go on her own, Marla most often, but she stopped it because men would 'pester' her on her solo visits.

They all much preferred the patio after work and during the weekends because it had the ease of home and everything was there. Brian had organised a system of shared costs for drinks and meals they had together. They all chipped in. Melissa was often delinquent in her contributions. They grumbled in turn as they made up the difference; she would promise failingly to repay them.

Playing Long Odds

It was soon after the incident on the beach, when they were all together on the rooftop, Shakira was to initiate something that was to impact them later that summer. She had seen a lottery advertised online to win a two-week African safari from a Canadian company, Dashir Lodge, that had long organised tours of photographic shoots on Tanzania's plains. For an entry fee of $50, you had the chance to win the land portion of the safari for two people. It covered treks in the Serengeti, Ngorongoro, a climb up Mount Kilimanjaro, chance of a balloon ride over the veldt and a beach weekend in Zanzibar. You were billeted in the luxurious Dashir camp before and after the safari.

"No airfare?" asked Kelly.

"No, no air," said Shakira. "But not a problem, girl! Troyan's always flyin' 'round in his company jet. We's gonna borrow it 'nd go to Africa in style, baby, Do you hear *me*?"

"There *is* a problem, girl," said Brian. "Maybe you better win the thing first."

"I will, Bry. I'm gonna enter online today. Who wants to come?"

Melissa frowned. "Wouldn't you want to go with Troyan, Shak? What a getaway!"

"That's Gucci, Mel. But it's not his scene. I'm bulletproof on that."

"Let's all enter," said Joanna. "Improve our chances."

Melissa, Marla and Joanna all agreed they wanted to go and entered the contest that day. The lottery had been online for some time and had an imminent closing date; the winner would know by mid-month. The other two begged off: Brian had already been on safari; and Kelly had absolutely no interest in it. Besides, she was toying with adding a holiday on to a buying trip in Florida and then Grand Cayman Island for an international fashion show and buying mart. It was happening around the same time.

It was promising to be a long, hot summer. It meant the GITH were happy to be home, yes, but also bounding with youthful energy to be out and about.

Melissa was jubilant with the group that very Saturday morning she had met a man. He was a lawyer who caught her favour at a pre-conference function she had helped organise for her company. The patio would be lucky to see her very much with dating about to take over her life;

Marla was there less than half the time, and where she was otherwise, except work, some feared knowing;

Brian was among the missing, with showings on three houses, including a listing on one of those estates on Moncrieff Crescent that alone could make him fat with cash;

Joanna had a work schedule at the shopping channel so helter-skelter that every day was a surprise guessing-game.

Kelly was playing spot-and-dash with her short buying junkets; and

Shakira was arcing that June moon with Troyan who wanted to share his elevated lifestyle with her very unreluctantly self.

So, it was very much catch-as-catch-can for the residents of cosy Covington as the hot days tumbled to pursue them. It got so the GITH would almost have to book a time to all be together. But each of them felt the same enjoyment climbing the stairs to see with whom they might be sharing a moment or an hour – that pleasure never went away.

Such was the case when Joanna climbed the stairs to see Kelly sitting and reading one weekday afternoon. She had fixed herself some lemonade, music playing on the radio, as she tried to get more colour on her khaki, oiled skin.

Oprah lay sleeping at her feet on the deck chair. She looked up lazily at Jo, flicked her tail and slumped back into slumber.

"Kelly! How're ya doing?"

"Not bad, Jo. The bastards gave me a day off. Have some lemonade, just made."

"Thanks. What're you reading?"

"A novel called *God's Gentleman.* Basically, it's about a guy who rises from his own ashes being some kind of Samaritan. What are you doing home?"

"I'm off 'til tonight. I've got two hours of *Natori* to sell from eight-to-ten. God, I'm whipped doing these weird shifts. I'd much rather have a bite up here, get a little drunk and hit the sack."

"Something eating you?"

"Nope. Just the grind."

They sat quietly for a moment, drinking their lemonade, when the News came on:

... the latest of the city's gruesome serial killings was discovered last night in a dumpster behind Cordovan Leather Works factory on the waterfront. Police say all eight victims now have been men, leading to speculation the serial killer might be a woman ... (Police say great proficiency with a knife was used in carving up ...)

"Shut it off, Kel. I don't want to hear that stuff now."

Kelly turned off the radio. "A woman. Sounds like a strong clue in your case, Jo."

"Yeah, well, I'm not so sure anymore. You were right – it's just speculation to think it's Marla. Seems a way-out possibility now. Still watching though."

"Me too. But I've gone the other way. I'm beginning to see you were making pretty good sense. So, let's make a pact, Jo. If we find anything like, concrete, we gotta call the police."

"If we're not dead first."

"You're beginning to sound like me, you poor sap."

"That far gone, eh?"

"Look, I've got a radical idea. Why not put your theory into action? Isn't that what you snotty college types do?"

"This can't be good."

"Try me. Take Marla to lunch. Ask her where she goes nights. Is she out with men, and if she is, why don't we see any of the guys? Take Melissa. She makes small talk seem like real conversation. You might pick up a hard clue or two."

"Too risky. If she's the one, and she gets suspicious, I'll be a corpse by morning."

"That would be a giant step forward in the case," Kelly smirked.

"That's not funny. I'm serious. You saw how she beat the hell outa that burly guy at the beach. I wouldn't have a chance. But I'll think about it. She's sharp. I'd have to keep it pretty vague. Right now, all I'm seeing are a lot of knives on the table."

Kelly couldn't know that you don't give Joanna a challenge – a tough one, a dangerous one, an impossible one; she could never resist taking it up. She needn't have worried. It proved to be no challenge at all. Marla was happy to oblige and Melissa gushed at the chance for a Girls' outing, suggesting they shop for clothes and sundries in the morning and then lunch to finish. Marla even suggested the lunch place, The Rogue's Gallery, an eatery and bar on the waterfront, half a block from the leather works, site of the latest homicide.

Joanna noticed Marla's particular interest in the Cordovan building both coming and going. But at lunch, she freely volunteered how this was her favourite haunt at night, where she met and danced with boys, but never met one she liked well enough to bring back or introduce to the GITH.

Before the entrée arrived, Marla had answered most of Joanna's unasked questions. And anything she left out, Melissa small-talked innocently out of her. Just like on the beach when she went alone, Marla explained blandly being the centre of attention of every man in the bars she frequented; sometimes, the passion-pressing contests for her favour got a little rough. Yet she told it all in a flat, uncaring tone.

Joanna was somewhat relieved at how forthcoming Marla had been with the details. It settled in her head that she may have been wrong about her. Melissa's help was immeasurable because she could ask questions that never seemed to raise Marla's suspicions. What gave Melissa's input such a ring of normality was the conversation soon turned to her own affairs, specifically her love life with Jeremy. She was overjoyed to have an audience to air her high jinks with 'Jiggins'. It so transported her she even offered to look after the bill.

They should have known. Her card came back NSF after being maxed out that morning clothes-shopping. The two paid the bill, threatening never to do it again until Melissa looked after the string of past debts owed to the GITH.

They Shoot Horses…

Being a bright and sunny day, they decided to walk the few blocks home, some of it through parks and neighbourhoods. It was in Brigham's Circle, a pretty downtown park, the Girls witnessed Marla commit a murder.

It was one of those freak things you couldn't make up. A car was approaching the park in the fast lane, speeding a yellow light, when it blew a tire. A car behind it was going even faster, as the light went red, causing it to crash into the first car. The impact sent the lead car careening into the bike lane where it hit a mounted policeman head-on. The horse screamed wild-eyed and pitched over, throwing its rider 10 feet into the park's flower beds right in front of the Girls. They screamed and jumped back. Marla reached down and with one arm brought the police officer to his feet; he seemed dazed. The other Girls stood agog, their parcels strewn around them. The horse was braying in pain and flailing two of its legs. Marla went over to examine it. She tried to hold its neck, but it jerked out of her grip. She went back to speak to the policeman.

"This horse must be destroyed now," said Marla. "Two legs are broken and it's got some broken ribs and probably some internal bleeding …"

"Are you a veterinarian?" he asked.

"No, but I've killed lots of animals. This horse is finished. It's got to be put down. Now."

"I can't do that. I'm not authorised. I'll call the city's emergency animal services. It's their …"

"You can do it," pleaded Melissa. "The horse is suffering. You've got a gun. Don't let it go on. He's in pain."

"Now back up, ladies, this is police business …"

"Give me the gun. I'll shoot it. I know exactly how to do it."

"Do it. Give her the gun," said Joanna. "You can't wait. Don't make the poor creature suffer any more."

Marla held out her firm and confident hand. "Now."

The policeman hesitated, taking in her strong, stoical presence. He unlatched his holster strap and handed her the pistol. Marla took the gun, released the safety, cocked the trigger and hid it behind her back. The policeman spoke to the mounting crowd to back away. She went over to the horse. Pressing her hand down hard on his upper neck, she quickly put the gun to the sub-orbital depression in the forehead and fired. The horse flinched sharply a few times, then lay quiet. Marla stood up, put the gun on safety and handed it back to the officer, heft out. She smiled at him! Joanna's eyes widened as she saw her blithe composure.

"Thanks. You weren't kidding. You have done that before," said the policeman.

"Yup. I worked in a slaughterhouse."

"I'll need you to come down to the station."

"You'll have trouble explaining how a civilian killed with your gun," said Joanna. "Better say you did it. We'll be your other witnesses."

"It'll be all right," added Marla. "I'll back you up. I've lived with most kinds of animals. I know when something has to be killed."

He thought for a moment. "You're right. Okay. What're your names?"

The policeman called Animal Services to deal with the dead horse and took Marla to the police station. A witness gave the licence number of the hit-and-run driver who had cravenly flapped away with a flat tire. The Girls were told they may be called for statements later and were then released to go home. First thing, Joanna headed for Kelly's room.

"How'd the lunch go?"

"You'll never guess what happened."

"What?"

"We saw Marla *kill* in broad daylight. She's with the police now."

"Sure, and my name's Carmen Santiago."

"Melissa's getting the others. Come on upstairs."

"Hey! You're serious? Tell me what the shit you mean!"

Joanna was first up. She opened a chilled Soave and poured while they assembled.

"Where's Brian?" she asked.

"Open house, probably," said Melissa. "He'll be home soon."

"Okay, let's not wait," said Kelly. "What's this all about?"

Melissa bubbled in, "We saw Marla kill a police horse in Brigham's Circle and she did it with the cop's gun. She took it right off him and shot the horse in the head."

"Jo, can you translate what Melissa just said?" asked Kelly.

"Yeh, a car hit a police horse in the park. We were there. The poor animal was past it. Marla told the cop to shoot him, said he was beyond help. The cop said no, against regulations; so she said 'Give me the gun, I'll do it'. It went back and forth; finally, he gave her the gun, and she shot him between the eyes cool-as-a-cucumber. I watched her right after and she was totally deadpan, no emotional reaction at all. I told the cop he'd be in big doo-doo for giving his gun to a civilian to kill his horse. So, he took Marla to the police station as an expert witness to tell the powers-that-be that *he* killed the horse. We gave our names as witnesses, and he let us go."

"Slaughterhouse Sally strikes again," said Kelly. "Holy bloody shit!"

"She's one cool tool, that Girl," pulsed Shakira. "First that big bro on the beach, now the steed of champeens: who's she gonna Tik Tok next?"

"She deserves a medal for what she did," said Melissa. "She should, but she won't."

"Who deserves a medal?" asked Brian, just arriving.

"Marla," said Kelly. "She shot a cop's horse with his own gun and pegged it on him so he wouldn't get in trouble."

"What? That doesn't make any sense."

Joanna then gave him the long version. His jaw was stuck at open. Shakira handed him a glass of wine and he took a giant swig.

"That's amazing. Where's our very own horse killer now?"

"With the police, saving Blue Boy's ass," said Kelly. "He'll probably get a medal and she'll get 30 days and a steady diet of baked beans."

"I hate baked beans," said Marla, striding in with a loose gait and slight smile.

"There she is, the killer of the hour," said Brian. "Quite a step up from rats, honey."

"Rats're a step down, *honey*. What'd you think we killed in the slaughterhouse – possums?"

Shakira diaphragm-laughed. "They jus' don' git up and go kill no possums in that big bad abattoir, baby!"

That night, around 2 am, Joanna suddenly woke up to see a large dark figure standing by her bed. It was Marla, her form unmistakable.

"Marla?"

"I want you to tell me the real reason for taking me to lunch."

"Do you see something sinister in it?"

"No tricks. Answer."

"Curiosity. You obviously meet men or maybe women when you're out so much, but no one comes back. The Girls were curious. That's all."

Marla stood there, silent. Joanna knew to say nothing more. Moments went by. Then Marla quickly put her face close to Joanna's.

"I won't be happy if I find you're spying on me. Be careful, Jo."

"Relax, Marla. You're imagining things. The Girls all share things. You're one of us. Why shouldn't *you*?"

"Be careful, Jo."

She drifted swiftly away. When the coast was clear, Joanna ran to Kelly's room, shaking badly. She woke up Kelly to tell her what happened.

"Holy shit. She's paranoid. Doesn't mean she's the serial killer, but … shit."

"This is just what I was scared of, Kel. Now she's watching me."

"It's okay, Jo. It's okay. You gave good answers. Great answers. You kept your cool. But you're still shaking. Get in with me, sleep over. C'mon."

Joanna climbed in beside Kelly who held her for a time until the shaking subsided and she fell asleep. When she awoke, Kelly was up with coffee and toast and sat on a bedside chair; Joanna propped up on pillows. They reviewed the incident and what it meant. There were a lot of 'What ifs' and 'I wish I'd saids'. But they agreed in the end Joanna probably assuaged Marla's suspicions. Yet doubt remained.

Celebration

One week had passed. It was Saturday night. Short ribs were grilling in serious hot BBQ sauce, and Brian was standing holding a flute of champagne as the Girls ascended to greet him. Oprah sat in front of him, as if the coming procession was in her honour. She knew it wasn't when Marla surfaced; she vanished. Three of the Girls came with boyfriends – Troyan, Jeremy and a new face, Yonxin Ma. He dealt in jade jewellery and was hawking his trinkets as a vendor on the shopping channel with Joanna.

She introduced him to Brian. "Just call him Ma. He's used to that."

Kelly and Marla came solo and had specifically asked Brian not to ask Jake or Hoppy. Even Kelly's questionable taste in men could not savour the likes of those two.

They took a glass of bubbly and together toasted Brian for scoring two house sales that week – well above asking – and with closings by month's end.

"Thanks, it's been a great week, no one can doubt it, but the jewel in the crown is that big fish on Moncrieff. If I can land that one, I'll buy this old elephant of a building and we'll all live happily ever after."

"Don't bank on it," said Troyan. "Living ever after …"

"You just heard the voice of the enemy. He's one of *three* amigos now who're going to break up this sweet gang of mine. It's happening. I can feel my Girls slipping away …"

The Girls chorused an "Awww".

"We'll come visit, honey boy," said Shakira. "Don' you go cryin' and screamin' 'bout it."

"He can scream all he wants. But if he goes hoarse, he'll get one to the head," quipped Kelly.

"Not from me!" cried Marla.

Brian knew Troyan well from poker, and had met 'Jiggins' on more than one occasion; Ma was new to him, but Brian had an inkling he might be amenable to being part of a plan he was devising about the Girls. He got to each of them separately in the party and arranged a boy's night out later that week at the Beaches' only English-style pub, *The Feather & the Firkin*. The Girls didn't think anything about it. They were always making plans with one another in Brian's presence.

The champagne flowed and the ribs were a hit, cooled by tzatziki dolloped on grilled bakers and a kale and cucumber salad. Someone turned up the volume signalling a time to get up and dance. Predictably, Shakira's fondness for stepping out saw her in a pressing twirl with Troyan and the others soon followed. Brian took turns dancing with them all, especially Kelly and Marla, and was always surprised how supple and surrendering Marla was when she danced with him. He asked her about the outcome of the horse affair.

"Burt, that's the cop, he got off with a slap on the wrist for killing the horse … the one he didn't kill."

"That was down to you, 'saving Blue Boy's ass' – Kelly's words."

"Yup. The Chief believed me. If only he knew. Burt was pretty happy. He said he was knocked out by something I did hundreds of times. Then he asked me out."

"What'd you say?"

"I said I had a mean and jealous boyfriend. Brian wouldn't like it."

Brian laughed. "That's right. If he does it again, *I'll* ask for his gun."

"If you do, I'd make you my boyfriend. The offer stands."

When he picked up with Shakira, he was met with unbridled joy. She was her super self around Troyan. Even while they danced, she kept glancing over as he danced with Kelly.

"If I can ever tear you away from your *man*," said Brian, "we have a date. Remember?"

She looked at him with a twinkling curiosity. "We do? Oh, a game. Sure baby, you got money now. I'll fleece you goood."

"You can try, *baby,* but maybe you better get yourself ready to touch Troy for the loan of a lifetime."

"Ha, in your white dreams. More like you get yerself ready to take an 'L', bro."

"Take an 'L'?"

"Loss, my honey. A big, money-packin' loss."

"R-ight. Then I guess I better sell that big mansion on my listings."

"That's cursed. You're gonna need everythin' you got and much, much more."

That was long enough out of Troyan's arms, and as Brian took Melissa's hand, he saw Shakira and Troyan looking at him and laughing.

"Look how happy Shakira is, Melissa. Who could tell she's about to take a 'D'? (Shakira does a diaphragm-jerk.) That's a *dive*!" (She jerks again.)

"What's that about?"

"Oh, a little competitive play over a golf game we're going to have soon. So, what's with you and Jiggins …"

"We're starting to get serious, Brian. At least, I am. We're seeing each other all the time now. He hasn't said anything yet, but I hope he does soon."

"The three of us guys are going to have a beer later this week. I'll see if I can find how far along, he is. If he's about to break his water, I'll tell you …"

"Oh, Brian, if I didn't know you …"

"I think you might end up with everything you wish for."

"I don't trust wishes much. 'If wishes were horses, beggars would ride'. I want something I can take to the bank."

"It's time we decide on a song together, Melissa," said Jeremy, cutting in. "Have you got *Can I have this dance for the rest of my life*, Brian?"

Melissa looks at Brian and nods as if to indicate this is what she wants from Jeremy.

"Yeah, actually, it's on this cycle. You won't have long to wait, not for the rest of your life. Kelly, let's twirl."

"You're having a good time, Bry. So you should. You deserve it."

"I'm waiting for the 'but'."

"Not tonight. I know how I am. But you're giving me nothing to work on. So, it's a night off."

"Nice. But I may need you at your most cryptic soon."

"Why?"

"Stella's coming to visit. She's bringing my two sisters. They're grown up now, but they still treat me like …"

"Shit?"

"Your favourite word and perfect here."

"Who's Stella, the nanny?"

"Probably," said Brian laughing. "Actually, she's our mum. She's great. You'll like her."

"Uh-hu, I can see *you* do, poor mama's boy."

"Joanna, come rescue me …"

"Why do you need rescuing?" said Joanna, stepping easily into Kelly's place.

"I was just telling Kelly my mother and sisters are visiting. You'll be interested in studying the sibling rivalry my two sisters have with me. They're a tough act."

"Not unusual. But the rivalry usually mitigates when the siblings grow up."

"Not these two."

"Interesting. I'll observe and report back, Bry."

"By the way, Ma is joining the men next week for a few drinks at the pub. I'll get a chance to see what he's like."

"Then you observe and report back too. A man's view is something I can't replicate, so knock yourself out."

"Since he's your pick, I can sort of tell what he's like …"

"Let's have it, kid."

"Serious, studious, thoughtful and … careful."

"Hmm, in other words, dull. No, don't worry. You're 68 per cent right. Other people provide enough excitement around here."

Joanna was looking at Marla when she said that. Brian half turned and stopped. The horse killer lowered her head and gave them an enigmatic look through her sculpted brow. Did she hear?

The two Girls hadn't yet got around to telling Brian about their fears over Marla. But he did wonder if he might catch Marla at the pub, attracting men like iron filings when he dropped in mid-week with the Girls' boyfriends. Not to be. They ordered pints at the bar, then found a long table.

Troyan felt it would help to tell the other two men a little about what to expect from a man who lived with five women who included their girlfriends.

"Shak tells me the Girls find you pretty iconic the way you fit in at an all-girls dorm."

"The secret," Brian replied, "may be the food. Not long after I invaded the place, I cooked for them all. I also took up baking bread. An easy way to draw them in was to leave my door open and let the smells of bread in the oven fill the Hall."

"That does it for me," said Jeremy. "Bread's one of my weaknesses."

"Really? Then Melissa has probably shared some of what I bake for the Girls."

"Yeah, I've tasted your brioche and Zop, is that right?"

"Zopf. Yeah, that's a favourite, a braided bread from Europe. Great for breakfast. So, you're still there in the morning to eat it then."

They all laughed as Jeremy nodded. "Guilty as charged. And I want my life sentence to be that I can be around to taste it *every* morning."

Troyan furthered. "Me too. The Multigrain is my breakfast pick. I may have to buy you a bakery to keep my morning loaf comin', bro."

"That's two confessions. What about you, Ma?"

"Nope, not yet … glad to know I've got it coming. I never thought fresh bread would be the metric for morning-after confessions."

"If you get your bakery, Brian," said Jeremy, "keep the Ciabattas coming as well. Mel likes to make paninis."

"When do you find the time?" asked Troyan. "Shak says you're always working. When do you find time to supply the entire building with … baked goods?"

Brian laughed. "It's the way I relax. I make four loaves at a time and wrap half a loaf in foil. And I label their names on them. The Girls come in every morning now. They like the ones you guys like, so I bake them most. They don't like Soda Bread or Sourdough much, so I get to eat those."

"So, the reason they let you live a bachelor's paradise is you're useful," said Jeremy.

"Yeah," said Brian, "and happy to live a fabled life with the Amazons."

"One of 'em sure is, that Marla, oooeeee!" said Troyan. "She's GOAT!"

The others nodded with concentrated stares. Whatever spell Marla cast over men also charmed the four around this table with her abracadabra.

"Yeah, she's pretty unique," said Brian. "There's something a bit scary about her, but she's the one I like the most. We seem to understand each other."

"Unique isn't the word!" said Troyan. "She shoots horses, doesn't she?"

"Yeah, she did. Used to slaughter animals. We kill the rats in the building too. Oprah has pretty much taken over that job now."

"Amazing," said Jeremy. "You'd never guess that back story from the way she looks. She's a *babe*! And I've never used that word before."

Ma wasn't going to commit. He just smiled wanting to agree.

"Okay, guys, I've actually got something I want to talk to you about. Unless you want to make it all about Marla."

"No, it's pointless," said Ma. "We're unavailable … and something tells me she's unattainable."

"I agree," said Brian. "So, let's move on."

"I presume you want to talk about something pertaining to the Girls," said Jeremy.

"Yeah. A little while back, Shakira came across a contest that would send two people on a safari to Africa. They loved the idea and three of them entered. No word yet. But I've been thinking …"

"… winning's a long shot, so you want us to ante up to make it a sure thing," inserted Troyan.

"In a word, yes. I'm on the verge of a windfall commission and might be able to handle it all myself. But I thought you guys might want to participate in what will be a last blast for the Girls together …"

"… before they're married off," inserted Jeremy.

"You're making this too easy for me. If one of them does win the contest …"

"… thousands-to-one against," inserted Ma.

"R-ight, but if it happens, two of them are looked after. Otherwise we've got four to send off on this two-week junket. When you ask? July.

What does the contest cover? Only the land portion, not air. What'd you think? You want in?"

Troyan already had it worked out: "I want in. I've got an executive jet that can take them there and back …"

"Shakira mentioned that," said Brian.

"She did, did she? Already the Diva of Bailey Street, and no ring on her finger."

"She knows her man," said Brian.

"The plane and Shak. That's my part."

"That's great. Either way, the 'air' is a big boost. What about you two?"

"Too early for me," said Ma. "If you asked me in another six months … the way things are going … I'd say okay. But not now."

"I don't want to put any money into this," said Jeremy. "And the reason is I'm secretly – get it? – secretly saving for our first house. Her family may want to give us one, but I won't let them. How's about I invest in a party when they come back. I could help with that."

"I'll help too … with the party," said Ma. "Jo's worth that much."

"I can't wait to tell Joanna you said that!" said Brian.

Ma laughed. "She won't care. She'll think it's funny."

"He knows his Girl too," said Brian.

"One codicil I'd add," said Jeremy, "Melissa's parents. I can't help but I can ask Mel to speak to her parents. They'll pay her way and she can probably get what monies you need to help otherwise."

"Sounds good. You speak to her first. I'll have her in tomorrow night."

"Leave it with me. It'll mean she'll have to be put in the loop though."

"Yeah, she will. Anyway, Shakira and Melissa are now looked after. That leaves me and maybe Melissa to pay for Joanna and Marla."

"What about Kelly?" asked Troyan.

"No, she's got a buyer's trip, so that lets her out. The other thing I should mention is I want them to think they won the trip regardless … that we had nothing to do with it. That way, they won't feel any obligation. I'll arrange it with the company in Africa."

"The contest is for two," said Ma. "How are you going to explain a win for four."

"Lie. I'll get the company to tell them the contest got such a big response that they decided to make it for four people."

"This is complicated," said Jeremy. "What happens if the real contest winners are bragging about the free trip they got and the Girls are around to hear it? You're busted."

"No, I'll screw that down and all the other loose ends with the company. Their entire staff will have to be sworn to secrecy. No leaks."

"No wonder you survive living with five women," said Jeremy. "Sheer cunning."

"It's nothing. It comes with the satin sheets."

They grappled to grasp what that meant; he smiled slyly.

"Let me know when you'll need the jet. I'll have to reserve the time."

"Sure, as soon as I've got it in motion," said Brian, "and thanks."

"One question," said Ma. "Are you going?"

"No. I've been. And I don't want any other man going with my Girls."

"Listen to this guy, *my* Girls!" said Jeremy.

Troyan laughed. "If you can roast chicken with Marla, and good luck, you won't be cuffing with our Girls. RIP to that, bro."

"I don't know what 'cuffing' means, but RIP I know and I'll add *res ipsa loquitur*," said Jeremy.

"Your code words don't protect you, they betray you. It's clear as paint that you two are ripe-to-rotting for the altar."

The next evening, Brian had Melissa in to speak about the holiday. Jeremy, as promised, had already called her about getting help from her parents.

"I think it's a wonderful thing you're doing for us, Brian. So generous and kind. I'm sure I can get my parents to help. I asked Jigs why he wouldn't help and he said he couldn't. I don't believe that …"

"He told me why, Melissa, but I'm sworn to secrecy. Believe me, if you knew, it would make you cry."

She stared at him emotionally. "Oh, then it's something for us?"

"Let me put it this way. I told the boys about baking bread for all of us. And I tricked him into revealing he was eating the Zopf at breakfast with you. Then he said, 'I would like to be around *every* morning to eat it'."

"He said that?" Melissa put her hands to her face overwrought, then she broke out into a laugh. "Wow, wow, wow! Thank you, Brian. You said you'd find out if he's ready, and he is, he is, he is! (She throws arms up.) Wheeee!"

Brian smiled broadly at her, saying nothing. He gave her a few moments to enjoy her feelings of elation. When she was ready, he outlined his subterfuge that would send the Girls to Africa.

Weeds in the Garden   **5**

It is a truth universally acknowledged that a single man, in possession of two older sisters, must be in need of relief. To them, Brian would always be embryonic, unchanging and limp. Ironically, they were the ones who reverted: catty teenagers belittling a brother who had advanced well past their stuck mind-set of him. He anticipated little change but held out hope when they came with Stella for a visit.

The doorbell sounded. It rang only in Brian's suite, something unchanged from the time the controlling old grouch had lived there. He ran down the Hall and into the waiting arms of Stella who gushed a happy greeting.

"Oh, my boy, how lovely, lovely, lovely to see you."

His sisters, Tracy and Lorilyn, stood waiting their turn. When he opened his arms to embrace each of them, one punched him in the arm.

Tracy: "Hello, fat brother, still as ugly as ever."

And the other pushed him hard in the chest to avoid a hug.

Lorilyn: "Living with other girls still 'as done nothing for your fashion sense, I see."

"You promised, girls, be nice to your brother."

The sisters were both dressed in patterned sun dresses, very suited to their figures, with carefully chosen accessories. Their appearance was calculatingly perfect. Wedding rings adorned their fingers, but no husbands draped their arms.

"Tracy, Lorilyn. I think you'll like the Girls I live with. And you'll get to meet them all. (He was leading them down the Hall.) I know you'll like this, Stella: The Girls research and read uplifting stories to each other.

Joanna has her turn today. She's a psychologist, so we're curious to hear what she'll come up with."

"Oh boy," said Tracy, "he's found a bunch of Pollyannas to shack up with. This is going to be rich."

"And I bet they just love, love, love our baby brother," added Lorilyn. "Poor, blind mice."

"Girls?" admonished Stella.

"Where's Dad?"

"He's down with the flu, dear," said Stella, holding his arm affectionately. "He's very sorry. But he said he'd take another trip when he's better, just you two."

"Too bad, I've missed him."

"Not as much as your adorable sisters, I bet," said Tracy.

"Yes, I'm sure you just *pined* away for us," added Lorilyn.

They both giggled to each other. Stella gave them both a stern look.

"Well, I have missed you, my darling, more than you can know."

"Thanks, Stella. You're never far from my thoughts."

"Mother always loved you best," said Lorilyn.

"Brian this and Brian that all our lives," said Tracy wearily.

"Stop that, just stop it," said Stella irritably. "Keep to your promise – no more of your cut-up."

That subdued them until they reached the patio and met the GITH. Stella was amused with Brian calling out 'Man on Deck' near the top of the stairs. The Girls had put on light kimonos and crochet kaftans over their bathing suits mainly for the visiting guests. Brian sat his family down with drinks. Stella led the conversation praising the rooftop set-up; the Girls told her it was her son's handiwork. The sisters glowered.

"Thanks for waiting, Girls," he said. "I think we're ready now. Joanna?"

"Thanks Bry. Well, my story is a sad fantasy with a supernatural element. I know you expected some deep psychological saga from me, but this story is a favourite of mine. I think you'll be touched by it too."

The two sisters looked at each other and rolled their eyes.

Never Too Late to Say Goodbye

"Single-mother Brenda had been making heartbreaking trips to the Metropolitan Childrens Hospital for six months to see Harper, her ten-year old boy. He was all she had in the world and the thought of losing him to cancer was unbearable, but all too real. 'm afraid there's no hope," Dr Doumouras said to her quietly. "I'm sorry, the end is very near. It's time to say your goodbyes."

Brenda went to sit by his little hospital bed and held his hand. Tears streamed down her face. Her very will to live was ebbing from her. Harper was in a coma and couldn't consciously hear her last words. Dr Doumouras had her hand on Brenda's shoulder as the boy slowly slipped away. The young mother grabbed up her son in her arms and held him tightly, sobbing uncontrollably. The nurse turned off the whining monitor.

In a few minutes, Brenda released her son and put his little head with those golden curls gently back on the pillow.

"Goodbye my darling, my darling boy. Take my love, all my love with you. O Father, look after my child, my treasure until I can be with him again."

"Stay with him as long as you like, Brenda," said Dr Doumouras. Both she and the nurse were mothers; the loss of Harper was unavoidably personal. They left the room wiping away tears.

Brenda sat by his bedside, mercifully in a numbing state, watching her son's little face take on that soft light, the radiance of peaceful death. She had no words then; the intense, painfully intimate togetherness would shatter with words. This soulful communion would end all too soon, but not quite yet. Just a little longer.

In a few minutes, the nurse came back in. It broke the spell.

"Oh, I'm sorry, do you need more time?"

Brenda roused herself, "No, I've had my time with my sweet boy." She bent over and kissed his forehead. "Goodbye, goodbye, my own heart." Her tears wet his brow. She wiped them away.

"I'm so, so sorry for your loss," broke the nurse.

"Thank you," Brenda nodded grimacing as she gathered her purse and a bag the staff had stuffed with his favourite things from home. At the door, she couldn't decide if she would turn and look at Harper again or just walk on, so as not to prolong the pain.

"Mummy," came a small voice.

The nurse reacted with a cry and rushed out to get the doctor. "Harper, is that you?" she cried, rushing to his bedside, grabbing his hand.

His eyes were open and he looked at her smiling, the soft light of death still on his face.

"They let me come back, Mummy. They let me come back and say goodbye to you."

"Oh, my sweetie, my sweetie, stay with me, never leave me, don't go."

"I can't Mummy. I have to go back. But I wanted to come and tell you, I'm okay. No pain anymore. I feel great. No, I feel terrific!"

Brenda laughed almost boisterously, "That's wonderful, my darling. I'm so glad."

"It's amazing over there in the other place. You'll really like it. I asked the angels to bring you over, but they said it's not time for you yet. I told them I want to be with you. So, they said go back and say goodbye, but that's all."

"Thank them for me, darling. It means everything to have this last time with you."

"I love you so much, Mummy. Everyone does over there. But not as much as me. I love you best."

"And I love you best, the bestest of the bestest."

"Me too, the bestest of the bestest. Oh, they're calling me. I gotta go. Goodbye Mummy, goodbye."

His eyes closed, his mouth went into a seraphic little smile and that pastel light shone from his face.

Brenda stroked his face. The little miracle had filled her heart with a contented solace. She stood up and turned. The staff burst in and stared, but there was nothing to see. The little miracle was private, just for Brenda and her darling boy.

"That's a delightful little story, Joanna," said Stella. "Wherever did you find it? Just delightful."

"A story any mother would love, even ours," said Lorilyn.

"With Harry Potter for a son," added Tracy.

"What's Harry Potter got to do with it?" said Kelly, dabbing her eyes. "It's just a tender story of a mother who lost her son."

Tears wet the cheeks of all the Girls, except Marla and the sisters. Kleenex was passed around with a light laughter. The box was handed to Brian who also wiped. The Girls smiled at that. The sisters pointed at him and tittered.

"I'm glad you liked it, Mrs Upjohn," said Joanna. "It was in one of my texts at university. It was a fantasy example used to show the importance of ritual endings in the grieving process."

Stella nodded. "It would be the hardest thing in the world to lose a son. I can't imagine losing Brian. It would be like losing my very heart."

"We feel the same way, ma'am. We love Brian," said Melissa.

"What, like a mascot?" asked Lorilyn.

"Or a cheerleader in pants?" asked Tracy.

They twittered. The Girls frowned.

"Girrrrls," Stella threatened.

"Say, Joanna, have we met before?" asked Tracy. "You look very familiar."

"I get that all the time. I work for the Shopping Channel. You've seen me there."

"Do you hear that, Lorilyn?"

"We know tons of people who buy off the Shopping Channel. No one who *works* there!"

They giggled. Joanna stared at them incredulously.

"What's so bad about that?" asked Kelly. "It's a good job. What do you girls do?"

"Nothing," they both said.

"And proud of it," said Tracy.

"Very proud," added Lorilyn.

"We're all working Girls, and we're proud of *that*, aren't we, Girls?" posed Melissa.

"Doin' nuttin', sittin' around tryin' to look pretty ain't my idea of a life, sistas," said Shakira.

"Oh, we agree," said Lorilyn. "*Trying* to look pretty is no life at all."

"Not our problem, dears," said Tracy smugly, producing another mutual giggle.

Brian was serving his latest idea – a caviar and boursin-filled scone. Lorilyn took one with a napkin and nibbled at it daintily.

"Aghhh, Brian, what'd you put in this?" cried Lorilyn.

"It's gone off!" said Tracy. "Don't eat it, Girls. Our brother'll poison you."

Lorilyn: "Still useless. Can't put flour and milk together and make a simple scone."

"That's not true!" countered Melissa. "Brian is a wonderful cook and a wonderful baker. We just love the great breads he makes for us, all kinds too. In fact, we never buy out anymore."

"I pity your taste buds if you eat his bread," said Tracy. "Mum tried to teach him lots of times and all he could come up with were rocks!"

"Now, now, they were good first attempts," said Stella. "Don't be so mean Tracy. These are excellent, darling. Very creative."

"Thanks, Stella. And you too Melissa. But, you know, I probably wasn't much good back then. Tracy isn't all wrong. I think my baking's improved though."

"Don't put money on it," said Lorilyn.

"We would, Lorilyn," said Joanna. "Brian's so good, he could open a bakery. We'd all be his permanent customers."

"Get this sistas," declared Shakira, "Our Bry's no oaf with a loaf."

"No oaf with a loaf, where'd that come from, Shak?" asked Kelly. "That's good."

Lorilyn noticed Marla, who was passive and contained. "You're obviously the strong, silent type. What do you do?"

"Oh, this is gonna be good," smiled Kelly.

"I'm a butcher. I tether up large animals and knife out choice cuts of meat while the animals are still alive and screaming so your meat is fresh when you buy."

This horrific image stunned the sisters but broke the tension enough for the rest of the company to burst into relieved laughter. Marla wasn't laughing, of course, instead giving Lorilyn that enigmatic look under her brow.

"Marla's just joking, Lorilyn," Brian laughed. "But she *is* a butcher. She provides all the meat for the household from a high-end butcher shop down the road."

"Creepy!" said Lorilyn, nodding gravely with Tracy.

"Come and sit by me, Brian," said Stella. "We need to chat. I want to take something back to tell your father about what you're up to. He'll want to know. And so do I, of course, my darling."

The Girls were not particularly pleased to be left with the sisters, knowing they were in for a full session of Brian-bashing and, quite unsolicited, they got it.

"It's so funny to see Brian living with so many girls," said Tracy. "He could never keep a girl for long …"

"He smelled, you know, real BO. Dad used to say, 'Brian, you stink like a stag, hit the tub now'!" said Lorilyn. "No girl wanted to be inside ten blocks of ole stinky."

"Remember this Lor'? We'd hear him in his room, calling some girl's name and groaning away. We'd bust in and he'd duck under the covers, so we couldn't see his little prong!" (They laughed, one patting the knee of the other.)

"Of course, we always did and we'd laugh about it after. Oh, fun times."

Kelly, who was the most cynical of the Girls, seemed the most outraged.

"We don't want to hear these stories about Brian. We like him and live here with him. If you have to talk about him, say something nice. Okay?"

"I agree," said Melissa. "Brian's a fine man. He doesn't deserve this. I don't care how he was as a boy. He's great now. Isn't that what's important?"

This was met with a little disappointment between the sisters, who pouted slightly. After a pause, they started up again.

"Let's see, something positive," said Lorilyn. "Well, he doesn't stink anymore."

"And his skin has cleared up nicely," said the other. "Thank *God*!"

"Oh, Trace, remember everybody avoided him like he had a disease."

"Yes, his nickname was 'Brian the Boil'."

They laughed wide-mouthed at that. The Girls started to shift in their chairs and looked at one another with true irritation.

"I still remember the rhyme we made up," said Tracy. "Say it with me, Lor'."

"Acne, Acne on his face,
The worst, the worst of any case,
Father, Father, give us grace,
Lost, lost to the human race."

At that, the sisters applauded with tiny claps as they laughed over such a happy remembrance.

"Girls!" said Stella. "You have broken your promise to me. Now stop it or we'll have to leave."

The Girls surely thought what a wonderful idea that was. They already loved Stella but had no time for her daughters. They looked at Marla, knowing she didn't suffer fools gladly or anyone much else for that matter. So, they wondered how she was taking this assassination. But she seemed impassive to it all.

"Brian," Marla called, "shall I get the lamb burgers from the downstairs fridge?"

"Yes, thanks Marla. Bring up the buns too. They're on the counter."

By the time she came back, carrying the trays, the sisters were back on a roll.

"No normal pack leader would lead a boy scout troupe and get lost for two days on the most famous hiking trail, *The Lion's Head*, with signs every ten feet …"

"They had to helicopter them out. Or how about that sailing regatta at the cottage when we were 18?"

"Oh, what a riot! He used to go on what a great sailor he was and then in the big race, he swamped his boat and caused damage to two others …"

"That isn't true," said Stella. "That happened, but Brian wasn't responsible."

"No, Mum, he was always there when disaster hit. Everyone blamed him. Look at how he broke everything he touched in the house …"

"I don't remember him breaking anything, Tracy. You're imagining all that. As I recall, you were the one who broke things most of the time."

"No, Mum, it was Brian. I remember it like it was yesterday."

"Brian," said Marla, "shall I fire up the grill?"

"I can do that, Marla."

"No, I'm happy to do it."

Lorilyn stood up and wandered over to where Marla was getting out the lighter. She looked over the paddies on the tray.

"Oh, Trace, you ought to see these."

"What about them?"

"They look like meadow muffins. More Brian Specials."

The sisters giggled, not knowing that Marla had clicked on the lighter and 'accidentally' set the hem of Lorilyn's dress on fire. Soon, she started to scream. Brian was up and over to the large metal bucket of ice that had tinned beer and pop in it.

"Quick, Marla, grab one end and we'll pour it on her."

The two grabbed the bucket, strained to lift it; Marla managed to hoist it higher, both surrendering – too heavy. Lorilyn's dress was more than half up in flames, her screaming shrill, the Girls over with towels. Stella elbowed through them, grabbed Lorilyn and pushed her forcefully on the bucket. She fell back into the bucket, her legs awry, her frilly underwear immodestly exposed, amid the sizzle and smoke of the dying fire. Tins and ice were displaced around the bucket. One moment later, Stella grabbed Lorilyn under her arms and lifted her up, looking in her eyes.

"Are you burnt, dear, are you in pain?"

"I … I … don't …" Lorilyn broke down in tears.

Tracy grabbed a beach towel from one of the Girls and placed it around her middle and started to take her down to Brian's bathroom. Stella turned to face Marla.

"I saw what you did, Marla. And I know it was no accident. It was a wilful and deliberate act. I know it and you know it. I know my girls have been a trial today, but Lorilyn didn't deserve this. You should be ashamed of yourself. What have you got to say for yourself?"

"She got in the way of the flame before I could move it away. And I was about to push her in the bucket when you came and did it. That doesn't mean she didn't deserve it. They both deserve whatever they get, a couple of brainless little bitches!"

Stella then smacked Marla hard across the face. Marla hardly moved from the blow but looked at Stella with a look of amazement and seeming pleasure. There was a definite stifled smile. Brian then stepped in. He put his arms around both their shoulders.

"All right. It's done. Let's leave it there. Stella, why not go down and see how bad the burns are. There's some Polysporin in the bathroom cabinet. If it's bad, I'll drive you all to the hospital. You can find some lounge pants and a sweat shirt of mine she can wear."

Stella looked at Brian. She softened and kissed his cheek. Not looking at Marla again, she turned and strode downstairs. The Girls gathered around Marla.

"Well, shit, Marla. I wouldn't have done it," said Kelly, "and you shouldn't have done it. But I'm fucking happy it happened."

The Girls finally had a turn to laugh after an afternoon of frowns and frustrations.

"Kelly," said Brian, "you don't mean that …"

"Oh yes, I do," she responded. "I'm sorry. And I think all the Girls feel the same way. Marla was right. I'm sorry. They're both a couple of shitty little bitches."

Brian shrugged, as if not disagreeing.

Melissa started, "I don't know how you lived with those two all those years…"

"I didn't have much choice, love …"

"No, but you turned out to be a great guy, despite them," said Joanna. "Good on you, boy."

"Those salty, small sardines are Extra!" said Shakira. "That's the only word for it. But you're GOAT, Bry."

Shakira hugged him. And the other Girls took turns hugging him too. Marla was the last to do so …

"A little tight, sweetie," said Brian. (She took her arms away and he stroked her cheek.) "You know, Girls, they're not usually so bad. They're performing today."

"I know what's going on here," said Joanna. "Simple reversion. Seeing you brought back all those memories and reflexes for them from years ago, and they simply relived them. It happens in families all the time: you stay stuck on how a person was and think that's how they still are. It's never true."

"Thank you, doctor," said Kelly. "You can explain it away all you like. To me, they're both two shit-fed little bimbos."

Stella came back up.

"Lorilyn's all right. A little redness, a little sore, but she's not in any pain. We were lucky. But they want to go. Go down and say goodbye Brian. (He nodded and left.) I know the girls have been difficult. It's a long story. I see how much you like Brian. How could you not? Such a dear boy. I know I'm his mother. And I didn't like what they said any more than you. That didn't justify setting her on fire, Marla. That's a criminal act. You had better watch yourself in future …"

"Yes, you better, you fucking monster," said Lorilyn, who slipped up to the patio's entrance in Brian's clothes twice too big for her – pants and sleeves rolled up – but still in her elegant high heels. Her coiffed, golden hair was transgressed.

"All right, Lorilyn, time to go …"

"Look at me, Marilyn. Look what you've done to me. My wonderful sun dress is burnt to shreds. Ruined forever. I've got to go back looking like this. How could you? You're insane, you're a physiopath. You ought to burn …"

"Lorilyn, now!" said Stella, leading her away. "Good bye, Girls."

"Good bye, Mrs Upjohn," they all said randomly.

"She could-a killed me, Momma. How could anyone be so horrible? Tim will have a fit."

Her exclamations faded as they descended. The Girls sat down and said nothing. Two of them shook their heads.

Kelly suddenly said: "She should be happy she didn't get any crispier."

The Girls laughed at that, then protested with 'oh-no' admonishments.

"What you don't know, Girls, I would've saved her, just like Stella. I wouldn't want her to die. She's got years and years of suffering and setbacks to live through. I would never want to deprive her of those."

Brian didn't come back after his family had gone. The GITH went ahead and had dinner without him. Somehow, they understood. They imagined he had been very embarrassed by it all. Unlike him to disappear like that, so they felt pretty sure that was it. Later than night they had cause to find him endearing in a brand new way.

Silk Trappings

They checked periodically but gave up at 11 o'clock for his return. Then, around one or two in the wee hours, they were awakened by loud banging at the front door. Marla, who was closest, got up and went to investigate. The others soon joined her.

Marla asked through the outside door, "Who is it?"

"Brianski. Friend of the Covington Five!"

"Brian!" said Marla. "Must've forgotten his keys."

She opened the door. The others crowded behind her. No one was there. Brian had collapsed in a pile beside the front steps. They were concerned at first, but seeing he was hopelessly drunk, rushed to help him. Marla and Kelly took Brian's arms around their necks and put their arms around his waist and heaved him up for the journey to his rooms. Joanna and Shakira followed them. Melissa went ahead, turning the lights on in his suite and pulling the covers down on his bed.

"Ah, my Girls, my Girls. Thank yooo. Ha. I knew yooo'd come rescue moi and my drunken little ass …"

"Boy, are you squiffed, Bry," said Kelly.

"Yuppy yup, my lovely. Blotto is more like it … Mmmm, who's got me by the waist? I likey …"

"Likey all you want, big boy. You won't remember what happened with your Girls in the morning."

"Oooo. Are all my Girls taking me to bed? Not sure I can handle IT! Oh, there's Marla. Mmm, you're a ripe bananana."

"Thanks Brian, didn't think you ever noticed."

"Oooo, yeah! You fill the screen, peach face."

The Girls were laughing in mock-shock. They got him to his bedroom and lay him gently on the bed.

"I love all of my vuunderful voluptuous … lovey … dovey …"

He was gone and snoring arrived.

"This is new for me," said Melissa. "Do we take off his clothes?"

"He won't know," said Marla. "But women would feel violated."

"Right on, Marl," said Shakira. "C'mon, he's our boy. Let's look after him."

"And what does that look like?" asked Joanna. "Covers over him fully clothed?"

Kelly: "Normally. But for Bry, let's make it more comfy – down to his undies."

Marla: "Agreed. I'll strip off his trousers."

Shakira: "I'll rip off his shirt."

Joanna: "I'll tear off his shoes …"

Melissa: "I'll shed his socks …"

Kelly: "I'll grab his dutch oven."

Melissa: "Woo. What's that when that's at home?"

Three together: "A pot to puke in!"

They went about removing his clothes. When they had him down to his underwear, they all laughed. Brian was wearing *silk* underwear in a pinkish, lavender hybrid colour. Hidden elegance by accident. It touched and tickled them.

"Silk underwear!" said Shakira. "That's Gucci in more ways than one."

"First time for me," said Kelly, "and I've seen some pretty fancy duds."

They got the covers over a grunting Brian. Each of them bent over and kissed him:

"Good night, Bry."

Melissa said, "Nighty-night, Bry, in your sweet, puce silk undies."

The Girls stood watching him when Marla asked:

"Why didn't he use the fire escape? He wouldn't've locked the patio door."

"We don't use the fire escape when we're sober. Imagine, drunk."

"Good, Mel," said Kelly. "He was so out of it, probably didn't even occur to him. But you're right, it'd be suicide."

Before they filtered out, Joanna picked up his keys on the counter to show where he had forgotten them.

Marla: "We better check on him in the morning."

Joanna: "Don't think so. Better make it one or two in the afternoon."

Kelly: "No, I'll drop in first thing and make sure he isn't swimming in his own vomit. He might miss the pot."

Melissa: "What if he chokes on his sick? Maybe someone should stay with him …"

Joanna: "He'll wake if he upchucks."

Marla: "Unless you want to stay with him, Mel …"

Melissa: "No, no. I didn't mean that …"

Their laughter trailed off as the Girls went to their apartments with 'good nights' dropping at every door. Marla took her key out of the front door's deadbolt, then glided along to her place. Happy silence settled over the scene. Nearly. Someone with acute hearing might have picked up that undulative sound of snoring coming from the far room along the Hall.

Was it an apology to the GITH? By 9 am that day, the not-so-subtle sniff of a Caramel Pecan Sweet Bread with a pulverised chocolate and icing sugar topping suffused that hallowed Hall. It brought the Girls to Number 1, with their plates and tongues out. Not a word was said about all the bubble and squeak the day before, for life was now thankfully, tastefully restored by good baking. It seemed to put everyone back in that happy slot. Except Brian wasn't there. He baked it the day before for the party and heated it up and added the topping that morning before going back to bed for the day.

The Game's Afoot

A day or two later, a long-awaited threat came to pass. A silver Acura swirled around the circular drive at Delhaven Golf Course and came to a stop. Brian got out and climbed the front steps to be greeted with a gangly embrace.

"Your day of doom is here, bro," said Shakira smiling.

"Those about to win, salute you, sis," said Brian, smiling back.

The fated golf game between the two would be played just as an offer on his big listing on Moncrieff Crescent was being reviewed by the owners. He could shrug if the game went south because he was a cell call away from hearing his fat commission went north. The sale was as good as inked. But he was told he had a free day because the sellers meant to deliberate in their decision. Shakira took him to the pro shop for a set of clubs.

"Ah, yes. I get the trick clubs to guarantee you pros win your nassaus."

Shakira diaphragm-wrenched. "We'll switch bags, honey. Doomsday doesn't care."

When he saw Shakira's swing at the first tee, he feared he was going to lose most of the holes at 20 dollars a pop. Delhaven permitted this practice with their pros because the club took nine of every ten dollars gambled. Despite his bravura, Brian had fully expected she would dominate play. What he looked forward to was talking to her as they played. He saw Shakira as having a distillate savviness; she could capiche, consider and conclude with the best of them. Brian wanted her viewpoint about what the future held for their happy band.

She explained the change for the GITH started when he brought the 'brothers' in for poker. Doors started to close. When the Girls met boyfriends, the girls' open-door circus was further curtailed. Then when those boyfriends started to go behind some of the closed doors, *laissez-faire* moved out.

"So it's men that fouled our happy nest," said Brian.

"Yeah, baby. When we don't *need* 'em, that's iconic. Then, bang, we *want* 'em, that's scabrous."

The front nine saw five birdies for her to his nine pars. Brian was not disgracing himself because Delhaven was not a difficult course. It would never hold a pro championship on its turf. The two played on.

He asked if she thought they'd get to Africa. She said that Troyan agreed to provide the plane and pay her way but wouldn't pick up all the costs. Melissa could get the money. But for Marla and Joanna to go, they'd need to win the lottery.

Brian noticed that, except when he broached her on a subject, she concentrated on the play. She had all the earmarks of the pro; she'd use a three wood off the tee (to his driver) and still go longer, liked hybrids for approach shots, long-viewed either end of the hole before putting and she'd help him, despite money on the game, with best club selection and reading the greens. In the end, it was the game, not money.

Then Brian pressed her on another thing he was curious about: in her view, how did the GITH feel about Marla?

"She's one dangerous chick, Bry. Sure, she looks snatched, but somepun ain't wired right there. Beatin' up that bozo on the beach and lightin' up your sister, that's scary. It's brewin' for a bruisin' and we ain't gonna like it. Jo's doin' her psyche trip on her and tol' us to step light 'round her. We're all woke to that."

Holing out on the 18th, Brian did better on the back nine, owing her a hundred and fifty dollars. When they went to the clubhouse for a beer, his call came in. The house sold. He gave her fifty more. She wouldn't take it. A deal's a deal. He liked her a lot more for that.

Up, Up and Away 6

The African safari lottery winner was announced. It was Joanna Zhou. That was the Upjohn version of events. (The contest for two would actually be won by someone else.) But first, before the 'fake news' could come out, Brian had to convince Dashir Lodge to go along with a bogus winner. He had to further bend the ear of the Lodge managers to accept the barefaced fib that the trip was for *four* people due to an unexpected flood of fee-based entries. That change could never happen in a real-life contest.

Regardless, the vital African connection was successfully made. Brian then set to work with Melissa and Troyan to make the safari a reality. He met them at the *Feather & the Firkin*. Melissa had been able to touch her family for the money to send two people, and Troyan was able to get the jet for the times needed.

"You're going to like the plane, Melissa," said Troyan. "It's a Gulfstream G650ER, the fastest exec-jet around. It's got just enough fuel to get you there, but we'll get 'em to refuel in the Azores just to be sure. Two attendants should be enough to serve up the meals. The seats and divans turn down to beds. And you've got the usual movies and stuff."

"Sounds pretty swish."

"It's iconic, Bry. You're bathed in beige luxury with dark wood accents … I sound like the brochure. It's beautiful. Great for long hauls. You get there fresh."

"I'd like to pay for all the meals and drinks on the trip there and back. I owe the Girls that."

"Straight fire, Melissa. Brian and I'll bite the other hard costs. You good to go on that, Bry?"

"Absolutely. As for the two Girls in question, Melissa, I'm looking after Marla and you pay for Joanna …"

"And I've got Shak," added Troyan.

"And I'm okay for Jo. No squawks on getting the money. Wow! This is going to be a great memory for our time at Covington."

"You make it sounds like it's almost over," said Brian. "I love what we've got in the Hall."

"We do too, Bry. But we're all getting on. Frankly, it's time to show our knitting."

"So you can double stitch for a permanent weave?"

Melissa laughed. "Seems so. Three of us have now."

"You wouldn't be 'jigging' me?"

"Not about Jiggins."

"What are you two talkin' about?"

Melissa and Brian looked at each other and smiled:

"Marriage!"

"Got it. Boy, I do got that."

"I hope so," said Melissa, "because Shakira wields more than a mean golf club over someone I know."

"Don't remind me. I just played with her last week. I'm definitely 'lighter'."

"You were warned, Bry."

"It's all right. I only lost five grand."

Melissa's mouth opened. "Holy … oh! Brian!"

"R-ight," Brian chuckled. "I guess we're ready. I'll get the Lodge to send Joanna notice of her big win and we're all dummied up about it, like forever?"

"Right."

"Right."

"Good. We'll have a party when it happens," said Brian.

"Amigos too?" asked Troyan.

"Of course," said Brian. "She'll get the email next Saturday, early afternoon. So, be waiting. It's amazing how careful you gotta be to run a con. Crooks must have stressful lives."

Celebration

The bulletin for Joanna couldn't have come at a better time (being prearranged). All the GITH were on the patio sunbathing on that sultry Saturday afternoon. Brian had just prepared a platter of cold melon slices and cheese, half-listening to the television news that put the number of men killed by the neighbourhood serial killer at 10. Brian shook his head and climbed the stairs.

"Man on deck!"

He appeared and went straight to the table to put down the snack where Joanna was working at her computer. The others were lying out on lounge chairs or on towels glistening from the oil on their supple, already well-browned skin.

"Brian," said Kelly, "we've been talking."

"Oh-oh. What've I done?"

"Listen to that paranoid guy. We've just been saying how much we love that you're not running around naked in a wide-open kimono trying to tantalise us all the time. But we gotta know: is it because you're *gay*?"

They all rose up and looked over at him. A silence hung in the air. Brian looked at them sternly, then broke into an open smile.

"No. I'm not gay. I mentioned to you before, Kelly, I work too much to have a girl. And I probably get all the female companionship I need from you guys. You met my sisters, so you've got to know how much it means to me that we all get along so well …"

"That's so sweet, Bry," said Melissa.

"Natch, I'd sometimes like it to be different with someone. I miss being intimate, if you know what I mean?"

"Haven't a clue what he's talking about," said Marla. "Do you know, Girls? Tell us about it."

"Yeah," said Joanna, "in-tim-ate. Nope. Draws a blank. What's that?"

"Oh boy, crash course starts on Thursday. I'll draw up a timetable. Whooee! I'm really going to get off on this ride."

"Keep it in the thong, boy," said Kelly.

"Cold feet already? That's okay. Keep your feet. It's the rest of you – Zazazooom!"

"Suddenly, we created a flamin' white Godzilla, sistas," said Shakira.

"The big question is: have you got what it takes?" asked Joanna.

"You mean …"

"Yeah, Mel, that's exactly what she means," said Kelly.

"Before we agree to anything," said Marla, "you better drop 'em, Bry. We need to inspect the tackle. No deal if it isn't triple A."

They all giggle.

"Yeah," said Shakira, "drop them shorts, bro. Let's see those chukkas."

Brian laughs. "Only too glad to oblige. First though, are you tackle-worthy? I'll need proof. Off with those skimpy bottoms, Girls. Melon, anyone, cheeeese?"

They laughed at that, not knowing why, when Joanna's computer sounded about an incoming email. She opened the email and read the message with a short intake of air. Then she screamed. The GITH rose up en masse and stood watching her.

"What?"

"What is it, Jo?"

"What happened?"

"I won the frickin' lottery! I won! Hey! It's for *four*! Four people, not two."

They all rushed over, crowding to read. They screamed.

"We can all go! We can all go!" repeated Joanna, seeing Kelly. "Kelly?"

"No, no, Girls, I'm off on a buying trip. So perfect!"

All five started to dance with each other, flouncy, abandoned, spirited and singing something unknown.

"Read it, read it out loud, Joanna," said Brian.

I am pleased to inform you that you have won a two-week land safari for four people, not two, due to an overwhelming response to our subscribed lottery. The trip is from August 15–30. It does not cover the air fare, but transfers, meals and accommodations are included. Please read the attachments on the requirements you will need for Africa, such as vaccinations, visas etc. etc. Congratulations. Please review and be in touch with us as soon as possible. Darryl Peters. Dashir Lodge, Arusha, Tanzania.

"Champagne!" cried Melissa. "We need champagne and lots of it!"

"Someone call the hounds," yelled Kelly.

The three suitors were waiting outside the building. Moving to one side, Brian took out his cell and called Troyan.

"Give it five, then join the mayhem," he whispered distinctly into the phone over the continuing whoops.

Melissa had grabbed a bottle of champagne from the fridge and handed it to Brian to open. Marla went to the kitchen for flutes. Oprah had come to the top of the stairs wondering what all the screaming was about. She saw Marla coming toward her, jumped in fright, and bolted back down and under Brian's bed.

"Grab the pages downstairs, Marla," shouted Joanna. "I'm printing them out now."

The Girls were only one sip into their glasses when the three amigos thundered up to the patio.

"Hey, what's going on? The three of you here in five minutes?" asked Kelly.

Jeffrey whispered to her, "We're here for something else. You'll see."

Joanna greeted them. "Guess what guys? We're all going to Africa, Four of us. I won the contest for a free trip. How about that?"

"Damn cursed, damn bloody cursed," said Troyan, hugging up Shakira.

"Spectacular!" said Jeffrey, kissing Melissa. "You'll have a spectacular time!"

"You really won?" asked Ma. "Fantastic! Are you lucky like that?"

"Yes, I am! I found you, didn't I?" said Joanna.

Ma melted in her arms with a happy groan.

"A Call in the Hall!" heralded Brian, as Marla was handing drinks to the men. "Raise your glasses, everyone. This is a special moment for the Girls. Kelly's not going. She's got a business trip to the Cayman Islands, so we're very, very sorry for her! But the others are off to Tanzania for a two-week safari. Happy Hunting, Girls."

Troyan had been looking at the email and then said, "You were told the trip doesn't include air. Oh-yes-it-does. Did you *hear* me? I will book my company's jet to take you there!" (Cheers filled the patio.)

"And I'll book my company's jet to bring you home!" (More cheers.)

"Happy Trails to the Girls in the Hall."

Brian started up the music from his iPhone, finding an old 1950s' tune called Happy, Happy Africa.

It was then Jeffrey's turn. "Your attention please, I need your attention."

Everyone stopped. Brian turned down the music. Melissa froze, wondering, hoping, half-expecting …

"You may wonder," Jeffrey continued, "why we all showed up so fast after you just heard about the trip. Here is the reason."

Jeffrey dropped to one knee in front of Melissa and presented her with a ring in an open box. "Would you, Melissa Prebys, do me the honour of marrying me?"

"Shit! Yes!" yelled Melissa, covering her shocked mouth with her hands. "Oh, sorry, sorry. Yes! Yes, I do, I mean I will!"

Wild cheers went up as the couple kissed passionately. She threw her head over his shoulder and wept uncontrollably. A minute later, Jeffrey pried her off and slipped the ring on her finger. She looked at it, displayed it to the crowd – laughing, crying – then coiled around him again and held on.

Her squeeze outlasted the applause, then the genders segregated, the GITH surrounding and hugging Melissa, Brian and the boys congratulating Jeffrey.

"I know her family is old school," said Jeffrey, "so I called her dad last night and told him I wanted to propose today. He gave me his blessing and promised me a bounty, which I put the kibosh on. That's what's done, I was told, you politely decline, and then down the road, you take it all. Not that I will."

"Of course not," said Brian. "You want to do it all yourself. Make your own way. As a lawyer, you will. But let him buy you a house. I'll make that happen."

Then all the men hugged and kissed the bride-to-be, and the GITH gave 'Jiggins' an in-house embrace. Brian and Melissa were especially tender. He put his hand on her cheek.

"I'm so happy for you, Melissa. You two are going to have a wonderful life together."

"Thank you, Brian. You're such a sweet man. Always such a great support and a friend to me. Thank you."

She kissed him on the lips for a moment, then wrapped him in a tight hug.

Jeffrey smiled, waited, then cut in. "Can I have this dance … (the three finished it) … for the rest of my life?"

Brian found and put that tune on, the original Murray version.

Marla and Kelly were now at the table, sorting out the pages of the African itinerary. Shakira and Troyan who loved to dance were shimmying with the affianced, and Joanna and Ma sat in adjoining lounge chairs, animated in conversation. Brian looked around smiling. This was his happy family. He could see the cracks fissuring the Covington Compact, but this, this was a special day of their lives in the Hall.

Jeffrey and Melissa trailed off, with two glasses and a nearly used bottle of champagne, presumably to her suite to savour their new esprit. It gave Brian his 'out' to go down and bake bread, Marla sitting with him. Kelly went to her digs to pack for her trip that was nearly upon her.

Shakira and Troyan decided to go for dinner out. And the lottery winner and her beau fell asleep on the lounge chairs, fully bubblied and talked out. When they woke, they found the breeze had scattered the pages of the trip's itinerary over the entire patio.

They spent some time reshuffling the pages because they'd need them to decide what they wanted to do on the trip.

When the Girls came in singly for their bread in the morning, a sign on the counter confronted them:

Breakfast on Africa
In the Treetops.

An array of outfits made an appearance on the patio. Lounge shorts and camisole (Joanna), light sweats (Kelly), a patterned nightshirt (Shakira), red satin pajamas (Marla) and baby dolls with lace cover up (Melissa). Their nightwear defined their personalities so exactly, one didn't give it a second thought. What was different was the three amigos were with them, had never left them, and all were having their first Covington breakfast together.

On the serving table was cut-up fruit, cold cereal and yoghurt cups. Coffee was plugged in. Warming in the grill was the baking from the night before: almond croissants.

"I hope you don't expect this from me when we get married," said Jeremy.

"Oh but I do, darling. Brian has set the bar for all you men," replied Melissa.

"I hopes yuh don't have lax wax, Troy boy. Did you hear? It's the Upjohn Eats for us or I bogey your ass."

"You don't bogey no man's ass, sister girl, 'cause I'm gonna birdie your big ole butt all the live-long day."

Shakira did her diaphragm-jerk.

"You know, Girls, you never know what you're going to get," said Marla. "It could be a man who bakes for you *or* a naked man in a wide-open kimono hoping for cheap thrills."

The Girls laugh. The men just stare.

"What's *that* about?" asked Jeffrey. "Who's the naked guy in the kimono? Not Brian, I hope."

"No, it's a privates, uh private joke, Jeff," said Joanna.

"Let's get back to the topic at hand, like an African safari!" said Brian.

"Right on, Brian," said Troyan. "I got great news. The jet is gonna take you. I reserved it last night."

The Girls whooped it up. Shakira threw her arms in the air and around him triumphantly.

He continued, "You gals are going to be able to stretch out. It can carry 18. You'll have two flight attendants to serve you meals …"

"… and champagne. I'd like to pay for all that," said Melissa. "I owe you Girls."

More applause. This offer really impressed the GITH. Even Kelly saluted to her.

"And I'll pay for the crew," said Brian. "I don't owe you Girls. But I want to."

"Hey, does that mean I get the jet too down to Florida and the Caymans?"

Silence.

"Thanks, a shitload."

"The flight goes direct to Arusha, no stopovers in London, or plane changes in Ethiopia," explained Troyan. "If this wasn't Africa and a safari, I'd say getting there would be more than half the fun. You're going to love it. Trouble is, Girls, you'll never want to go back to pathetic and sad ole 'economy' again!"

"If it's so fancy-dancy, boyfriend," said Shakira, "you better come fly this bird."

"I don't fly no bird no how, lover girl. I just sit back in the plush and lux-ur-iate!"

"I like Shakira's idea," said Brian. "It would be fun for the rest of us to come along for the flight, if it's such a one-off experience. But I haven't even got the time to discuss the itinerary with you."

"Where're you off to, Bry?"

"Doing an Open House for a colleague. I'll be back for dinner to hear what you decided. Could you feed Oprah, Kelly?"

"I'll do it," said Marla, smiling under her brow.

After Brian left, they got down to it. Joanna led the discussion. They decided to spend the first couple of days at the Lodge and visit some local sites. Then head out for seven days in a land rover to the three main parks: Tarangire, Serengeti and Ngorongoro. The first is home to large elephant herds, as well as dazzles of zebras amid the giant baobab trees; Serengeti is noted for encounters with the big cats and the migrations of plains wildlife like wildebeest; the last is a giant crater encircled with forested slopes and interlaced with trails to view thousands of animals and birds.

In all three, they'd be staying in upscale tented camps, with western-style beds and running water. The last night at Ngorongoro, they'd be put up in a traditional old colonial coffee plantation fashioned into a rather grand hotel.

"What about climbing Mount Kilimanjaro?" asked Melissa.

"Drop it," said Marla. "I got no interest climbing some damned mountain. Shak?"

"Likewise, Marl."

"That leaves the sunrise balloon safari," said Joanna. "You rise with the sun and float where the wind takes you. Afterwards, you sit down in the bush to a full English breakfast served on china with linen and silver. It's optional, so it's an extra cost, $500 a head. What d'you think?"

They all voted to include it and pay for it themselves. The boyfriends had already decided in their minds to look after that cost but discreetly said nothing at the time because Marla would be the only one paying it herself (she didn't).

Joanna typed up the itinerary and sent it off to Dashir Lodge.

"Okay, that's done," said Joanna. "Now, I've got to see how the weather's going to be in a month, so we can get our clothes together. The other thing is shots. We don't need any, but have to start a round of malaria pills two weeks before we leave. And don't forget to put Imodium in your toiletries bag in your packed luggage. I'll print out the forms we need for visas and all the info on what you need to know. You'll all need to buy travel insurance. I'll organise that. That's it."

"That's great, Jo," said Melissa. "This is going to be exciting. Sure wish you could come, Jeff."

"We'll have a honeymoon somewhere special. You can be thinking about the wedding on your trip."

"I'll be doing that, all right. What about you, Kelly?"

"No, I won't be thinking about my wedding on the trip …"

"You know what I mean "

"Yeah, I'm half-packed. Leave tomorrow. I've decided to tack on a vacation to the trip. Maybe I'll meet a guy."

"Don't!" All four women said at once.

"Thanks. I want you bitches to be happy too."

"Say, Girls, let's go out and pick up a random guy off the street for Kelly," said Marla. "We couldn't do worse."

"I'd tell you to FO, Marla, if I didn't think you're right. Okay, let's all hope I don't meet a man. My friends."

Inevitably, balefully, she did.

Scuba Do

The Florida buying trip went well; she placed a lot of orders and spent her free time in a rented car exploring the Keys. Then she flew to Grand Cayman for the merchandising conference. It was a one-week conference cum show, so she dropped in and out of it; this meant she could use the majority of her time there as a holiday. A big attraction is scuba diving, one of the world's best places for it. She had a diving certification for 50 feet from a previous trip to Cancun, and went to look for a good dive shop to rent her tank and take her out to the reef. That's when she met Trane.

He had operated the Paradise Dive Centre for five years and was obviously well-established with three employees and a shop stuffed with scuba gear. Trane had been a free diver, but was now a technical diving consultant, teaching specialist courses. When Kelly walked in, she caught his eye.

She was not a siren like Marla, but had initial appeal for a lot of men because she was extremely tidy in her appearance: fake blonde hair on a nice-shaped head, grey-blue eyes, and a trim figure. Just so tidy. But, as witnessed, her personality put the dash in her appeal; talk flowed out with that cynical edge men found amusing. Her tongue is what did her in, however, for the wrong men were most drawn to her baiting wit.

"Can I help you?" asked Trane.

"Don't tempt me. Forget that. I want to dive."

"I'm your man."

"Not this trip …"

"Sorry?"

"I'm here for a week and would like to do some diving. Here's my certification."

"Okay, what kind of diving would you like to do?"

"There are different kinds? Don't you just do a dunk with a tank on your back?"

"No. There's night diving, nitrox, deep diving and reef diving. Your card says reef is what you're used to."

"Just for fun, let's do all of them."

"All of them?"

"Yeah, problem, Aquaman?"

"No," Trane said laughing, "but that's a few hundred dollars. Are you sure?"

"No, are you sure?"

"I'm sure. You'll get your money's worth."

"Then, let's go."

Because of her cynicism, it would be easy to imagine that Kelly was somewhat impervious to the opinion of others. The very opposite was the case. She was stung by the Girls warning her off a travel romance. Long time, she had been aware of her problem with men; after all, she lived with the consequences. So, she was going to make sure it didn't happen here.

But Thane proved to be a very good trainer and companion in the water, such that she was warming to the idea of him out of the water too. The night dive only happened once; the underwater world is an eerie and frightening place at night and takes getting used to. Kelly didn't like it. But in their daytime dives under his masterful control, she was developing a greater ease with each passing day; she was going deeper and even working for her nitrox certification. Her rented underwater camera took as many shots of Thane as the more colourful creatures beneath the waves.

After a few days of his constant coddling as her guide, Kelly found herself giving way at the hinges for this man. The GITH were still saying, "Don't!" in her head, but her heart was starting to say something else. The last day, she asked him out to dinner. Her feelings had already directed her to make a reservation days earlier at the Upstairs Restaurant. It was a five-star spot, so she just got in as it was. If she was so damned certain to book so far ahead for dinner, maybe she'd better book for breakfast too, just in case. So she booked Laurens with its legendary reputation for Eggs Benedict – something rich and gooey for the morning after. Thane jumped at the invitation for dinner, no one knowing if his secret wish and her forward plotting would be a match. It was.

Their table looked out at bending palms and the turquoise sea they had spent so many happy hours immersed in. Soon, they were tipsy on the rum flight and each other. The six course menu-tasting with a wine/rum pairing followed, floating them to her rooms in a soft haze of booziness and rapture. Kelly had not been with anyone since Keith, so found Thane's athleticism enduringly welcome. When they awoke, she was happy to endure it all over again. They debated forgoing breakfast and loitering in prolonged propinquity for their last hours together. But they roused themselves and went off.

"I wish we'd started earlier," said Thane. "Last night was so great."

"It happens when it happens. Call it the topping on the omelette sibérienne."

"What?"

"Oh, the guy who lives down the Hall bakes. He spoils our ass."

"He must be gay."

"We wondered. No girlfriend. But no boyfriend either. Jury's out."

"I want to see you again. When can you come down? Would love to spend more time in the water with you, before hurricane season."

"Next year. Maybe I can swing another buying trip down here … maybe."

"A year. Anything can happen. Maybe I'll surprise you."

"How?"

"Can't say. It's been a trip, Kelly. You're really something. Promise you'll write."

"You've got my address, you write too."

After a hurried packing, Kelly waved a poignant goodbye to Thane as she boarded her plane for home. On the flight, she thought about him non-stop: when can I get down again? I would have to give up the last week of vacation time. Go for it. Thane's awesome, so patient and responsive. Just what I needed. And he's got all that staying power above and below the waves. Last night was yummy. More of that S.V.P. Lots of laughs, easy mixer, seems good with his female staff and the boat captains. Natch, Kelly, he has to get along with them; he works with them. No girlfriend. I wonder why? Attractive guy, great bod, good teeth. Living in paradise, bikinis everywhere, what guy would want to tie himself down to one girl? Now that I think of it, his eye never stopped roving. He flirted with every girl he got near. We met for drinks at night, then he'd be off. Where? Oh yeah, I asked him what he did nights. He was evasive. Went home mostly, relaxed. Yeah, with who? As if I didn't notice when he flirted with those girls, their body language wasn't saying the cheque's in the mail. I figured it's the culture down there. But is it? Who're you kidding? Oh wake up, girl, Thane's a player! Shit, another basic unit. Another love-'em-and-leave-'em lothario. And you got right in line, you idiot! Did you get that he wants you to come down to *him*? Write to *him*? Service *him*? He played you the whole time and made you pay for it. Eight hundred smackers. I even bought dinner. And breakfast. And come to think of it, all the drinks at night. And the lunches around the dives. No, I tell a lie. He bought one frickin' lunch. You picked a ripe one this time, Kel. But at least, you're out of it. It's over with. He's behind you. Now you're free to do it all over again! I better not tell the Girls. They'll gloat. Not that they don't deserve to. What a shitfest! Hey, remember, you've always got Brian. His frothy lalla rookh pie is almost better than sex. Almost. Yeah, he's a ridiculous boy scout but, count to five and come alive, that's getting to look like a plus. He's no goddam trouble and you'll never go hungry. Maybe a badge boy is just right for me, my golden guy …

How golden was he? He was there to greet her at the airport gate with flowers. She'd forgotten she gave him the flight information when he drove her to the airport. She exhaled in his arms; here was comfort, here was home. He proved it with the first words out of his mouth.

"I've baked your favourite pie for your homecoming, Kelly."

She exhort-laughed. "That's amazing. I was even thinking about it on the plane."

She'd only been back long enough to take a second bite from that pie when the dreaded question came.

"What's his name, Kelly?" asked Joanna.

The other Girls laughed. Kelly was amused and irritated at the same time. She sighed resignedly as if this was something to get past.

"Thane."

"Son-of-a-bitch?"

"Son-of-a-bitch."

Joanna nodded. Something unwritten but compelling took hold to end the subject. After a pause, Brian reset the conversation.

"Successful business trip, good conference?"

"Yeah, Bry, all that went great. Great inventory. Bought a ton for fall. But what's up with your trip, Girls?"

"We're packing, Kel," said Melissa. "Dashir sent us a checklist of essential items. Whatever had to be paid for, like visas, is done. Troyan's providing a stretch limo to take us to the airport. You've got a good man there, Shakira."

"Yeah, he's a home boy. But I ask you, 'Can I keep 'im there? Can I keep 'im wantin', cravin' this same sweet truly yours'? Spill it, Jo. How do I keep holt?"

Keep Him Wanting

"You want tips?" asked Joanna. "You always mock me when I do. But if it's flash psychology you want, here goes, Shak!"

"Lay it on me, girlfriend."

"How about a perfume that smells like a grilled T-bone?" Kelly interjected.

"Ha, Kel, that would do it," Joanna laughed. "Sight, sound and smell are all important cues to attraction. A lot of small things make all the difference. For instance, saying 'I love you' is more powerful when you whisper it in his left ear. But if you want him to be more willing, ask in his right ear. As a woman, if you want something from him, then you sit side by side. You're more persuasive if you sit on his right. Be on his left side for an ask that's more intimate."

"This is for you, Bry, when you want to make an impact with a woman, sit face to face because that's how women communicate. You want to be more attractive and confident, Shak, then keep dancing, stand erect and make eye contact. Smile a lot."

"We all like happy people. Happy people smile 40 to 50 times a day compared to the average Joe – that's me – who smiles about 20 times a day. Smiling with eye contact makes a man feel special. You want to step up your appeal, close down your mouth; the less you reveal, the more mystery surrounds you. That'll keep 'em there. Then pick an ear."

"What about clothes?" asked Melissa. "Clothes matter."

"Same principle. Don't reveal too much. Women are sexier in red. And sure, something we all know as women, how you dress is linked to your mood. So dressing to your mood and taste really adds to your happiness. You happy, he happy."

Marla asked, "What do we do about brains? Men can be good at things, but they're also pretty clueless."

"You mean like they know, 'The price of everything and the value of nothing'," said Melissa.

"No, Mel, they're shit stoopid." Kelly cut in.

"That's not true, Kelly. Single-focussed, not stupid. But women with higher IQs have a harder time finding a mate."

"If that's right, Jo, then I'm the only one here with half a brain," said Marla.

"Are you sure you mean that?" asked Joanna to delayed laughs, including Marla's.

"How come I feel both beaten up and left out?" asked Brian.

He got a big 'Awwww'.

"Don't you feel that way, bro," said Shakira. "You're the main man. You're the boiler-plate!"

The GITH murmured assent as Brian gave her a smile and nod.

"I included you, Bry. I told you how to talk to us girls. That's more than 95.3 per cent of what all men know. But if you want lifestyle advice for both genders, the best I've heard is this: Don't act without thinking and don't think without acting. That's all you need to know."

"Wow, I've got to remember that one!" said Melissa. "This has turned out to be your second story to us, Jo. Fascinating. I can't wait to experiment with Jiggins."

"She's going to jerk her Jiggins," quipped Kelly.

"That sounds a little coarse, Kelly," said Melissa.

"Relax Mel. Shit, haven't you two even had sex yet?"

"Of course we have, we're engaged. And don't be so uppity. You can't even keep a guy long enough to propose to you."

"Ooooo, Melissa's grown some teeth," Kelly laughed. "Good one, Mel."

Melissa wasn't laughing but, being who she was, the little frown on her brow was winsome.

Departure for Africa was imminent, but the time leading up to it had been a bit hectic. The Girls had to contend with the usual surprises that always seem to arise at work before a holiday. Then the million details. The pills, the cash, the toiletries, the documents, but most of all the clothes. The Hall had been abustle every night to refine what to take to handle hot days and cool nights. And Brian helped with boyfriend anxieties. He hosted a couple of dinners upstairs and even took the men off to the pub to quell their imaginings of a beloved being dragged into the bush and devoured by lions. He had been there, so they listened to him.

During one of the dinners, Brian handed out paint chips to the Girls. While they were away, the building was to undergo some improvements: a new runner down the Hall and all the suites re-painted. The Girls could choose what they wanted among 30 colours. Brian was amused they all chose two colours each for their rooms. They all wanted their bathrooms in another tint.

Now There Are Three

The coming apartment upgrades also offered a possible opportunity to advance Joanna's informal investigation into Marla. She and Kelly both thought it now a perfect time to bring Brian in. When they approached him, he was not terribly surprised. His own rising doubts had prompted him to ask Shakira about her on the golf course. Joanna outlined the pattern she was seeing that made her think Marla was very likely a *psychopath*. That thought sat very badly with Brian. Of all the Girls, he was most fond of her. They knew that and tried to soft-pedal the hard pill they were making him swallow until he got used to the idea.

Then, Joanna went through the list of big and little incidents and indications that led her to her prognosis. There was the bozo on the beach, setting Brian's sister on fire, Keith's murder (Kelly volunteered that one), the horse killing, all the rats, Marla's beach story, Oprah's paranoid fear of her, the verbal threat to her …

"She attracts every man on the planet," offered Kelly, "but never has one of her own. She's gotta know *you* like her a lot, Brian, but it doesn't faze her a bit."

"She has no emotional life. Have you ever seen her actually happy or sad, angry, even annoyed, offended et cetra, et cetra? She laughs, she jokes, she carries on as one of us, but is it just an act? Is she covering for what she's really up to?"

"Jesus, Joanna, what are you saying?"

"Is she the serial killer?"

Brian froze in a wide-eyed stare unable to speak.

"I know what you're feeling, Bry. When Jo approached me, I was dumbstruck too. But she brought me around. You will too."

"You don't have to believe me. But I want you to help us. And during the trip is the perfect time to do it."

"Are you two out of your bloody minds? How dare you. Marla's one of us. She's one of the GITH. How can you accuse her of something so, so … horrendous?"

Joanna and Kelly looked at each other and almost smiled at his defence of her as one of them, but they pressed on.

"We love that you love us, Bry," said Joanna. "But if we're harbouring a killer, and we know she is …"

"… of animals under controlled conditions. That's a big difference to slaughtering *people* in cold blood."

"It seems like a giant leap, we get that. But I'm a trained psychologist. I've studied psychopaths, and she ticks a lot of the boxes on Dr Hare's checklist for the disorder."

"And have you noticed that most of the men killed are from our part of town? There's 11 of them now. Will the murders stop when she's off the continent? We're betting they do. And if they start up again when the Girls are back, she's our assassin."

"We'll have to see about that. I don't believe what you're saying. The things you talked about, the incidents put together like that, well, it's weird. I don't deny it. Marla's not your average girl next door … don't laugh. There's nothing funny about this. But all of them, together, don't add up to what you're saying she is."

"We get it," said Joanna. "We don't want it to be true. But what if it is? Will you help us?"

"Yes, I'll help. You want me to check her room for evidence, don't you?"

"Yeah, we do. She'll have tucked it away carefully. You'll really have to look."

"I'll be around," injected Kelly. "I'll help you search."

"That's if we find anything. She's no dummy, y'know. If she knows we're going to be painting her suite, wouldn't she get this incriminating junk out to a storage locker or something?"

"No. She doesn't know we're looking for it," said Joanna. "All the rooms are being done. She has no reason to suspect us. She'll think about it, of course, but figure it's all right. She may move it to a new place in her room, but I'm counting on her leaving it there."

"You gals have really got me spooked. I like Marla. This is really hard…"

"Yeah, we know, Bry," said Kelly. "But if she's killing men all over town, do you really want her in your bed?"

"She's not in my bed! You know, sometimes, Kelly, you put things in a bitch way, you know that?"

"Sometimes?" asked Joanna.

"I'm sorry, Brian. But let's face facts. You don't want a relationship with someone like that, do you?"

"No. But we don't know she is."

"No. But you're going to help us find out if she is. Right Kelly? Right Brian?"

"Don't 'right Brian' me, it isn't right. But I'll help, sure, to prove you wrong."

Farewell My Lovelies

The day arrived. The long Lincoln limo moored in front of Covington Place.

Troyan stepped out, passing all the luggage standing like sentinels along the Hall, and joined a champagne farewell on the roof.

They raised a glass to a safe trip, the men kissed their girls and soon, they and their bags were stuffed into the spacious interior of the limo en route to the airport. Brian and Troyan squeezed into the front seat to escort the travellers comfortably onto the jet. When the car pulled up on the tarmac beside the aircraft, baggage handlers took the bags and the party ascended into a saloon-like luxury, which evoked cries of pleasure. Customs officials came aboard and asked for passports. That meant Troyan and Brian had to get off, so they made a hugging farewell, then jumped into the car for the trip back.

On the highway, they caught sight of the jet climbing into the clouds.

"I'm suddenly feeling a bit sad," said Brian. "I haven't been away from the Girls day-in and day-out since I moved in."

"You guys are tight" – Troyan chuckled – "I get it. Keep tellin' yourself they're in for one sweet time."

When the Gulfstream reached its initial cruise altitude, the captain went on to welcome the Girls and tell them he was turning off the seat belt light.

"Wine!" cried Melissa. "Let's have a wild party."

"What's happened to that meek and mild, proper young lady, Mel?" asked Joanna.

"Later. I want to break out and have some fun. It doesn't have to be radical. Let's just be freeee!"

"You caught the spirit, girl!" said Shakira. "I wanna fly on yer wings."

The two flight attendants came out and gave each of the Girls a circular, wood-simulated box with their names inscribed on top. They were cool to the touch.

"What's this?" asked Marla. "A kit for snake bite?"

One flight attendant said it was nothing quite as good for their health. The other attendant read from a paper she held:

"Sweets with sweets war not, joy delights in joy."

The GITH all shouted at once: "Brian!"

"That's a sonnet … from Shakespeare."

"Don't recite it, Mel," said Joanna. "Let Brian have the last word."

They opened the boxes. Inside, there were four round compartments. Two had Peach Castellas and the other two were filled with Hersey's kisses. Under each lid, a small silver fork was attached.

The Girls seemed sadly happy, heads shaking. Marla frowned.

"The guy never lets up."

Melissa: "You're the dreamiest of dream men, Bry …"

Shakira: "… who we'd never marry but …"

Joanna: "… that's why you'll stay our dreamiest man!"

They laughed. The attendants rolled the drinks/tea trolley down the aisle.

"Bry's one scary *mofu*," said Shakira. "Does that brother have any flaws?"

"He better have," said Melissa. "A perfect guy would give us nothing to work on."

"Nahh, if we're not around, who knows what he'll get up to? Something mischievous, I hope … we all like them *bad*."

That remark showed blind prescience from Marla, given Brian's intent to root through her room for evidence of mass murder.

Father, Here Art Thou

But he was for the moment otherwise engaged, getting the new runner laid down the Hall. The painters were in the building too, prepping the rooms for a re-paint. It was mid-week by then; the Girls would be spending their first days in the wild animal adventure. Brian was about ready to sit down to dinner with Kelly on the patio when his cell lit up with a surprise call.

"Dad! How are you? … Yeh, sorry to miss you too … Are you coming to see me? Stella promised you … Good … Friday? Sure, what say I get a tee time at Delhaven and we'll play a round? … Perfect. I'll let you know. You're going to miss the Girls, except Kelly. They're all away in Africa … Yeh, pretty wild. Why not come Thursday night? I've got a bed for you. That way, we can get an early start … Great, Dad, great to hear from you. Bye."

"Sounds like you get on pretty well with your dad," said Kelly.

"Parents. Never great. Stella was amazing. She wouldn't put up with any crap, but she was always trying to save me from my sisters and help me with my girlfriends. Dad's another story. The guy's a lawyer. Everything's a legal wrangle. Even for big holidays when we were young, he made us sign a legal contract that we'd behave. And argue. He just loved to argue. If he can't argue about every little thing, it isn't worth thinking about."

"What a bore. You wouldn't want to say anything or you'd set him off."

"R-ight. He didn't do it with Stella. She'd say, 'Daniel, stop!' That was the signal and he'd give it up. I couldn't do that. And I was the only boy. Was I going to follow in his footsteps? He assumed I was. Automatic. That bugged me too. I think what he was doing was preparing me mentally for life or something. We argued all the time. He couldn't understand why I got so mad at him in these arguments. I never won, not in his mind. It *was* a bore, stressful as well. I may be able to talk to him about it now. Maybe I will. It's bound to end up in an argument. He'll like that."

"You should. He might be able to hear you now."

"What's with you? Where's your bitch-edge? That's what I need from you now."

"No good. Dealing with family, it just eats you up. I had a shit time with mine. Don't get me going. I'm a goddam bitch because of them. Maybe if I stay away forever, I might actually come out okay."

"Can't be *that* bad!"

"How about divorce at five, trailer camp, single mother slut, alcoholic 'step dads' to fight off, constant screaming fights, constant poverty and no escape."

"Jesus, Kelly, it *was* that bad. But you did escape. You've got hard edges and no wonder, but I think you turned out great. So, have dinner with us tomorrow. He'll probably go home after that. We're both workaholics, so he won't be around long. And he'll be civil with you here."

"Sure. I'll be here. I'm intrigued now. I'll like to see how you deal with him after what you just told me."

"Well, it just occurred to me we could put him to work. He might be able to give us some good advice about Marla, if we tell him the story. From a legal point of view. If we seek his counsel, he won't argue."

Daniel Upjohn arrived late enough on Thursday night to do little more than have a drink with his son and be shown the building, still in upgrade disarray. His father particularly liked what was done to the patio that had a welcoming glow lit up in the dark. Then they hit the hay for an early morning tee time.

The young man's need-to-feed prompted him to set his clock an hour earlier than agreed, so he could cook them breakfast before they left. If Daniel was impressed by his son's baked bread and special way of doing eggs, he didn't say, noting only how good the coffee was. They took mugs of it with them on the way to the golf course. They kept up a lively flow of inconsequential talk – outside things – mostly their work. Not having seen each other for a while, Daniel kept it light trying to gauge how much his son had matured or changed and Brian guarding his words for fear of sparking an argument.

The two men were not evenly matched. Brian had a 10 handicap but, if he had played only with scratch golfers like Shakira, it would have been lower. Daniel rarely shot under 100. So, golf was a means to an end, never a sporting challenge between them. Their first tee shots proved that well enough. But it signalled a conversation could start.

"You know, Dad, I expected to hear from you sooner. I figured you'd want to take action against one of the Girls for setting Lorilyn on fire."

"Lori and her husband – you remember Tim? – They came to me. I deemed what had happened was a hybrid offence that could go either way. I persuaded them not to proceed. Frankly, not enough damage, and too hard to prove if the perpetrator had intent. Stella thought so, but it's only her word. The Girl could have argued Lori got in the way. The real offense, I heard, was how Lori and Tracy treated you."

"Well, it wasn't indictable, Dad. I didn't mind it personally; it was the same-old for me. But I was really embarrassed the Girls had to hear it. I took that hard. We're all pretty good friends."

"You know, both girls are actually all right when they're with their husbands and kids. But with you, they start to behave like empty-headed teenagers. It's quite peculiar. I gather Stella tried to control them …"

"They were gone, beyond her superpowers."

"It must have been very upsetting for Stella to see it. She came down hard on them when you were kids, mostly over you. And she knew how to do it; tough love she learned from her father. He was very strict with his four daughters or so she said."

"I find that hard to believe. He was always so nice to me."

"You were the son he wanted. He didn't know what to do with girls. But Stella remembers with real fondness how he always fulfilled his obligations to them."

"Like what?"

"Straightened teeth, a good pair of skis, an undergrad degree, and one wedding each. That's it."

"That can't be right. Not the same person. Gramps was so generous with me."

"And if I hadn't been scrappy, fighting for the right to be a husband and father, Stella would have relegated me to the same strict treatment you kids got, copying her dad, you see."

"Did you need your teeth straightened?" (Daniel just glanced sideways and smiled.) "I don't think Stella was so strict with me."

"Understandable. You see her as your great defender because the girls were so silly with you."

"'Silly' is not the word I'd use. 'Mean' is more like it."

"Have you noticed that just as Stella did with the girls, and the girls did with you, you are regressing with me in constantly disagreeing with everything I say?"

"No, I'm not." (They looked at each other and laughed.) "Well, you taught me."

When they got back to the Hall mid-afternoon, Kelly was not in her suite, so Brian assumed she was up in the patio. She likely wanted to get away from the painters who were busy at work. They started up the stairs, and before the top, Brian gave his usual clarion call.

"Man, on Deck!"

"It's okay, Brian. Oh, wait, your dads with you, right?"

"R-ight."

"Then wait a sec, let me put something on."

"'Pretty good friends'? That's what you said."

Brian smiled and shook his head. "Not what you think."

Kelly met them in a robe, then went downstairs to change as the others snapped a couple of Krombachers. She soon re-joined them in shorts and a tank top a size too small. That was the sort of oversight that roused the wrong sort of men.

"Why aren't you on the safari, Kelly?" asked Daniel.

"Not my thing. And I just came back from a working trip in Grand Cayman. I added a holiday on while I was there. How was the game? Who won?"

"Brian. He's a much better golfer. But it gave us a chance to have a good conversation."

"Isn't that why men play golf? They need an excuse to be together?"

"Don't, Kelly," said Brian. "That's an argument-maker."

Daniel laughed. "No, no, she's right. Men need shared activities."

The icebreaker out of the way, they soon got down to the subject they each had a private reason to discuss. Daniel naturally wanted to get as much first-hand information he could on the woman who set his daughter on fire; Brian wanted advice on how to proceed with the 'case' and Kelly was interested in a fresh view of Marla from someone 'official' outside their circle. Daniel listened carefully without commenting when they filled him in on all of Marla's machinations.

"One of the Girl's is a psychologist. She's convinced Marla's a psychopath," said Kelly. "There's a serial killer loose in town – 11 murders so far – and Jo thinks it's her."

"I think they're talking crap. But we're watching if the murders stop when she's away. I think it's a huge leap that someone who used to kill animals in an abattoir is automatically a mass murderer."

"I lost a boyfriend. He was one of her murders …"

"We don't know that, Kelly." Brian cut in.

"No, not exactly. But it's shit close to home, and the way Keith was killed is the same like the other serial killings: he was slaughtered!"

"I'm very sorry to hear that, Kelly. But so far you've got circumstantial evidence at best, mostly speculation. This won't work," said Daniel.

"Yeah, well Jo wants us to rifle through her room for any evidence," said Kelly. "Now's the time with her away."

"Marla seems definitely unhinged from what you say. Searching her room constitutes a break-and-enter infraction. But with the room in renovation, something could be unearthed accidently that's suspicious. First step, take photos of whatever you find. Then put everything back … exactly. Even with anything that could be strongly tied to the people killed, it's still too weak to get a conviction. Unless she can be linked directly to an actual murder or corpse, what's needed is a confession. You say you're the closest to her, Brian, even if she's not close to *you;* it's possible she could open up."

"How would we get her to do that?" asked Kelly. "When she opened up to Jo about where she went at night – and that's nothing compared to this – she later got really paranoid and threatened her."

"No guarantees, I agree. Get the police to wire you, Brian. Then hope a conviction results from that evidence. If it doesn't, you better move out."

"Thanks, Dad. Your concern for my welfare is touching."

Daniel laughed. "Wire technology is advanced: it could look like a shirt button. You won't be waving a microphone in her face. And if you find anything solid in evidence that's verifiable, you might get her in prison and do the interview from there. That might put her off-balance enough to improve your chances for a confession."

"Or make her really clam up," said Brian. "Joanna says she's disconnected emotionally. I don't think she knows fear at all. She'll just stay stuck and make you prove it right to the end."

"That's always the gamble when you're dealing with human personalities. But getting her on record is going to be the only way to stop her, unless the police get lucky from something sloppy she's done. Not likely. She's seems very meticulous."

"And dangerous, deadly dangerous," added Kelly.

"There *you* go! You two! Imagine how eager I am now to cosy up and kiss a confession out of her."

"Look, why not make a search right now while I'm here?" said Daniel. "I'll have a nap for my trip back. Then, Brian, you can cook for us, and I'll be off. Look behind all the pictures, under the bureau drawers, in shoeboxes, even in shoes, in the inside pocket or, better, feel the lining of her coats, inside the pillow protectors. If it's not there, she may have moved it off-site, knowing people would be in her room."

"The Girls seemed to think she wouldn't," said Brian, "because all the rooms are being painted. No reason to suspect."

"I'm game to look now, Bry," said Kelly. "The painters are probably gone by now. Let's go see what we can find."

Daniel went to lie down while the others went to Marla's room. It was the first to be painted, so the dust covers had all been removed and furniture put back. They went through everything in vain. About to give up, Kelly tried to open Marla's locked jewellery box, sitting on her vanity. They looked in the drawers for a key. Nothing.

Then they recalled what Daniel had said about drawer bottoms. Brian looked under the vanity drawer and saw a taped-on tiny envelope, the kind you buy at a hardware store for washers or screws. In it was a key that opened the jewellery case. It was full of showy paste which Kelly had never seen Marla wear. She removed the top layer in the box; a second tier was missing that would have rested on a flat, removable satin pad. She dug up one corner. The cushion came away. Lying underneath was a round, brown envelope.

Happy Africa

The Girls' land rover had by this time driven through Tarangire, the park that is notably home to herds of elephants in the African scrubland. Drivers would radio one another about the best sightings and the trucks would descend on rivers and streams where the big animals would tend to gather. Their first view of elephants had actually come when a long line of them heavy-footed it through the Tarangire escarpment, a low valley that panoramaed two miles below them from the patio where they sat drinking cocktails at their first tented lodge.

Once in the Serengeti, the Girls bounced along on pot-holed roads; to pave them, it was argued, would ruin the natural environs with unwanted commercial transport. Wherever they could, their driver Jeremiah would stop at watering holes for a chance sighting of hippos or other wildlife where predators and prey would often shoulder alongside to drink. In the central plains and heading north, encounters improved for seeing the big cats as they trailed wildebeest, zebra and antelope in the current migration. By the time they reached their encampment in the north, near the Mara River, the Girls would be unsettled in their sleep by the loud moans of the wildebeest as they paused ever closer to the tents in their summer trek.

The next morning before light, they were ripped from their beds for a quick breakfast then chivvied into the Rover for a bounce to the Balloon Safari launch site. They would watch by torch light as the whisper burners inflated the massive balloons that had lain flaccid along the ground. Then as the sun rose, the balloons floated up with their passengers to wander at the whim of the winds. The pilot, however, controlled the altitude – sometimes almost grazing the treetops, sometimes at 1000 feet for a wide vista of the plains. As the Girls' balloon ascended, someone played the sonorous music from the film *Out of Africa* on their iPod; it added an emotional pitch to the otherwise silent soaring but left a trace of something missing when the music ended. The flight showed the magnificent line of country more than the abundance of wildlife, so visible from the ground. In an hour, they were jostled in the basket as it ran on its side for 50 yards on the ground, everyone hanging on for dear life, until it came to a grateful stop; the balloon was deflated, the flight over. But not their spirits; they were buoyed by champagne and a traditional English breakfast savouring the cool of the morning in the African bush. After another day and night of animal watching in Ngorongoro, they were homeward bound for Dashir.

On their first afternoon back, Joanna happened to overhear two of the other guests as they went by on the walkway past her cabin.

"I'm still pinching myself we're here, Sally. I'd have to save up for years to afford this trip. And would I?"

"Well, I'm just glad you asked me to come along or I'd never see it. It's a once-in-a-lifetime thing for me, Janet, I can tell you."

"You're lucky if lightning strikes once. It sure did for me."

"Yes, well, your invitation was mine."

Joanna frowned. She was bunking with Shakira who came out to the porch to sit with her.

"I just heard a couple of guests talking. And reading between the lines, I wonder if one of them – her name was Janet – if she didn't win a free trip too."

"Would they have *two* free trips? This ain't no chain."

"I agree. I'm going to ask Janet. If she won the lottery, what are we doing here?"

"Easy answer. She didn't. You better stop readin' between them lines."

But Joanna did ask Janet. Then she went to the camp's manager, Darryl, who faltered. Immediately, she called a meeting on her porch for the Girls.

"Okay, Girls, I just found out and I had it confirmed we didn't win the lottery."

"Then, we're not here," said Marla. "Unless …"

"Brian!" yelled three of the GITH.

Joanna looked at Melissa. "You didn't shout out, Mel. Are you in on it."

"Yes. It was Brian's idea. He organised it all. And there was a lot of time and planning to keep it secret. He got Troyan to volunteer the plane and pay your way, Shakira. He got me to pay for you, Jo, and he paid for you, Marla. I helped because I owe all you Girls; I know you've been upset with me over my debts, and this was a way of making it okay. But Bry did it all. And he did it because he knows we aren't going to be together much longer, and he wanted this trip to be one of the ways we could remember our time in the Hall."

After a moment for it to sink in, they all rose up at once for a group hug and cry.

"Thanks, Mel, thank you for paying my way," said Joanna. "You're both amazing."

"I helped, but it was really Brian. He deserves the lion's share of the credit."

"He's a hero to do all this and keep it secret. He's our guy!"

Melissa agreed. "Right, Jo. Our Boy in the Hall."

"Uber awesome. And what's smexy is he don't expect any drilling rights!"

"He never does," said Marla. "That silk underwear must rub out his libido."

"Let's get him something," said Joanna. "Something fun for the perfect guy. How about a small statue of a Maasai warrior with a 10-inch prick? Guys love that shit."

"Oh Jo, really?" Melissa doubted.

"Yeah, I like it," said Marla. "It says this is the Brian we've been missing."

"Easy, Marl," cautioned Shakira, "we don' want to make a wild waffle-maker outa our boy."

They got a statue of a warrior with a prominent spike and to taunt Melissa had *Our Boy in the Hall* carved in the pedestal. And when Melissa wasn't looking, the other three chose a Tanzanite pendant for her; Joanna paid the largest share for the pricey item as the major recipient of Melissa's largess. They decided they'd make her gift double as a wedding present from them all and they'd hold off presenting it until closer to the big day.

Bruises and Bows 7

Within two days of the GITH coming home, Kelly got a knock on her door. She was used to closing it because of the painters; they were packing up, having finished the rooms, and days after painting the Hall. The workmen had been in and out constantly, so the front and back doors were left open. Any visitor could gain easy access. The open doors might have been a problem with an 'indoor' cat, but Oprah had bonded so tightly with Kelly that she split her time between Apartment 2 and the ledge on the patio whenever Kelly went up. Kelly opened the door and her eyes widened with genuine shock.

"Thane!"

"Hi ya, beautiful."

"What are you doing here?"

"Surprise! Come to see you. Wrap yourself around me."

She pushed back as he advanced for a hug.

"Hold on, hold on there, boy! Just like that? You didn't even think to call and see if it was all right?"

"Wanted to make it a surprise. We left it good. I wanta pick up where we left it."

"I have no say? Maybe I *don't* want to pick it up. Did you think of that?"

"Hey baby, what's wrong? It was perfect on the islands. What's happened?"

"I … just got engaged … to be married."

"Shit, that was quick. You're some shape-shifter."

"Yeah, well, it's someone I've known for a while."

"Who's the cowboy?"

Brian had arrived for a last word with the painters; at that moment, he moved past the door.

"There he is. Hi, darling! Meet the diver I was telling you about on my trip."

Thane turned to assess the 'cowboy'. Kelly gestured wildly with a finger to her lips and flaying her hands. Brian did his best to take it in.

"Hi, I'm Brian. Kelly told me she had a lot of fun on that trip."

"Thane. So, you're the lucky guy."

"I just told him we're engaged, honey. I guess it came as a bit of a shock."

They both replied: "You can say that again!"

The men looked at each other and laughed.

"I don't get it," said Thane. "Why a shock to you?"

"It was unexpected. It sort of came out of the blue."

Brian went over and hugged and kissed her. Kelly didn't hold back. Thane looked on grim-faced. Brian then turned to Thane, still holding Kelly with one arm.

"So … Thane, what're your plans?"

"Hurricane season started early on the islands, so I came up to surprise Kel. We got on pretty good on Cayman and I thought we could hang out for a while."

"Sure, I guess that'd be all right," said Brian, looking at Kelly. "The Girls will be back in a coupla' days; that may change the picture, but sure, stay with us 'til that happens."

"You can sleep in my old room here. I'll be next door with Bry."

"Still looks like you live here."

"Yeah, it's convenient. I keep my clothes here and use the bathroom. Why don't you guys go up to the patio and have a brew? I'll tidy up the room for Thane."

"R-ight. C'mon. We spend most of our time on the roof."

"Okay. I'll leave my bag here."

The two men left, and Kelly closed the door.

She hissed and spat: "Shit! Shit! Shit! What a sonafabitching shit! One night and he thinks he owns me! Now I gotta move my clothes … oh, I need a ring. (Goes to her jewellery box.) No. No. No. That one. It'll have to do. Just shows up! You sure can pick 'em, kid. Give 'em up, just give 'em up. Poor Brian. The guy went purple. What'll I need? PJs, towel, toothbrush, change of clothes. I'm not moving everything. That shithead'll have to get out when I need the room. What else? Check the sheets in the spare room. Bry's dad was there last. Bet they weren't changed. Oh, bloody hell! You've really done it this time! We got to get him outta here. When the Girls get back, he'll have a field day. He'll try and make it with all of 'em. They'll blame me. Jesus, weather's probably bad enough, he *can't* go home. So, what? He'll be here forever? Hey! Marla! How could I forget? Let him tangle with her. She might get a *momento* from him too! So go ahead, punk, try it out on her! And you will! Every guy does. Then hurricane season won't just hit the island. Ha!"

For a woman who couldn't spot a jerk in her soup, Kelly was no fool in some of her predictions for this particular specimen of 'pond life'. But initially, Thane ingratiated himself, mainly because he was working with men – Brian and the boyfriends – to prepare for the Girls' return to the brightly refurbished Hall.

A Ball in the Hall

Flushed and excited, the GITH stepped down from the jet, anticipating a welcoming contingent of loved ones; they were disappointed to be greeted only by the chauffeur. But the Girls intuited something was in store for them. Suspense wrestled with expectations when the car pulled up in front of 255 Covington Place. No one appeared.

"Where are they?" asked Melissa. "I thought they'd all greet us here at least."

"We shouldn't expect anything more," said Joanna, "not after what you and Brian and the others have done for us already, Mel."

"Never mind about the bags, Miss Shakira," said the driver. "I'll look after 'em."

"All right, Lebron, thanks," said Shakira. "Leave 'em, Girls. It must be what my Boy Troy wanted."

"Don't let that one get away, Shak," said Marla. "Spear him to the wall while you've got the chance."

"Spear me no spears, girl," replied Shakira. "I got other plans for that gen-el-man!"

They entered the little foyer, again to feel a little let down. But when they opened the inside door, they were met by a bang and a spectacle! Brian was clattering his pans and stamping on sealed-full brown paper bags; the three amigos, along with Thane, Jake and Hoppy, were blowing noise makers and waving sparklers under a banner that said *Welcome Home, Girls.* The Hall was decorated in streamers and bunting, balloons everywhere, and posters on all the doors with African animals they deemed looked most like their residents. The Girls screamed their delight and started to run toward them. Brian put his hand up.

"Stop."

Then the men all sang a little, long-worked-on ditty to perfect the harmony...

"Happy to have you home,

Happy to have you home,

Hope you never go 'way again

Happy to have you home."

The GITH who had boyfriends were swept up in ardent snuggles. Marla gave Brian a tight squeeze, but the other men got *honoraria* that anyhow needed her considerable strength to pry herself free in turn. The Girls waited to have a private moment for Brian on the roof; he had organised a large party, including many of the staff from Telvan Realty, including Joyce, and the GITH's friends whom Brian had got to know well enough over the months to call and invite. Once the mingling had eddied and the drinks had softened moods, Joanna presented Brian with *Jeremiah*. Brian was predictably touched, including the caption, and wondered:

"I don't know how you Girls could have known to pick a statue with such striking anatomical similarities to my own."

Shakira spoke up: "An easy match, bro, for a stud who leaves his door and kimono wide op-en!"

The party resumed as guests started to small-team and lovers found far corners. Brian was at his typical spot grilling boneless chicken breasts, that were smoking from his special marinade, when Marla wandered over to him.

"I want to see you later, after the party."

"Sure, Marla. Oh, and Marla, it's great to have you back, safe and sound."

She gave him a look he couldn't read before she moved off in silence.

"Did you get our postcards, Brian?" asked Melissa, as she bent to put a hand on his shoulder and a kiss on his cheek.

"Sure did. Loved it. Came this morning. Maybe you beat one or two of them home."

"I must tell you, Bry, it all went well, a great trip, fantastic actually. But our cover got blown. Jo heard the real winners of the contest talking, and you know Jo. So it all came out."

"Well, probably too hard to keep that kind of secret these days. So, they know you pitched in."

"Yes, they do. They were pretty happy with that, I think."

"R-ight. And we got them all on the trip. That was the idea."

"Where's Kelly? On another buying trip?"

"Yeah. Timely trip too. Her fling from her last trip is over there. Thane. He suddenly showed up. She was really upset about it. Now she's gone again and he's still here. Watch out for him."

"Thanks, I'll pass it on."

"If you hear that Kelly and I are engaged, don't believe it. She made that up to put him off. She's been sleeping in my spare room."

"That's crazy. He's got to go. Can't you get the owner to throw him out?"

"Maybe. I was thinking if he ever leaves the house, I'll pack his bag and leave it at the front door. Lock him out. Trouble is, I'm working night and day at this point."

"I'll let the Girls know there's a man threat."

"Okay. Oh, send Joanna over would you, honey. I'd like to talk to her too."

"Sure," she said and brusquely pecked him.

Joanna came over without Yonxin, guessing what Brian wanted. She grabbed his arm and put her head against his shoulder in a gesture of affection.

"Hi, Joanna. So glad you're back. I missed my Girls."

"We missed you too. You're a big part of our life, Bry."

"Thanks, likewise. Look, we can't talk now, but I wanted you to know that Kelly and I found the mother lode."

"Oh! Great! We better meet after the party."

"No, Marla wants to see me after. I'm trying not to think she's on to something. I'm freaking out a little to tell you the truth."

"She can't, Bry. We just got home. We haven't even been to our rooms."

"You're right. Anyway, we've got to get together. Can we have lunch together, maybe tomorrow, away from here?"

"Yeah, good idea. I'm not due back in for a coupla days. Say, who's that creepy looking guy over there? Is he a friend of yours?"

"No, that's Thane. Kelly's latest. And she's escaped on one of her buying trips leaving him for us to deal with."

"Say no more. Call me about a time and place tomorrow."

Then she kissed him, just as Melissa had, and left.

"All right, my children," said Brian loudly to the crowd, "the Chicken Suprema is ready!"

Lebron left the Girls' bags along the hallway in no particular order, not knowing who lived where. When the partiers had gone, the GITH went down and rolled their luggage to their suites, hooting their delight at the repainted rooms. The only suitcase and carry-on left were Marla's; she had stayed back with Brian in his kitchen. He topped off her glass with red, and they clicked glasses.

"Welcome back, Marla."

Thane was still up on the roof, drinking the remnants of the drinks left in the partiers' glasses. He came down at that point and expected to join the two.

"Private meeting," said Marla.

"Oooo, a little nookey goin' on," said Thane. "Sure you don't want a threesome?"

Marla turned her body in a bracing action, but Brian cupped her elbow to stop.

"Look, Thane, the Girls just got back and we'd like to have a little time to catch up. So, would appreciate if you'd leave us to do that."

"Sure. Call if you need help. I can tell this babe's a real barracuda."

"You don't know the half of it, bud," she said.

He left laughing at what he probably saw as bravura. She turned her dark eyes on Brian. As hostile as she sounded, he was surprised that there was no vestige of emotion in them; she was somehow unaffected by the coarse intrusion which had certainly irked him.

"Have the Girls told you we found out it wasn't us who won the lottery?"

"Yeah, I heard. Too bad. I didn't want the Girls to feel any obligation."

"They might. I don't. It's just who you are. They should see it that way, if they don't."

"That's a very realistic point of view, Marla."

"I call 'em as I see 'em. So, I want to tell you this: in my whole life, no one has ever done what you did for me. I can't remember one act of kindness. Unless it was just to get something. Like that fool (pointing to Kelly's room). But I don't get that crap from you. You alone. The Girls are good companions, of course. But we both know they're totally out for themselves …"

"Nothing against the Girls, Marla. Remember you're one of them."

Marla smiled and nodded. The Girls had often spoken gratifyingly among themselves about how he wouldn't hear a word against them.

"All right, but you're different. I wouldn't believe you existed if you didn't prove it by being here. I'm still not sure you are what you seem to be."

"I am, and what's more, it's you I wanted to look after especially. Don't tell anyone but, of all the Girls, you're my favourite."

"Why? The others are nicer to you. They trust you. I don't trust a living soul. But I guess if I had to pick someone to trust – and I never could – it'd probably be you."

Brian was moved, then realised he should have been amused.

"If that's a compliment, thank you, maybe."

Marla didn't respond, but stared voidly at him. Then she grabbed him by the neck and drew him to her in a full, vivid kiss. He put his arms around her and returned the kiss. Marla was just the right height for him, so they comfortably melded into each other. He ran his hands up and down her back as they kissed gulpingly with faces turned one way, then the other. Aroused, he squeezed her tightly. She responded with a grip that took his breath away. He broke it off to take in some air; Marla smiled even if her eyes didn't.

"I'm staying with you," she declared and walked into the bedroom.

Brian closed his front door for the first time since he'd moved in and turned out the lights. When he entered the darkened bedroom, she stood looking at him with luminous eyes; she was stark naked; he breathed in, taking in a sight that bettered the naked image of her he had conjured in his mind for months; she got under the sheet and watched as he stripped off; he slipped in beside her; they coiled and kissed; as they made love, he felt the vibrant strength in her limbs; she would be gentle, somehow knowing her might, but as she got aroused, that strength would be constrictor-like; he'd murmur, a signal for her to loosen up. Marla liked that he was a long-laster; but as he reached the moment of truth, he let out a wolf's cry, a peculiarity of his that spoke to something primal in her; it brought her to climax; she screamed. A loud banging on the wall suddenly sounded from next door with a 'yehaw' ejaculation. Thane was listening with his ear to the wall.

"Christ! I'd like to see that guy gone," panted Brian.

Also panting, with her skin glistening, she looked at him, those black eyes glowing with a seemingly sinister accord.

Before dawn, Brian awoke to find her gone. He looked out in the Hall where he knew the Girls' bags had been dropped. Marla's were gone now too. She had returned to her suite before the others got up. Later, when the Girls came happy to be getting their breakfast bread again, Marla gave no indication that anything had happened between them. She met his searching eyes with that same impassive look he was accustomed to seeing. He watched her go without looking back. He sniffed with amusement and shook his head. There was no chance that he had dreamt what was so wonderfully real for him, something he had fantasised about from early on, despite a conscious deliberation not to.

The Carrot and Stick

Lunch later that day between Brian and Joanna was momentous. Joanna stared wide-eyed, with shock and a shiver, at the pictures Brian and Kelly had taken of Marla's secret stash. Among the items photographed was one she recognised.

"Hey! That's Keith's key chain. I've seen it more than once. It was something he flashed around because he liked it so much. He was always looking for ways to use the knife part."

"Okay, now you've confirmed it. When Kelly saw it, she freaked right out. Dad and I had to get her drunk. I checked this item online. You can order it up for 30 bucks. It's an Armour three-inch pocket knife with key ring. Point is, they're easy to buy, but I've never seen one before and you probably haven't either. We put keys on our fobs now."

"That's got to be his. That's proof to me Marla killed Keith and is sure to be the serial killer. Living right with us. How *petrifying* is that?"

"That's just a first reaction you're going through, Joanna. The knife doesn't prove anything. So far, it could just be a coincidence. We went through this with Kelly."

"That's right, Brian. Sorry, I should have got that. You're right. Poor Kelly. How's she going to face Marla when she comes back?"

"She wasn't getting much sleep over that very thing until Thane turned up. He proved to be a big enough distraction to put Marla on the back burner."

"Yeah, he looks pretty freaky. What've we got? Looks like the key chain, three watches without bands, four belt buckles, one fancy gold chain, two rings and a driver's licence. That's 12. There've been 11 serial killings reported so far, unless … any since we went away, Bry?"

"No, all quiet, no killings."

"More proof that points to Marla. She goes away, the killings stop."

"My dad would say still not enough, all circumstantial. He's a lawyer."

"Tell me about the driver's licence of this old guy. It seems to be the odd man out."

"Yeh, that's her guardian. He died in a fire. I looked it up when you were gone. In the articles I read about it, Marla was the only next of kin. The fire destroyed everything."

"And all the evidence of a brutal murder too."

"Maybe. She told me last night she's never received one act of kindness from anybody her entire life until I sent her to Africa. So, I imagine her guardian wasn't all that nice to her."

"You think? Of course, as a psychopath, it wouldn't matter if she came from a loving or abusive background. It's nature not nurture for that disorder."

"R-ight. Anyway, my dad told Kelly – after she got over the shock of seeing the key chain, knife, whatever – she oughta wait until you got back from your trip, then both of you take the pictures to the cops. His idea was they could speak to the victims' families and see if they'd ID any of the items in the pictures."

"And if they do?"

"It might be enough to put her in jail until a trial. But he said getting a confession would be needed to convict her. And you'd need a wire to get it."

"And who's the lucky clucky who's gonna wear a wire?"

"Me."

"You? Could you do that? This is Marla."

"I know, I know. The fact is, Joanna, I'm beginning to see a relationship with her is going to be more than I want to take on."

"Remember, it's not you, Bry. She has no feelings. The best you could get is that she'd fake loving you just to manipulate you. You'd be her glorified servant. And the moment you stopped being useful, you'd be out on your ear. Or, in this case, *slit* ear-to-ear. Sorry, not the best scenario!"

"I think I know that about her now. So, I'll help with a confession."

"That's very brave of you. It may save lots of lives in the long run 'cause this killer is clever, covers her tracks. We should have paid attention to Oprah. She knew all along. It takes one night-killer to know one."

"Oprah's had the full run of the place with Marla gone. As soon as she saw her yesterday, she did her disappearing act."

"Where'd you keep the photos?"

"At work. But look, if you want me to go with you to the police, I will. It's just that you and Kelly … it's your case. So, it's up to you."

"Great. We'll go, and I'll tell Kel when she comes back."

He Takes a Dive

The euphoria of homecoming for the Girls was short-lived. The buoyant gratitude they felt to be home was dashed by an unwelcome lothario who leered and flirted with them constantly. Thane had been there a little over a week but made it seem forever in the upheaval he caused in the Hall.

Probably by design, Kelly had escaped on that buying trip for 10 days but had told Thane in no uncertain terms – as only she could – to be gone on her return.

The Girls started to close their doors with him lurching around and stopped going up to the patio after work to eat and relax because Thane would sunbathe nude in the hopes of titillating them. He also sponged all of their patio supplies without any thought of payment or replacement.

He made his first pass at Marla predictably, but she pushed him so hard he hit the ground with a bounce. He screamed at her in his wounded pride but left her alone after that. Then he tried it on with Melissa late one night. She struggled gamely to wrestle out of his embrace, outraging at him that she was getting married and didn't want anything to do with him. Her screams brought all the Girls in, but it was Marla, not Brian, who pulled him off her bed. Thane might have fought her back this time but was more concerned with getting his pants up and covering his shame. Shakira, Joanna and Melissa had their boyfriends stay over after that to avoid any more predatory intrusions.

Brian was prevailed upon to 'man up' and get this free-loading sex nerd out. He would have done that without a prompt, but was working day and night on two big sales. Not being around, he mistook the disruption first as bad blood between Kelly and Thane; then he put flirting with the Girls down to the guy just being an insufferable jerk. The incident in Melissa's bed set him straight. Brian told him he was mucking up their lives and to leave forthwith; he said his plane ticket was set for two days hence, the Wednesday of his second week there, and he promised he'd leave then. That proved to be a lie.

At loose ends, with no one to hit on, he chanced to approach Marla again, a desperate choice but the only GITH without a man at the door. She alone kept her door open during what came to be known as the *Days of the Jumbo Jerk*; the fact is, she feared nothing and was intimidated by no one. Her open door was no doubt a temptation to him. But he had an educated inkling that if he tried to sneak into her bed, she'd very likely inflict some damage to a moving part of his body. He knocked on her open door and asked her out for a drink.

"Why bother with the foreplay? Why not just jump me like Mel?"

"Okay, I made a mistake there. I won't do it with you."

"Good, because you already tried it once and where did that get you?"

"C'mon, give me a break here. It's just a drink. I need some company."

"Try Brian. I think he still has poker once a week."

"Not interested."

"Yup, well neither am I."

"Hey, what's your problem? Don't make me …"

"… make you, what?" said Marla, eyes flashing. "Maybe smack me around?"

"No, I was going to say, 'Don't make me beg'."

She narrowed her eyes. Her laser focus made him shift his feet.

"Okay. I'm starting back to work tomorrow, so it can't be late."

"Sure, just a coupla drinks. Know a good bar?"

"Yup. I'll call a cab. We need it to get there."

Marla had him wait outside for the cab while she readied herself. She didn't want any of the Girls to see her leave with him. They wouldn't've. Thane's presence ensured the Hall was tomblike.

In the taxi, Thane needed to talk, so he talked *at* Marla all the way; not being a conversationalist, he made it all about himself. She listened patiently from long practice talking with men. When it came time to pay the driver, he didn't have the correct currency, so she paid.

"You're expecting me to pay for the drinks too?"

"I don't have any of the right money left. I got just enough changed for the taxi at the airport. Here, I'll give you a Cayman hundred. That should cover it."

She shook her head, but took it. They went in and stood at the bar. Happily forgetting Marla was picking up the tab, he downed three drinks in rapid succession to her one. He kept his patter up the whole time. Marla stood, listening to him but getting the attention of most of the men in the place. One or two came up to try and buy her a drink. Thane answered for her, saying she was his date. After about the fifth drink, he moved in on her, brushing against her hip. She pushed him back sharply with her fingers against his chest. He reacted a little hot and told her in a loud voice to stop being a 'prissy little prude'.

A large, lumbering man came over and asked her if everything was all right. Thane again answered she was his date and everything was fine.

"It didn't look that way to me," the burly man replied.

"I don't care how it looks to you," said Thane aggressively. "It's none of your business."

The big man started to move toward Thane, but Marla got between them.

"Thanks for your concern," said Marla to the man, "But it *is* all right. I can handle him. He's a marshmallow when you're not looking. So, I've got this covered."

Thane looked at her with suppressed rage, but her reply caused the intruder to look at Thane with pity and a chuckle. He nodded sagely at Marla and moved off.

"What's the big idea?" demanded Thane. "Why'd you call me a marshmallow? I'll show you marshmallow …"

"Cool off, hothead. I said it to get him off our backs. I know his type. He fools himself he's a protector of women just to make a score and maybe get in a brawl. Making you a wimp was an easy way to avoid trouble."

He stared at her, thought for a moment, and suddenly smiled. Pretty quick thinking. He relaxed, ordering another round. Predictably, he got pie-eyed to the point he even wisecracked with the men who continued to approach his 'date'. She checked her watch, time to go. She asked for the tab.

"I gotta piss," Thane said.

"Go. I'll pay up and meet you outside."

He stumbled to the bathroom. She tapped her card and got a receipt with every man's eyes watching her as she left alone. Several called to go with her.

"Sorry, boys, going back to work tomorrow. Need to sleep … alone."

A moan followed her out the premises. She waited for Thane. He emerged weavingly.

"Right back?"

"No, let's do something wild," Marla said suddenly.

"Okay! What you got in mind?"

"Surprise."

They were within easy walking distance of St Bartholomew Cemetery. When they got there, she guided him past the locked entrance gates.

"I know a place to get in," she said.

"There? Why?"

"There's a large, flat gravestone marker about six feet long …"

"All rrright! Let's go!"

They got in through a large gap between where two fences come together at a corner of the property. She led him to the long, flat, marble marker and lay down, opening her arms to him. He got on top of her and started kissing her sloppily.

At that very moment, Kelly entered the Hall with a sigh and a frown. She locked the door, then wheeled her bag to number 2, hoping Thane had followed her dictates and departed. She noticed the GITH had their doors closed. Recovery from Thane? To her relief, he wasn't there. She walked into Brian's apartment and up to the patio. No one. She breathed out a great puff of satisfaction. Maybe he was good and gone. Two minutes later, she discovered he hadn't, snapping out her favourite word repeatedly. She wasted no time.

Kelly put his things into his suitcase. She checked to make sure his passport and plane ticket (rebooked on his phone) were in the side pocket of his luggage. Rolling it to the front of the building, she left it on the stoop. She looked in Marla's open door to see she wasn't there. Could they be out together? She wondered. The house locked, she went to bed in Brian's spare room just in case, noting with a sniff the sheets were again unchanged, but this time her scent.

In the morning, Kelly got up to be greeted by Brian and the Girls over breakfast bread. She was predictably upset to hear about Thane's attacking Melissa but pleased to see he hadn't returned to the apartment that morning. Not out with Marla; she was there and betrayed no sign of anything out of the ordinary. On her way out to work, Kelly saw the suitcase. She went back in and called to all the Girls to be sure to lock the door when they left. Brian crooked his head around his door and waved to her.

"Patio too," he shouted.

The suitcase didn't move for two days. Now Kelly was concerned. She called the police. They had a missing person on their hands. The police went through the suitcase with her. She had checked her apartment and found nothing else of his. The police spoke to the people at Thane's dive shop on Cayman; they got its phone number from a dozen calls left on his cell. The shop was frantic because he hadn't told them where he was going and hadn't returned.

It wasn't long before St Bartholomew's put a call into the police. They had found a body of a young man in the mounded earth of a grave that had been freshly dug. The practice at most cemeteries is that earth is piled on a fresh plot and allowed to settle to ground level. Then it is grassed and a headstone or grave marker is added. It happened that two heavy rains fell in as many days, so the twice-disturbed earth washed enough mud away to reveal a human hand and a nose.

The man had been murdered. A broken neck. Kelly was called in to identify him and was soon after cleared as a prime suspect; her company confirmed she'd been away for nearly two weeks, and she had airline stubs and hotel bills to make for a watertight alibi. The police, however, were extremely spazzed that this was her second murdered boyfriend.

Joanna and Brian had already been to the police with the pictures of the mementoes for them to investigate. Now they zeroed in on Marla as the possible link between the pictures and this new murder.

They interviewed her and all the Girls (as they had for Keith's murder) about their whereabouts on the night of the murder: the GITH had seen each other that night and could vouch that they had gone to their rooms. Only Thane appeared to have gone. Brian was provably out with prospective clients. Behind the scenes, the police were tracking families of those serially killed to find any connection with Marla's keepsakes.

Everyone was badly traumatised by this second death, even if it were Thane. But the three involved in the 'case' decided not to bring Shakira and Melissa into the loop about the pictures. If there were a possible killer among them, why trouble the rest of them until there was something irrefutable? Brian also decided some distractions were needed. He approached Joanna.

"We need something happy to happen around here, Joanna. Things've got a little … gruesome. I thought I could have a small pre-wedding dinner for Melissa and Jiggins. Maybe ask her parents."

"Great. Start it with a cocktail party so we can give Mel her pendant."

"Pendant?"

"Yeah, we bought her a Tanzanite pendant – cost a mint – 'cause both of you really put out for our safari. Now we could make it a wedding present at your party."

"R-ight. She gets expensive jewellery as a thanks and I get a carved pigmy with a boner."

"Yeeeah, but we love *you*, Bry."

He looked at her quizzically, then smiled with a resigned shake of his head. When Joanna saw he wasn't going to respond to her, she laughed blushingly.

"Moving on, I think we need to do more than our usual get-together for meals. How about having a fashion show here on the roof?"

"Hey, great! I could borrow some of the clothes, get the company's models to show 'em off, and I'll do the narrative."

"Good. Telvan can provide all the lights and AV equipment we need. I can set that up for you, even get you a red carpet."

"You're smart, Bry. It'll be a great distraction. We can ask all our girls friends and I'll throw in a couple of man items if you want to ask the guys."

Brian started at once to organise the dinner. Melissa was overjoyed that Brian had thought of it, especially to include her parents – Andrew and Ashley Prebys. When she learnt that a cocktail party was planned too, she said she would arrange to have the drinks and nibblies catered; Brian would have enough to do with the dinner. He agreed. She wanted to know the menu. He was reluctant.

"Bouillabaisse, knowing you. And you'll keep to that theme. Am I right?"

"Go to your room."

"Then, I'm right. It's okay, Bry, we can always tell by the way you smell. I mean, in your kitchen, kitchen smells …"

"… I know what you mean, Melissa."

"All I'm saying is it wouldn't be a surprise for long, so c'mon."

"I'm not telling you. So you're going to have to wait to see how I stink."

She laughed at his making light of her gaffe and kissed his cheek.

"Okay, I'll leave it. But I'm really glad about the cocktail party. That brings in the Girls. I want them to be part of my wedding, and this …"

"Make what you're about to say my surprise."

"Oh. If you like."

Love for Melissa

When the day came, the patio seemed a little more crowded than usual with a catering staff serving canapés and champagne to the guests that numbered the GITH, boyfriends. some of their girlfriends and Brian. Melissa introduced her parents to everyone. Brian thought they were as patrician as he imagined they'd be. They were very gracious, of course, but with a 'remove' that showed outwardly in their perfect manners and tailored clothes; for the GITH, the divide spoke loudest from Ashley's jewellery – it was real.

"Melissa has spoken so well of all of you," said Ashley, "we feel we know you. What a wonderful community you seem to have here."

"We blame Brian for that," said Kelly. "He's caused us all to be so damned happy."

Andrew laughed. "Don't fight it too hard, Kelly. Melissa tells us she's been very happy here …"

"And very sad to leave it, I'm sure," finished Ashley.

"Not yet, Mum. But it'll be hard when it comes. It's been like a super college sorority."

"Except we got a smexy guy in the middle," said Shakira. "Smexy without the rumble – that boy's yeet!"

"That's a compliment," added Troyan, "in case you don't catch her jumbo."

"We like having Troyan around too," said Joanna, "as a translator."

"What you sayin', girl, the GITH don't pick my cotton all this time?"

"What we don't get," said Marla, "we just say 'yes' to. It works straight fire!"

"Gucci, Marla!"

"It took me months to realise when Shakira says 'Gucci', she wasn't talking about a handbag," said Brian, smiling at her.

Shakira did her double bend.

"May I have everyone's attention, please?" asked Melissa. "Brian very nicely let us have a little party before the dinner for Jigs, uh Jeffrey and my parents so I can make an announcement."

"We already know, Mel," Kelly cut in, "you're getting married."

"They know that, Mel," said Jeffrey. "I proposed right here."

"Oh, Jeffrey, that's just Kelly. A proposal is hardly something a girl forgets. No, tonight, I want to say something else: I want all the Girls in the Hall to be my bridesmaids!"

There was a sudden outburst of benign shock then pleasure. They laughed a little nervously then all spoke at once accepting in different words. Melissa's parents looked at each other and beamed. Melissa flushed and giggled.

"Oh, thank you, guys, we've all been such great pals. I'm really happy you want to be part of my wedding. Thank you. Thank you. And everyone else here, all our girlfriends, are invited, of course. Just in case, I already asked Jo to help all the GITH to get matching dresses. And it's okay, it'll be looked after. We're going to have our wedding at the InterContinental. And we'll all be there together for a couple of nights before the ceremony. It's going-a be a blast!"

The GITH and their friends gathered around her and buzzed with gleeful excitement.

"Who's going to be your maid-of-honour?" asked Joanna.

"Oh, an old friend from home. Name is Laura. You'll really like her. She's a lot like me."

"That's cursed, girl. I'm sure we's gonna *love* her. Two days in the Gran' Hotel, we's gonna love *every*body!"

"Oh, Shak, that's so you," laughed Melissa.

Then the Girls started to pepper Melissa with questions: how long have you known Laura … did you go to school with her … why don't you want a church wedding … where are you going on your honeymoon … are you coming back here or where are you going to live …?

Excluded from this klatch, the men formed one of their own around Jeffrey, and toasted him. He told them they'd be invited to the wedding of course, but he already had his groomsmen.

The Prebyses gravitated to Brian by default.

"It's so nice of you, Brian, to have this little dinner for us," said Ashley.

"It's my pleasure, though I'm sorry Uncle Daisy won't be joining us. We're having his favourite dish."

They looked at each other and laughed.

"Melissa told you about our family eccentric," said Andrew.

"Yuh, I was cooking Bouillabaisse one night and Melissa suddenly appeared like a moth to flame. That's how I met her, the first. Not surprising, she's the most social of the group. We've been great friends ever since."

"She raves about you, Brian," said Ashley. "She says she'd never met a man who's such a wonderful cook and … baker."

"You're about to see that for yourselves unfortunately. Speaking of which, I should get back to my pots and pans. Jeffrey! Yuh, Jeff, come and look after your parents-to-be, I've got to go downstairs. See you later."

"Nice boy," said Andrew watching Brian depart. "I wonder Melissa isn't going to marry him …"

"Shhhh," said Ashley sharply, as Jeffrey came up with an eager smile.

As a joke, Brian hit his remote on the stairs and music started to play on the patio: The Wedding March. Everyone froze.

The GITH shouted as one: "Brian!"

He came back to the entrance and joined them in laughter, turning off the music.

"Wait Bry, don't go yet," said Joanna. "Come back. We've got something…"

Brian threw his head up in remembrance and re-entered.

Joanna began. "Mel, the Girls in the Hall want to give you a wedding present, something we all pitched in for. What could be more memorable, we thought, than something from our trip to Africa? And since you're the first of our wolf pack to get married, it had to be something rarified. And this is as rarified as we could manage. With our love …"

She handed Melissa the gift-wrapped box. Melissa, verging on tears, tore open the wrappings. In it, was the pennant with a medium-sized Tanzanite stone, quarried from the last, nearly depleted African mine.

"Thank you, girls. I think I know what it … oh God, I love it! I love it! Jeffrey, put it on me. Oh girls, it's fantastic! I'll treasure it forever. A great way to remember our time together. Our *wonderful* time together. (She paused.) 'So long as men can breathe or eyes can see, so long lives this and this gives life to thee'."

Andrew gave an approving cry and applauded; his wife flushed with pleasure and laughed. The GITH looked at the parents, then at each other with suppressed smiles. They knew the 'source' of Melissa making literature available to the masses came from the ones hooting their approval. The Girls applauded and gathered around Melissa, who held the pendant, staring at it, wiping her tears away with her frilly handkerchief. The GITH had given her something of true value to her.

 The cocktail party would wind down and the guests thin out after Brian dimmed the lanterns and hit a gong to preface that dinner was coming. He got Jeffrey to pour the wines from the opened bottles of Fuissé that stood on the BBQ lid. As everyone bade goodbye to the party guests, Brian brought up broiled oysters with garlic breadcrumbs.

"I hope you're going to join us, Brian," said Ashley.

"No, I can't cook and eat at the same time. But thank you. If I had thought to make one of the Girls a sous chef, I could have. But I didn't think of it. I'll join you for the dessert."

"Oh, Bry, I want you with us," said Melissa concerned.

"I'll be at your elbow all night, Melissa, and I'll sample one of the dishes with you."

"Ha. You're serving Bouillabaisse, you sweet man, I can smell it."

"That's next. And I'll want your hardest critique on it."

"Gee, the way you two carry on," said Jeffrey, "I better learn to cook."

Melissa told him he could start by helping Brian up with the dishes. He was happy to oblige, already cognisant that to marry a mondaine meant ever-new acts of usefulness would be expected for life. The first course was well-received and, when the two men brought up the soup, Melissa verged on giddy. Brian had included a small bowl of the bouillabaisse for himself and tasted it with Melissa, who took her time before saying anything. The others waited until they had discussed it.

"Still no octopus."

"Never."

"He told me a great story about his encounter with an octopus that put him off eating them. You must tell it, Bry. My parents would love it."

"Verdict, Melissa. Stop stalling."

"What would you give it?" she asked.

"Seven. You've had 'summers' more experience with it, so you should give it less."

"I need a full taste. Come back tomorrow."

"Coward. Please start everyone."

Melissa's parents had had the fish soup many times and declared to Brian they would give it more than seven. But they would, wouldn't they? Jeffrey was having it for the first time and declared there were too many conflicting flavours; this brought a round condemnation from Melissa. But there was a positive consensus on the main course – creamy coconut lime salmon with a watercress salad. And no complaints with the dessert, which was a tuxedo cake, each piece adorned with a necklace of vanilla cream rosettes. As promised, Brian sat with them for dessert and coffee when talk quickly turned to real estate from a response he made about what he did.

The Prebys family were all large landowners and thought nothing of asking if Brian owned as well as sold real estate. He made the quick decision to tell them he owned 255 Covington.

"Whaaat?" burst an astounded Melissa. "You own the Hall?"

"Yes, I do, Melissa. And I'm swearing you to strict secrecy about it."

"Wow. You own the Hall. But why are you keeping it secret?"

"It's my business and I only share what I want. What is the point of the Girls knowing I owned the building?"

"Oh, I get it. You didn't want to be treated like the Super."

"Good reason. Our secret?"

"Our secret. You never stop impressing me, Bry."

"Did I tell you, Mel," said Jeffery, "that I'm buying the Foxmore Building that houses our law offices?"

"Really?" she said, surprised, then realised. "Oh. Aww Jigs, it's okay. You're still Job One for me."

But her parents pressed Brian to continue about his career, which led him to recount his history of buying and selling properties toward making his fortune. This was not idle gassing on his part; he was prospecting. And before the night was out, he had landed a fish as tangibly as what they had dined on. He would be the agent to find the house Andrew and Ashley were buying for the couple. Jeffrey looked knowingly throughout this discourse. For Brian had planted the seed of such a possibility in his brain some time before. At one point, he nodded his admiration at how smoothly Brian had manoeuvred the transaction without it seeming like one. Once he made his sale, Brian turned the conversation to the couple and away from him. It was their night and an enjoyable one at that. A great success, in fact. But it was in grave risk of erupting into complete disaster when the family stepped down into Brian's apartment on their way out.

Sitting at the counter, twiddling a toothpick in his mouth, with a nearly empty glass of wine in his hand was the chauffeur, Augustus. When the driver saw his employers' shocked, then disapproving expressions, he stood to attention.

"Augustus! What the hell d'you think you're doing, man?" demanded Andrew.

"That's my doing, sir," said Brian. "I knew he was waiting in the car for you, so I got Kelly to ask him in for a bite and one glass of wine. I hope you don't mind. It seemed like a harmless gesture at the time."

"Oh Brian," gurgled Melissa, "what an absolute sweetheart you are."

She flung an arm around his neck and pecked his cheek.

"That was a very nice thing to do, Brian," said Ashley, softly. "Very thoughtful."

"Good man," said Andrew brusquely. "Nicely done. (To Augustus) Only *one* glass of wine, I hope."

"Yes, sir," said Augustus. "The chef made that clear."

"The *chef*!" laughed Jeffrey. "The highest accolade yet!"

"And indeed you are," said Ashley. "A wonderful dinner, thank you, Brian."

"He bakes too," said Melissa gleefully. "He gives us fresh bread every morning. Have you got any Mum and Dad can take home?"

"Melissa, you know better," scolded Andrew.

"No, that's all right, I'd like to. But as a penalty, Melissa, they'll get half of your allotment for tomorrow."

"Okay, that's okay. You'll love it. We just feel so spoilt by this man."

Brian had by then got out her bread, cut it in two and foil-wrapped half which he handed to the chauffeur. Andrew gave him his card and said to call him. As they were about to step into the hall, Brian put out the call:

"Man in the Hall."

They all laughed.

"Let me see you out. We double bolt the doors here. Don't want anything to happen to my Girls."

"There's *my* Girls again," said Jeffrey. "I'm sure glad I've got a ring on your finger, Mel."

"It's an endearment, Jeffrey," said Ashley. "No need to worry, I'm sure. It's so nice to know someone's been looking out for our Melissa."

She patted Andrew's crooked forearm in reassurance. He nodded in response.

"*I'm* not so sure, Ashley," continued Jeffrey. "I'm beginning to think I'm going to have trouble getting Mel away from here."

"No, Jigs, I love Brian. He's amazing. But I'm marrying you."

"Make her keep saying that to you, Jeffrey," said Andrew, turning to Brian. "It's been a great pleasure to meet you. A good surprise. Thank you. Come on Jeffrey, we'll drop you off."

"Thank you," replied Brian, "I've enjoyed it."

"We have too, Brian, thank *you,*" said Ashley, kissing his cheek.

Andrew embraced his daughter. "Good night, princess."

"Good night, darling," joined in Ashley, kissing her.

Jeffrey's turn. "Good night, Boffins."

"Nighty-night, Jigs. I love you."

"Good grub, chef, thanks," said Augustus.

They all laughed as Melissa gurgled and sent them kisses. He locked the door and escorted Melissa back to her room. She linked his arm and pressed against him.

"That was just great, Bry. Mum really likes you, I can tell. And Daddy was impressed. He likes go-getters. (Hushed) Imagine, you owning the Hall!"

"Speaking of owning, time to own-up. Tell me your score on the Bouillabaisse."

"7.5."

"Better than I expected. Maybe you're a good influence on me."

"Oh, Brian."

She hugged, then smiled at him as she closed her door. He nodded and walked on to spend the next three hours clearing and cleaning the night away.

Arresting Moments 8

The next morning, Joanna was last in the bread line. She waited until everyone had gone. Brian figured she was ready to talk about the fashion show.

"How was the dinner?"

"It went fine. Everyone seemed happy. Melissa's parents are great. By the way, she fingered that necklace all night. She's nuts about it."

"Great. We sure thought about it and had a fine time keeping her away when we bought it."

"It'll pay off, Joanna."

"What'd you mean?"

"Melissa can be very generous for the right reason, so expect pretty nice bridesmaids' gifts."

"Oh, I didn't even think of that."

"Why should you? So, fashion show?"

"Hey, yeah. I'm ready. Picked the clothes, got the girls, and thinking out my spiel now."

"Okay. I've ordered the AV, carpet, lights, and we'll need extra chairs. Haven't picked the music yet. Almost set."

"When are we going to do it, Bry?"

"Tonight?"

Joanna looked shocked. "I can't do it that fast, are you joking?"

"Yes, I am." (Joanna noticeably relaxed and laughed.) "How's about next Monday? That'll give us a week."

"More like it. Great. Are we keeping it secret?"

"No, you Girls will want to ask your friends. I'll get the boys."

"Ergo, extra chairs. Good thinking."

"Let's tell the GITH about it tonight."

No sooner had Joanna left Brian's apartment than her phone rang. The display showed it was the police. She wheeled right into Kelly's and answered it. Kelly was eating her Covington toast with her coffee and looked up surprised.

"Hello? Joanna Zhou. No, I'm with Kelly now. What's happened?"

Kelly got up and went over to her, all attention. Joanna was listening intently, occasionally nodding but not saying anything.

"What? What?" asked Kelly.

Joanna put her hand over the speaker. "It's the police, just a sec. What'd you say, officer?"

Her eyes darted at what she was being told; Kelly gestured impatiently; Joanna waved her off. Her eyes widened. She grabbed Kelly.

"Got it. Okay, inspector, I'll talk it over with Kelly and Brian … I get that you want it now, but we need a plan. We know where the evidence is kept. But you've gotta know what danger we're under if Marla's spooked. So, let's talk and then we'll meet. Yeah, today. Okay. Great. I'll call you back, detective. Right away. Bye."

"What's happened? Tell me what they found out."

"The worst. She's it, Kelly, she's it!"

"Shit! We're living with a fucking serial killer!"

"The cops want to meet us. They want to use a search warrant to get their hands on the actual items in Marla's jewellery box. Their investigation with relatives got very positive results. The items were almost all recognised …"

"That's the scariest thing that can happen to us. A killer among the doves."

"It looks like we've been right all along. But, Kel, we've gotta be careful. I've been threatened already …"

"You're right. We've got to play this very cool. Can't let on we know anything. What else?"

"The detective said if they can show the real items to the relatives, they think that's confirmation, and it'll help cinch the case. But if the police take the stuff now and she's still around to discover it's gone, we're sitting ducks. She'll assume we were working with the cops and we'll be the next on her list."

"Right. Let's go talk to Bry before he leaves."

They went into Brian's just as he was coming out of the bathroom, wearing only a towel, unembarrassedly. The Girls looked at each other and smiled.

"You're back. Hi, Kelly. You want to talk more about the fashion show?"

"Fashion show?" asked Kelly. "What fashion show?"

"Never mind that. I just got a call from the police. About the stuff."

"Oh-oh. Sit down, Girls. I'll put on a dressing gown."

"What fashion show?"

"Bry and I are arranging a fashion show next Monday. We're telling everyone tonight."

"Here?"

"Yeah, upstairs. We thought the Girls needed a little boost after Thane."

Kelly nodded intensely. Brian then joined them, and Joanna filled him in on the phone call. He looked stricken at the news, and exhale-sobbed when she finished. The women looked at each other, concerned.

"Sorry, Bry," said Joanna, "I know you like her …"

Brian was hot: "Yuh, I like her. We've been through that. But now we know she's a goddam killer! And she's been using us – don't you see that? – hiding in plain sight. We've got to get her out of here. Tonight! And I want her arrested right in front of us. We need to see her taken away in irons or we'll never sleep again."

"The detective wants to get the box now. He doesn't want to wait. We can't stop them, can we? Isn't that withholding evidence?"

"Of course. They'll grab it with a warrant. But they've got to protect us from this assassin! So, they've gotta get the goods and arrest that murderous bitch in front of us."

Kelly almost laughed. "And you think showing a few trinkets to the families will be enough to hold the murderous bitch?"

"This isn't funny, Kelly. What's the matter with you? We now know for sure this woman murders and she murders for a hobby …"

"And we're in the direct line of fire," added Joanna.

Brian didn't reply, but stared hard at Kelly. Kelly just nodded calmly. He was right to be annoyed, she thought, given the shock of knowing the woman he loves is Jill the Ripper.

"I get you're upset, Bry. You have a right to be. But the question is still out there: can they hold her on the real evidence or not?"

"I don't know, Kelly. I'm not a lawyer. How do I fucking know? Shit!"

Impulsively, he grabbed a cushion beside him and threw it across the room. The Girls had never seen him like this, so equally impulsively they got up and sat on either side of him and each took a hand. He slumped back and said nothing more.

"You're right, Brian, we need to call a lawyer," suggested Kelly. "It could be Jeffrey. No, your dad. He knows the details. He said before you'll need to get a confession out of her to put her away. If they have that, they won't release her."

"I could call him. But what's the point? He's had his say. He'll just repeat it."

Breakthrough

"Oh, wait a minute," cried Joanna. "Wait a minute. I just thought of something …"

"What?"

"We may have new evidence, guys. Something from Thane's murder. Kelly, is there anything Thane had, something he carried with him, that Marla would make a keepsake?"

Kelly thought for a moment and shook her head. "No."

Joanna continued. "Because that would be something that won't be in the photos. If it's something you could recognise, that'd be proof. That's new evidence."

"Only if it's something obviously his," said Brian. "A belt buckle wouldn't do it."

"Yeah," said Joanna, "it would have to be something unmistakable. Can you think of anything, Kel?"

"How ... about ... something ... something from Grand Cayman," guessed Kelly. "Something like his dive card, or any ID from the islands."

"Yes, yes, that would do it," said Brian, forgetting his anger. "There's one way to find out."

The Girls looked at each other and at Brian.

"Didn't you say Marla could tell if anyone messed with her stuff?" said Joanna.

"I did. But I'm not anyone. I've done it before and she couldn't tell. We could wait for the cops to nab it or we could know now. Marla's probably gone. We could go down and check. If she's still there, we could tell her about the fashion show ..."

"... which, with any luck, she won't be attending," said Kelly.

"Let me get dressed. You guys due at work?"

"Yeah, but not for an hour and a half."

"Not 'til 10. There's time."

Brian went into his bedroom and closed the door. They sat. A visible shiver went down Joanna's back. Kelly took her hand.

"This is scary stuff, Jo, but we'll get through it."

"Yeah. Never seen Brian act like that, have you?"

"No. Can't blame him. He loves her. And he's going to be the one to put her away. How hard is that?"

Joanna just nodded. "I hope we find something new. It would really help."

"It sure would. *And* we've got a body this time, right?"

"Hey, that's right, Kel. Maybe ... God, I hope it'll all be enough, so Brian doesn't have to wear that wire."

"That'll be up to the cops to work out. A confession would make it a slam dunk. But why would Marla want to let the cat out of the bag? Suicide."

Brian returned, and they went down the Hall to find Marla gone. They saw the jewellery box in its usual spot. They found the envelope and took everything out carefully on Marla's bed. Kelly stiffened when she saw Keith's key chain, though she had seen it there before. Then she let out a cry.

"That! That! There it is, what we're looking for!"

She pointed to what looked like foreign currency. It was the $100 bill from Grand Cayman that Thane had given to Marla when they went to the bar on his last night.

"R-ight," said Brian, "it wasn't there before. That's it."

"There's our proof. Okay, Bry, let's get the stuff back just as we found it."

Brian did so under their joint scrutiny. They returned directly to his apartment where he made some tea, and Joanna was about to call the detective when her phone rang.

"Hello? Detective Hastings. I was just calling you … What? Outside? Now? (to the others) They're at the front door. Let 'em in, Bry. (To phone) Yeah, detective, we're coming. We've turned up some new evidence. Yeah. We're excited and we're also scared out of our minds. Okay, we'll meet you at Marla's. Let's go, Kel."

Brian greeted the detective and two other policemen at the front door. He turned to see the Girls coming down the Hall. He waved them over and took the police into Marla's. They got there as Brian was getting the key to open the jewel box. He took it to the bed.

"We just had a look and found something that wasn't in the photos. You know Joanna, and do you remember Kelly? Her boyfriend, Thane, was the last to be killed. We found something of his in her stash. This. It's new evidence; it wasn't in the photos."

He showed them the bill.

"He is … was … a dive instructor on Grand Cayman Islands," said Kelly. "That's a Cayman bill. She's got to have taken it off of him after she killed him. I was telling Joanna; you've got a body now. He must have tried to rape her and she killed him and took it as her *momento*. Just like the others. She killed him and took it right off of him …"

"Kel, Kel, slow down, take a breath. It's all right," said Joanna, giving her a side hug.

Kelly paused. "Okay. The key chain. That's Keith's. Keith Radowski…"

"… the gym owner who was murdered at his place of business," added Detective Hastings.

"Yeah. Y'know he was my boyfriend too. He loved that chain. Remember it was in the big photo of him at the entrance to the gym."

"Good work," said Detective Hastings. "We'll take all of this and start showing it to the families of the deceased …"

"Just a minute, detective," said Joanna. "We can't risk Marla discovering her stuff is gone. If she does, we're dead meat. She'd kill us all in our beds. She's already threatened me. I'll be the first."

"R-ight. We thought if you came with a warrant tonight, with a story of some new development, pretend to search all the rooms, get the stuff and arrest her, we'd be safe. Otherwise, Joanna's right. She'll know we were in on it and start slashing. Even I wouldn't have a chance against her."

"I understand. When are you all back home?"

"By 6 o'clock. I'll make dinner for everyone, including Marla, up on the roof garden. We wanted to make an announcement about something else anyway."

"All right. I'll call you on your cell just after six. You come down and let us in. I'll give you the warrant. My officers'll do a fake search and get the evidence. While they're doing that, I'll come up and explain the situation to the tenants. Then, when my men bring up the evidence, we'll arrest Marla and take her with us."

"That's perfect," said Brian. "Keep your gun handy. You may need it."

"I'll do that. What else do you want to tell me?"

"It's got to be a complete surprise. Her blood runs cold, so she can act fast and think fast. You'll be up against someone who is very strong and fearless."

"How is it you know this about her?"

"We've seen her take on a big guy at the beach. He didn't have a chance. And I know her better than any of the others. I know her strength."

"How is that?"

"I'm in love with her."

The detective looked at him curiously, then nodded. The Girls gave each other a serious stare.

"I'm still prepared to wear a wire and get a confession out of her if I can. But it'll only work if I'm not compromised."

"We'll let you know when the time comes. As … Kelly … pointed out, we've got good evidence and a body, but we don't have any witnesses. So, we may still need you. That's for the court to decide down the road … anything else?"

Brian looked at Joanna and Kelly.

"Just remember," said Joanna, "If you can't keep her locked up, she'll come after us."

"Don't worry. We've been after her for some time now. We're not going to let her go. She'll probably put up a good fight, if what you say is true about her. So, we can keep her in custody for resisting arrest. You've done well. You've really helped crack this case."

"What'd you call her, Kel?" asked Joanna. "Something pretty poetic for you – she's the killer among the doves?"

"Shit, yeah. An' she wants to keep us 'doves'. She's killed *two* of my boyfriend's so far. No wonder I wanna stay single."

The police laughed.

"We'll try and do something about that, Kelly," said Detective Hastings. "So, are we clear? Wait for my call and have them all up on the roof at six."

"R-ight. Oh, one other thing. No stakeouts. Marla sees everything and she's always on guard."

"And she has most of the markers of a severe psychopath. So, don't underestimate her," added Joanna.

"Joanna's a psychologist," explained Brian.

The detective nodded. "Good. See you tonight. And don't worry. She won't get away."

They left. The trio went back to Brian's apartment and flounced down.

"Shit. I need it, I need it long and hard, right now, right up the kazoo."

Brian and Joanna laughed.

"I'll do you one better, Kelly. I'll bake you a cake."

"You're the only guy on the planet who thinks cake is better. But yeah, Brian, give it to me. With all you got. Make me a cake."

"Hey guys, let's call in sick. I can get Greta to cover for me. We'll get sloppy drunk. What'd you say? Like you, Kel, I need to let it all hang out."

"Great idea, Joanna," said Brian. "I'm with you. And we're in for a helleva night. We need to get totally blotto."

By 10 a.m., they were falling-down drunk. Once past the hysterically happy stage, they slowly wore down until they passed out on Brian's bed, hugging each other for sheer comfort from the horror to come. Oprah lay heavy-lidded at their feet.

By 3 p.m., the Girls roused as Brian disengaged himself to take a desperate leak.

By 6 p.m., they were all up on the roof – the BBQ smoking, music playing and nearly everyone being stupidly normal. The three seemed to huddle together, as if their closeness would somehow shield them from the inevitable unfolding of a frightening presentiment.

Rooftop Rumble

"Hey, everyone," said Joanna to the group, "Bry and I have an announcement to make. Next Monday, we want to have a fashion show up on the roof. Ask everyone you know. I'm providing the clothes and models and Brian is going to stage it. You don't need to do anything, just be here and bring lots of others. We'll make it a scream."

The announcement was met with casual applause and noises of approval.

"If you need a model for large sizes," offered Marla, "I volunteer."

"Thanks, Marla," said Joanna, "but we'll have a range of sizes for all the items and we can only show one."

At that moment, the dreaded phone call sounded. Brian answered it. He spoke briefly in the phone; said he'd be right back and left still talking on the phone.

Joanna and Kelly were careful not to stare at him or watch him go, but stayed close to each other. There were questions about the fashion show to keep them occupied. Luckily, Joanna had a trained mind and could focus; Kelly kept tipping her glass as if thirsty but otherwise did her best to control her rising gorge.

Brian was gone for about five minutes at which point Marla asked where he'd got to. Joanna replied that it was probably a work thing, the guy was a workaholic after all. A few moments later, Brian emerged with Detective Hastings. He made a shrugging gesture to the group as if to say he had no idea why the police were there. Marla discerned instantly he was a policeman; she quickly looked at the fire escape and started to edge toward it.

"Sorry to be so long, Girls. This is Inspector Hastings. He's got something to say to us."

"Sorry to disturb your evening, ladies, but I've got a search warrant to search your rooms. We're doing it now. Don't be alarmed: we'll be as careful and discreet as we can. We've got new information from a witness on the case of a Mr Thane Dubois, who resided here I believe. (He handed Brian the warrant.) If you'd be good enough to stay up here, we'll be finished soon. Nothing to worry about. Strictly routine. Thank you."

"Would you like a cup of coffee, Inspector, or a soft drink?"

"No, thanks."

The Inspector cast his eyes over the Girls and smiled at them benignly. He made sure not to stop at Marla, who had inched ever closer to her escape.

"What's the new information about Thane's death, Inspector?" asked Melissa.

"I think the usual phrase is 'I'm not at liberty to say'. But we have turned up a witness with a solid lead and we're just closing off all obvious possibilities first. This is the spade work police must do in every investigation. And the investigation into Mr Dubois' death is still very much open."

"You already did us about that dumb dude," said Shakira. "You think one of us *bruk* his neck? 'Cause we all wanted to. Right, Girls?"

There was a general murmur of assent.

Inspector Hastings laughed good-naturedly. "Don't incriminate yourself, ladies. We're starting here because this is where he was staying. We need to do a thorough search. It's something specific. If we can find it, it may help our case. That's really all I can tell you. Sorry."

Two policemen suddenly entered, one waving the envelope.

One of them said, "We've got it. Marla Bauer."

When her name was called, Marla was at the fire escape. But a policeman appeared at the top, blocking her. She lunged at him. He lost his grip, dangling by a hand; she kicked at it. He groaned but held fast. The two other plainclothesmen ran at her. She grabbed the first by the lapels and pitched him at the fire escape; he took some of her blouse with him as he grappled at the railing from going over. The other detective tackled her to the ground. She was up first and sent a shoe into the Inspector's groin; he buckled. The tackling officer grasped her shoulder from behind; she snapped his hand backwards. He screamed. She sent several blows to his head; he fell. The cop on the fire escape joined the fray, billy clubbing her. No effect. She sent her fist hard into his throat. He staggered back, choking, coughing; she kicked him in the midriff. But he caught her foot and hoisted it high. She fell. All four of them piled up. Marla was growling like a wild animal. The men undulated up and down on her as she flexed mightily. Two of them fell off – with a free hand she'd scratch deep chasms in a cheek, snap a finger of another, almost pluck out an eye; they all piled back, smothering her until the Inspector put a gun to her head.

"Stop! Now! It's over."

Marla stopped struggling. She heaved to get her breath, her mouth frothing.

The Girls in the Hall stood frozen in place with their mouths open. Brian's cheeks were wet with tears. Joanna noticed and side-hugged him.

The corps of police got Marla roughly to her feet, cursing her. They were injured and angry. The Inspector handcuffed her.

"Marla Bauer, you're under arrest for the suspected murder of one Thane Dubois. Anything you say may be used as evidence …"

"I'm not saying anything to you swine!"

"Come with us."

The police led her past the still-silent group whose wide eyes she met with disdain. She glanced at Brian to see he'd been weeping. She had a look that could pass for concern, but blinked it away with vacant disregard.

As Marla was escorted out, Joanna was still holding on to Brian as they watched her go.

"See the police out, Kel," said Joanna. "Maybe get her another top?"

Kelly nodded and ran after them. The others looked at one other still in shock.

"What just happened?" pleaded Melissa. "Is this real or am I in some crummy nightmare?"

"You'se awake, Girl," said Shakira. "Our horse killer's that big bad people killer too."

"That's right, Shak," said Joanna. "She's the serial killer."

"Scabrous!"

"Hiding in our midst the whole time," said Melissa. "What a monster."

"Yeah Mel," added Shakira, "a killin' monster serial *bitch*!"

"You in there, Bry?" asked Joanna. "Go get yourself a heavy shot."

The other two Girls suddenly saw how affected he was, too wrapped up in their own dismay. They went over and all three hugged him.

"Oh, poor Brian …"

"Yeah, we thought you was OTP. Boy, a lucky escape from that pirhana."

"OTP?" asked Joanna.

"One true pairing. You need to get ginglin', girl."

"Shak's right. She would have destroyed you, one way or another," continued Joanna. "You know that."

"Yeh, I know that. Did you see how she took all those cops on? I couldn't believe what I was seeing."

"What a fully packed shitcase!" said Kelly, returning. "Count your blessings you're alive, people. Marla damn near beat the cops down. If she did, she'd of killed us for sure. She'd have to. D'you see that?"

"God!" said Melissa. "We came that close. How horrible!"

"I'm woke to yah, Kel. Bitch!"

"Even you, Bry," Joanna said softly, rubbing his back.

"Even me," he replied, breaking from her and getting that drink. Kelly went over and put her arm atop his shoulders.

"You okay?"

"Gotta be. But this is going to be a dark hole in my life, maybe forever."

"Never forever, kid. Lovers come and go … in our case, it's murder in the name of love. But it's never forever. Shit, I hope not."

"Let's get pissin' drunk," said Shakira. "We need to get pissed."

Joanna, Kelly and Brian looked knowingly at each other.

Melissa screwed her face. "D'you think it'll help?"

"What'll help you Girls more than anything," said Brian, "is to call the hounds. We'll all get drunk together."

Troyan, Ma and Jeffrey were screeching their brakes in front of Brian's building within 10 minutes. They ran in and wrapped their arms around their Girls, exhorting to hear more about what went on. The GITH deferred to Brian to tell the story. What he omitted was any mention of the subterfuge that he, Joanna, Kelly had performed to unmask the killer among them. It would look now that the three were careless in their regard for the other Girls' safety instead of shielding them from what was relatively unproven. Sitting amidst the brightly lanterned and gay surroundings, the witnesses went over and over the arrest Brian had described graphically. Then it was time for the men to speak up.

"That's it, Shak," said Troyan. "You ain't stayin' 'nother night in this place. You better pack yer bags and lemme take you as far away as I can fly ya."

"I second that idea, Mel," said Jeffrey. "I don't want you to leave my sight for the next few weeks in case Marla is released … the cops may have to let her go on some technicality."

"I'm with them," said Ma. "Come home with me tonight. I'm frikin' freaked you were living with a cold-blooded killer all this time."

Brian answered them. "You want to protect your girls and so do I, guys. But the inspector told us they'd keep Marla in jail on resisting arrest and probably for causing bodily harm to the officers. We're not in any danger right now. So, instead of getting the Girls to move out, when there's no threat, why don't you all move in? You've been here a lot anyway during the Days of the Jumbo Jerk, so why not stay for a little while longer? It looks like the cops've got their serial killer. So, her case'll shoot up the docket for an early trial date. Jeff?"

"If that's the case they're making, then yes, very soon."

"What'd you say, men? Join us."

The GITH liked the idea and the boys agreed. By the time they had gone around the events of the day for a few more rounds, they were all heaped with exhaustion from overstimulation. They straggled off in pairs to bed. Brian and Kelly were left.

"I don't want to be alone tonight, Bry."

"Neither do I, honey. It'll just be the three of us."

They went downstairs and got into bed together. No sooner had they embraced and shared a reassuring word to each other than they promptly fell asleep. Oprah, at their feet, purred loudly into the darkness. She was happy, free at last to preside over her reclaimed realm.

Shatterproof

During the same time that evening, tensions had been building, not venting, at the police station. Marla was chained hands and feet in an interview room with the items from her envelope laid out before her. The police started with the $100 bill.

"Did Thane give this to you or did you take it from him around the time you killed him?" asked Hastings. "We knew he worked on Cayman Island and was staying where you live. So why not admit it?"

"Nope. I took a trip to Cayman a few years ago. I've got a passport stamp to prove it. It was money left over. I just never cashed it in."

"What about this key chain? It's the same as one owned by another murdered man, the first of two slain boyfriends of a girl you live with. You killed them both, didn't you?"

"No, I didn't, inspector," Marla said with a calm smile. "I bought that key chain on Amazon two years ago. I don't have the receipt – got it on line. I was told Keith had one like it. But I never met the man. The Girls will tell you. I like to go to pubs most nights. We never crossed paths."

They went through all the items systematically, and she had an innocent answer for all of them.

The Driver's Licence. "That's Zach's. He was my guardian, the younger brother of my dad. When my parents were killed in a car crash, I went to live with him on the farm. I was 12. Last Thanksgiving, I went for a visit. I asked for a picture. He brought me up and I realised I had nothing of his. He gave me a *ring* – this one – he said he wasn't wearing anymore and this expired licence. It was the only thing that had his picture on it. I was glad to get these things because last Christmas, a fire destroyed his house and took him too. You see that man's *gold chain*? That was my father's. Zach gave that to me on my 18th birthday. He was such a kind man and he loved my father. He knew I would treasure it as the only thing he could give me from my dad.

"That *ring* – that one there – is also precious to me. It came from a boy in high school. He was the first boy who wanted to go steady with me and he gave me the ring. Don't you give your heart when you give a ring? Anyway, after we graduated, we went our separate ways. The ring found its way to the bottom of my jewellery box, and I forgot about it. Then when I was making up this envelope of my special mementos, I had to include it. My first love.

"*Belt buckles* are something I collect. These four are keepers, especially dear to me. They represent intimate relationships of people who are no longer with us …"

"… the four you murdered, you mean …"

"Oh no, inspector, nothing like that," replied Marla still with measured, smiling control. "This one died of Ewing's sarcoma, this one a construction accident when a crane dropped a large window on him, this one hit a guard rail and went over a cliff, and this last one choked to death on a rib eye."

The examining officers looked at each other and almost wanted to laugh at Marla's imaginative fabrications.

"The three *watches* are easy to explain. All the straps are off for various reasons. This one, the Breitling Warhawk, I needed with clear numbers and waterproof when I worked in the slaughterhouse. The cloth strap didn't hold up in that wet environment. The Rolex I bought five years ago as an investment. I haven't got around to putting a better band on it that'd get me a higher resale price. This Tudor Black Bay was from my last boyfriend. We split up a couple of years ago. He moved to England and left it behind. I took the strap off because Jack had such bad taste. There you've got it, gentlemen. Before you, the story of my life."

"More like the story of your savage murders, a full baker's dozen. And the straps are off the watches, not for your reasons, but because of blood stains. That's obvious."

"You'll have to prove that, Inspector Hastings. I have given you very reasonable explanations on why I have these items."

"No, Marla Bauer, you have given us 13 fabricated lies on why you have these items. And yes, we will prove it. When we do, you will go to jail for the rest of your life."

The police kept Marla in custody on the two charges connected to the arrest. They got her old passport and checked the date stamp; the issue date on the $100 bill was more recent than the stamp. She was caught in a provable lie. The police also knew she was lying about all the other items (except the driver's licence) because the actual pieces were shown and categorically identified by the families of the murdered victims. And those families had no reason to lie about the possessions of their loved ones.

The inspector was pursuing another line of inquiry trying to put Marla and Thane together the night of his death; he had officers going to local bars around St Bartholomew Cemetery with pictures of the two; but so far, patrons at one recognised her immediately, but not Thane. She was with someone they recall, but none of them could vouch for her escort being the man in the picture. Her credit card transaction also pinpointed her at the bar with a man and dated four days prior to the discovery of the nearby murder.

The residents of Covington Place, new and old, were relieved that Marla was being kept behind bars. The GITH did their best to get back to their happy state. But the haunting image of Marla fighting off the police beset each of the Girls and disturbed her sleep. This, in turn, made their men anxious too. So, the timing of the fashion show and Melissa's marriage, soon after, were welcome events to offer balm.

The Fashion Parade

"We are about to start, everyone. So, welcome to the first Covington Place Fashion Show for the Girls in the Hall and their many, well-deserved admirers."

With these words, Joanna set the tone with a light touch for the chat-happy crowd strung along one side of the red carpet and bunched at the end of it. The runway was bathed in light; the models waited at the patio doorway; then music sounded for the first fashion to flash along the scarlet ribbon.

"We open with styles for the upcoming season, then give you fashion for any reason. So, winter coats we see, val-da-ri. Here's Nicole, in a Pajar Media Parka with Oversized Collar. Any colour if it's black and the price nudging $600 for sheer lightweight warmth. A quality price, you say, but affordable with easy pays over an entire year for many years of wear. It will flatter any setting and hey, eyeball those 'storm' cuffs and big side pockets."

"For milder winter days, you won't do better than Christy's Arctic Expedition Pullover Puffer Jacket for $129.90 in nugget gold, sundried tomato and black. Indoor/outdoor, breathable, water resistant and check that stylish high collar. It's Eco-Good too, if you care: the jacket filler is recycled plastic bottles. Wear this puffer and help the dump! Or if you prefer, Save the Duck, here's our own Melissa, in the Duck's Alexis Puffer Coat. A low $200 gives you a hood, high density 100 per cent nylon, in citronella, clay pink, frost grey or steel blue. Fits slim from XS to double XL. You wear it like you own it, Mel. Pay at the door.

"Now for something across gender lines, Brian's going to rouse you rabble with a Christmas gift to give *or* to get. How about both? Give the same gift and get a life. Here's why. You're watching Brian strap on the Oculus Quest 2 All-In-One Virtual Reality Headset. He can hit the la-la button for a mere $299 from Amazon. It's the top tech gift of the year: play games, watch flicks, take fitness classes or escape the humdrum and journey to exotic lands without leaving your satin sheets. If you buy two, you share the experience, not the headset. Suddenly you're in Bora Bora or Pago Pago together and you got there without dropping a stitch or spending a dollar. Where are you now, Bry, what do you see?"

"Call me a lunatic, but I'm on the Sea of Tranquillity with the Queen of the Acamarians skimming along in her stone boat with the warriors of Black Vindeloria hot on our heels. The Queen turns to kiss me full on the lips …"

"Say no more. I'm sold. Hey! Sell me this, I hear you say, for Nicole's back, flouncing in a desk-to-dinner pleated sweater dress from Marla Wynn. Two easies of $24.66 from XS to 2X, shibumi in the day, elegant at night, there's extra give in those pleats for that sexy swish-and-sway done just your way. Watch for it as Nicky whirls her dervish outa here. And heeere's Christy in a Kim & Co. Brazil Knit Short Sleeve Button Front Dress. For that café look, youthful, playful, a veritable one-stop wardrobe for a mere $80: open the 12 buttons, now it's a duster to wear with shorts or a denim legging; hourglass it with a patent buckle belt. Lose the belt, now it's a swing dress. Extra Small to triple XL, in hot pink solid, hot fuscia, blue animal or black purple. That's crispy crunch, Christy, crispy crunch.

"Home Girl Shakira is out of her golf clothes and sporting a two-piece top and pant matching lounge suit for a frugal $99 from Brian Bailey. Give it a wiggle, girl, you're not striding the fairway now …"

"I'm wigglin', I'm doin' my full sashay, girlfriend. Ask yourself how much swing-hip mojo can the boys take?"

"More, more," said two of the men in the crowd.

"Less, less," said Troyan.

"You see the mojo, but do you see the material in this head-to-toe gorgeous French Terry, in three colours? It's an ease-of-care, ease-of-wear ensemble with a 'lastic pull on, mid-rise, semi-fitted, long sleeve, sloop neck. And just look at that button detail down the sides to break the eye's plunge. Give it a big booty shake as you go, Shak. Brian, why have you put Kelly in that ever-so stylish rainwear when it's so clear and dry?"

"Because if it weren't for her Nuage Raincoat, she'd be clad only in the night. And who better to demonstrate it than our own Girl, Kelly, who we know is all wet even in sunshine?"

"Hey! Fill my order: hold the ham, hold the onion, hold the mayo, hold the shit."

"That's our Girl, Kelly, poopy as ever. Hose her down, Brian, and make her Nuage raincoat sweeten her mood with this haute couture surprise. Do you see it? That orange raincoat when it's wet goes zebra wild! Get the lime and it goes dotty, slip on the navy or pink and you get spring flowers. When it rains, a tone-on-tone pattern appears top-to-bottom on this full-length raincoat with hood, fully waterproof with taped seams for under 60 bucks. Hoof it outta here, Kelly Girl, you're clean and dry."

"I'm clean! I'm clean! No more Shitheads Anonymous!"

The fashion show continued in Joanna's glib patois through several more fashion stylings – A Mr Max terry knit polo dress, Diane Gilman's jeans and leggings, a Guillaume leather jacket, handbags from Coach, runners from Sketchers and shoes from Edleton and Camuto. Interspersed were Brian's picks from his own collection: A Bespoke Post Waterproof Backpack and a Truff Best Seller Pack of truffle sauces and oils, hot and not, from Amazon.

When it was over, everyone was invited to go down to Brian's apartment where the models and Girls had everything on show for Joanna to take orders on the merchandise. Then back up to party into the wee hours with Marla gratefully pushed out of mind for a time, at least.

Hard upon came Melissa's wedding – a second distraction that seemed more like an alternative reality. But not before the Girls went frantic in this reality, cramming work with fittings for their dresses and presents bought and wrapped for a bridal shower at a carefully chosen location with their favourite caterer. Somehow it all got done but left the Girls exhausted for the event itself; they were running on nerves and adrenalin, with only the official photos and gifted, one-carat diamond stud earrings to remind them they had stepped into an all-white, flower-festooned, unearthly dream of opulence and romance à la society wedding they'd never see the like again.

They would return to Earth with a thud. Joanna got notice she had been fired from her job at the shopping channel for the unauthorised use of staff and clothes for the fashion show. It didn't matter she had returned the clothes at dawn and made the company close to $3,000. No self-respecting organisation would tolerate the wildcard initiative she showed and so took the easy and exacting action of severing the troublesome limb from itself.

The Girls were devastated and promptly sent back all their bought items delivered to the Hall and instructed their friends to do the same. The Girls also stacked bags of groceries at her door twice a week for the short time she remained with them. She then went to live with Ma and spend her days looking for work. So, it was to come as a complete surprise when Brian emerged from his bathroom to answer the phone to see Joanna standing there. She answered it.

"Hello. Yeah, Jake, he's here. But I gotta tell you: I've never seen him like this. Wow!"

"*What? What? What're yah seeing?*" Jake asked audibly on the other end.

"I'll let him tell you while I watch."

Brian had slipped his towel around his waist and took the phone. She went to the sofa.

"Hi, Jake."

She could hear bits of lewd speculation crackling from Brian's device.

"*So who's the sexual predator now, boy? Wait 'til I tell your mummy!*"

"Stella would laugh you away, pal. It was accidental. She caught me. Big joke. At least, she thinks so."

"*Why a joke? Were you in the shower? Did it shrink to an inch?*"

"Not that I noticed. But then I wasn't the one looking. I'll have to call you back."

"*You're busted, Bry. Now I know it's been a Buckaladian orgy the whole time.*"

"Bacchanalian. Bye, Jake."

Brian looked over at Joanna appraising him; he held on to the towel girding him.

"You sure beat out Asian boys, Bry. I love Yongxin to death, but you're pretty exciting. Woo, and all that hair."

"I know what you're saying, Joanna. I've been in a locker room. Welcome back, by the way. Everything okay?"

"Yup. Even better now."

"Stop that. I'll be right back."

He headed for the bedroom. She seemed to like his ample bum. She whistled.

"Your mother didn't tell you this, so I will: when a woman whistles, the Virgin cries."

"Who? What Virgin?"

"The Virgin Mary."

"Oh, *that* Virgin. Doesn't She always?"

"Cry?" Brian laughs. "Yeh, I guess She does."

He returned in a tee shirt and lounge pants. She rose to hug him and kiss his cheek.

"This is sort of full circle. Remember I walked in on Kelly when I first moved in."

"I remember. But it's different with women."

"So we've been told."

"The risks are greater for us girls."

"I'd never disagree with that. But being exposed, vulnerable, embarrassed … men feel all that too until it quickly occurs to them being naked could help with the conquest."

"Scuzballs. You guys are scuzballs."

"You say that, but you'd hate it a lot more if we weren't interested."

"Don't believe it. If you took a poll and asked women if they'd prefer a six-month sabbatical every year from men's *quote* – interest – they'd vote 98 per cent 'yes' with a point 01 per cent margin of error."

"Is that you speaking as a woman or a master of psychology?"

"Take your prick, uh, oops …"

"So what brings you back to your bachelor digs? Tell me it's about your new job?"

"Sure, I'm at the university as an assistant lecturer while I work on my dissertation."

"That's great, Joanna. I'm happy for you."

"Thanks, Bry. The real reason I'm here is this. (She handed him an envelope.) We're getting married and I want all the Girls in the Hall to come, of course. And you. You were always like one of the Girls anyway."

"Today, you saw how I'm not."

"*Hot dog.*"

Brian shakes his head. "So bad."

"There's another reason I wanted to see you – to get the latest on Marla."

"Of course, as the ringleader who exposed her nasty little secret …"

"… and top of her list to get knifed in my bed."

"R-ight. Here's the quick version: the inspector tells me the prosecution liked the evidence we gave them but aren't sure it's enough to do away with 'reasonable doubt'. So, they want me to wear a wire and get a confession. God, Joanna, the closer to the day, the less I want to do it. And it's two days off now. If I can get her to spill on Thane, they think it'll be enough. But to be sure, they want me to come up with bonus material on the others."

"Bonus material? Jeez, Brian, we're not selling box sets of Downton Abbey here."

"You know what I mean. Anyway, anything I get from Marla's supposed to be hush-hush. But I don't care. I'm going-a tell it all to you Girls. You deserve that."

"Great. I'll be here and I'll call Mel. Not many left in the Hall now. Sad."

"Yeah, just Kelly and Shakira. The whole Marla thing has hit Shakira hard. She seemed to like her too. I didn't know that. It was sort-a funny, Troyan was here last night almost asking permission to take her away from the Hall."

"That's cute."

"Yuh, well, nothing lasts forever, does it?"

"This was too good to last, Bry. We all had a blast. Time to go. I'll leave invites for Shak and Kelly with you. I also have one here for Marla."

"Nice. But why bother?"

"You're right. But think about this: it might help you with her. So, give it to her, if they let you. As you like to say, the GITH have privileges."

He smiled that she remembered that, so he stood up and embraced her. She returned his embrace. She kissed him a little surprisingly on the mouth then, with a smile and requisite words of farewell, left the building.

Happiness and Heartbreak   9

Brian sat on a hard wooden chair before a hard metal table waiting for Marla to appear. He was supremely nervous. If he showed it, the game would be up. Seeing her again was going to be tough too. He'd missed her despite what happened, despite who she was; he couldn't help himself. And the waiting didn't help. Would she be glad to see him? Would she fake it? Or just give him that same smack-of-indifference look she did on that fateful night on the patio?

He heard the heavy iron door open behind him. He took in a deep breath. There was a rustle of chains and suddenly Marla stood before him, tethered in hand and leg cuffs. It was she unmistakably, but careless in cheap prison issue and pallid without the miracle of make-up. She stared at him, unsmiling, as a guard seated her across from him.

"Marla."

"Brian."

The guard left them alone, which was a break in protocol, but necessary to improve the chances of getting a confession.

"What are you doing here?"

"I had to see you."

"Why?"

"You know why. I've made my feelings clear to you. Don't pretend with me."

A slight smile twitched on her face, its paleness intensifying those black eyes as they burnt into him.

"What's the good of all that now?"

"You might not have a tap to turn on, Marla. But I can't just turn mine off."

Her eyes softened. She always liked his bulls-eye directness with her. His mother had taught him well about tough love. Other men might be rough with Marla to get her compliance; he was rough with her to get a connection. At some level, she knew that. She didn't care, but she knew.

"So?"

"All right, let's start with the practical reason I came."

"What?"

"What do you want me to do with your stuff, in case …"

"… in case I don't come back?"

"Yes, in case you don't come back."

"Give it all away. Ask the Girls if they want anything. I doubt if they will now. There's nothing I want."

"The alternative is to put everything in storage for you."

"No. The 'bugs' are determined. One way or the other, they'll get their way."

"If you're so sure of the outcome, why d'you fight them? Why not just tell them your truth?"

"I have, but it's all lies to them. You give a bug a taste, he soon contaminates the works. They don't need any input from me."

"Fair enough. But I'd like to know a couple of things."

"I bet you would."

"For instance, did you really set Lorilyn's dress on fire or was it an accident?"

Marla looked at him searchingly. Then she nodded imperceptibly. She put her head back and smiled in the recollection.

"I did it on purpose. And you know that. It wasn't what those silly little bitches were saying about you. I didn't care. It was funny in a pathetic way. But she started to crowd me and when I smelled her perfume, suddenly all her phony feminine wiles made me want to hurt her. So I lit her up."

"You could have caused her terrible pain and scars for life, even death. Didn't you think of that?"

"Sure. But I realised someone might have seen me, so I decided to save her for my sake, not hers. I'm glad I tried for another reason: your mother."

"Stella?"

"Yup. She knew I did it on purpose. When she said what I did was a…"

"'A wilful and deliberate act'…"

"That's it. Right then, I felt a strong urge to pick her up and throw her off the patio. It was there and so easy. But there was something about her that's like me: steel in her veins. And she wasn't going to back down from letting me have it about her kid. It froze me in my tracks. In my entire life, no one's ever stood up to me or *for* me, for that matter. Except you. Because you did step in and defuse it. She liked that you were doing your usual good-deed act. She went soft and gave up the fight. That's when she stopped being like me. I wouldn't have let up. It made me think later: if she had my life, would she end up like me? She had a sweet time of it, so she knows how to exploit that sweetness to get what she wants. But I liked she could be dangerous too. If her life wasn't all cushy, but born in hell like mine, would she, could she be a killer?"

"Killer?" blurted Brian, staring at her wide-eyed. "God, Marla. That's a giant leap. I'm her son; I can't see that. When I did some pretty cruel things as a boy, she took it out of my hide. But in some way, I think she liked it, because I was a boy being a boy and my cruelty was just a stage I'd grow out of."

"But you didn't. You love killing rats."

"I don't *love* it. I just don't mind it."

His remark brought a flash of recognition in her lustrous eyes. She smiled and her face was suddenly lovely.

"That makes us enough the same. I don't care either."

"Yeah, well, maybe the difference is I regret what I did as a kid."

"Like what? Give me the worst."

Brian paused, trying to call up what he had buried deep.

"I remember Stella beat the hell out of me when I would run bullfrogs' feet first through the ringers of a derelict old washing machine we had at the cottage."

Marla broke into a happy cackle. "And their guts would spew out of their mouths!"

"Marla! Would you stop? I'm trying to forget!"

They both laughed.

"Why forget?"

"Those memories are shit awful. I never want to think about them again."

"Too bad. If we were kids together, we could have gone on a wild killing spree. I started on small animals too."

"Yeah, well, talking about hurting things, there's another thing I want to know. If you wanted to punish Lorilyn for being a phony little bitch – but harmless – why didn't you take on that real sonofabitch Thane? If ever there was a man I wanted to put through the ringers, it was that bastard."

"Ha. No thrill there. He was a gutless idiot."

"He attacked all the Girls, not just Melissa. I know that."

"I was the first. He grabbed me and tried to kiss me. I threw him to the ground. He got up, ready to bash my face in. I stood waiting, smiling, hoping he would."

"He obviously didn't."

"Nope. He was full of piss and vinegar but didn't land a punch."

"I really disliked that guy. He leered at you. He obviously wanted you more than the others. Surprising he didn't try again."

"He was building up to it, after he had gone through everyone else. But it didn't work out for him."

"So he *did* make another pass. That asshole …"

"He tried, this time at a bar in front of everyone."

"What? Not our local?"

"No, we had to take a cab to get there."

"Have I been there?"

"I doubt it. It's uptown. One I liked. Went there a lot."

"I've been to a lot of them north of us. Which one?"

"The one at Beaufort and Trinity."

"Oh yeah, on the corner. What happened?"

"He got drunk. On my tab too. He didn't have any money; just bucks from Grand Cayman you couldn't cash. He moved in on me. I gave him the five-finger exercise. He got belligerent. So, I got him out of there, and we went for a walk to cool him down."

"He cooled down all right. He was found dead in a cemetery near there."

"That should have made you happy. It made me happy. Should have made the Girls happy too, especially Kelly. Boy, can she pick 'em."

"Yeah, Keith was the other one. Someone didn't like him either. Found lying in the gym's shower room full of holes."

"The touch I liked was his intestines were fanned out in a colourful frontal display."

"Jesus, I didn't know that."

"He prided himself as quite a player. Used to hold private training sessions with women at night. I heard. One of them obviously decided she didn't like her workout, so she eviscerated his bowel, slit open both jugulars, and left him to bleed out under a running shower. What I would call a clean kill."

Brian sniffed with uncertain amusement at the pun, trying to remember if all those details made it into the newspapers.

"Sounds like a professional hit. Hey, wait a minute. What happened with you and Thane. You got back, he didn't. Did you just leave him on the corner or what?"

"Yup. He wouldn't settle down. Kept groping me. I got him in a quiet spot and pushed him around a little. He finally got the message. We had enough of each other by that point, so I took a taxi home alone."

"We *all* had enough of him. Poor Kelly, she's two-for-two. She said the other day with her track record, she's going-a stay single."

Marla deadpanned. "Good choice."

"By the way, you missed Melissa's wedding. It was ritzy and very white. Sorry you weren't there."

"Don't be. I know you hate to hear anything negative about your precious Girls but, frankly, she's a real bimbo."

"She has her points. Leave her alone. I left an invitation from Joanna with the warden to give to you. She's marrying Ma, of course. I know, you won't be there; it's just a gesture. Did you know they fired her – the shopping channel – for putting on the fashion show? So, she moved out to live with Ma. Shakira is about to leave too. Troyan is champing at the bit to get her down the aisle. I didn't know Shakira had a special liking for you. Did you?"

"We got on. She gave me some golf lessons nobody knew about. Probably liked me 'cause I could drive the ball 50 yards farther than her. She was impressed by that kind of minor shit."

"Not minor, golf is her passion. Anyway, that's about it, I think. That's all my news. But I'd like to come and see you again."

"Why? Aren't you getting married? Everyone else is."

"Not unless you've heard something I didn't."

"Not likely. They've got me in near-solitary here. Gotta protect their hardened criminals from me. But they left you alone with me. Why?"

"They know I'm soft on you. It'd be like killing your mother."

"How hard could that be?"

"I want to come again. Maybe you can tell me about life with Zacharias."

"You're a complete idiot, Brian. Why would you want to step into that horror story? It's dumb-down dopey."

"Because it's your life. And I want to know you better."

"My life's all about abuse and killing. You don't want to know me better. There is no 'better'. Go play with your little Girls in the Hall … oh, I guess only Kelly's left. If she doesn't get you by default, she could only do worse."

Brian looked at her impassively. He was going to wait her out until she agreed. Marla raised her eyebrows. Then she realised she hadn't said more than half-a-dozen words during her entire incarceration. And she enjoyed chatting with Brian. A smile curled at the corners of her perfect lips.

"All right, Brian. You want to hear about that sonofabitch Zach, okay. But bring a sick bag and wear an incontinence pad. You're going to piss and puke your way through it."

"Gee, how often do you get an offer like that?"

"You won't gee-whiz about it after. I promise."

The police were waiting for him in the warden's office to remove the button wire. They said nothing about the conversation but were happy about another session. In the ride back to the Hall, Brian asked when they wanted the second visit. As soon as possible; he'd be informed. He asked who would be listening to the evidence and deciding on its use. No response. He asked if they thought it was enough to convict her. No response. He asked if she'd get life without parole if convicted. No response. But as he was getting out of the car, one of them wagged a finger at him and spoke almost angrily to him to shut up about what went on or there'd be consequences. It riled Brian.

"Hey! I'm doing this as a favour to you guys. I'm not the prisoner here. You remember that."

They stared at him bug-eyed. He got out and slammed the car door.

Brian walked down the Hall to his apartment. What a different feeling. No one was there. Kelly was on a buying trip and Shakira was probably off with Troyan planning their wedding. He sat down with a large Glenmorangie when a sadness suddenly engulfed him. Seeing Marla again was like a drug, elating him then deflating him. Just then, a trap sounded and the agonised fizzle of a rat. It was as if Marla was so right there that the moment needed a symbolic killing. He went over for a knife and a baggie only to find the rat had escaped. He was disappointed. Why? He wasn't doing it for her.

He looked up and Shakira was in the doorway. She was just picking something up and wanted to tell him she'd be moving her things out in a week or so. He asked about the dinner he wanted to throw for them as with

Melissa. She suggested Saturday night, three days off; her dad liked fish and nothing too fancy would work. He told her he saw Marla but didn't want to talk about it except to say she seemed all right. Shakira understood immediately, asking only if he was going to see her again. Brian said he was. She went over and kissed him, then hugged him. He couldn't help tearing up. She put his face in her hands and looked intently at him. She said she'd call him about Saturday and left. He fed Oprah, prepared some quick scrambled eggs for himself, and the two went off to bed. Oprah knew he was in a sad state, so purred him to sleep very loudly in his left ear.

Shakira's Turn

As before, a cocktail party for all the GITH preceded the dinner. All four came with their men – even Kelly with a tall, thin man who had a whiskered patch under his lower lip and darting eyes. The Girls looked at him out of the corners of their eyes; it would take the imagination of a cockroach to guess what each of them thought. Despite that, the GITH soon slipped into that soft-leather ease they had mellowed together. Melissa and Jiggins were back from their honeymoon and so physically demonstrative with each other, it had an infectious effect on the others with their men. In the midst of this hug fest stood Ben and Bessie Buckingham, Shakira's parents.

Ben had spent most of his adult life at Delhaven Golf Course as a groundskeeper and its superintendent for the past five years. And Bessie, the full-time office manager and outreach supervisor for their community church. Ben had fostered an interest in Shakira for golf that led to a short amateur career. He was convinced she was good enough to go pro, but Shakira loved teaching and was content with her life as assistant pro on her childhood course.

The Girls were naturally curious about Brian's meeting with Marla. He put them off, promising a get-together after his second visit. They were no longer traumatised by the dramatic arrest, but had been restive before their first visit back there together. No need to have worried. They'd had too many happy times there for one black moment to spoil it. Just before Brian was ready to serve dinner and hit the gong, spelling the end of the drinks party, he took the Girls downstairs for the sort of surprise they had grown to expect. He gave each of them a plastic-wrapped loaf of their favourite bread. The labels read: *A Touch of Home.* They were moved enough about that, but wept outright when they saw he had baked a lone loaf that sat unclaimed.

Troyan was actually to upstage Brian's culinary feast for Shakira and her loved ones. But it was not for lack of trying. Brian began with an unusual starter: Buddha Jumps Over the Wall, a delectation of quail's eggs, sea cucumber, scallops, chicken, ginseng and mushrooms. He had been warned that Ben liked simple food, so it came as a surprise to an irked Shakira to find out she was wrong. Brian went on to upset Shakira further by feeding them Ritz Carlton Creamed Finnan Haddie, asparagus with hollandaise, and jasmine pilaf, then finishing with a key lime cheesecake in a raspberry coulis.

"I tol' you Bry, poppa can't take this rich food."

"You settle, honey," said Ben. "… I never et better. You see me eatin' hamburgers and you think I love 'em? I don't. I hate 'em. I don' care if I ever see a burger on my plate to my dyin' day."

"Poppa! Are you pullin' my taffy? Did you know this, Momma?"

"No, child, I'm as flabbergusted as you. Twen'y-five year and he hate the burgers. (She chuckles.) I suppose you hates the hot dogs too?"

Ben nodded. "Worse."

They are completely shocked because Ben is serious; then they suddenly break into unrelieved laughter.

"I guess we won't be eatin' them no more, Ben. Is that what you're sayin'?" asked Bessie.

"You eat 'em all you want, Bess. I'll eat here."

As they were speaking, Brian offered second servings of the cheesecake, then said, "It seems, ladies, you'll be coming to Brian's international cooking school Saturdays at two if you're going to keep the old man happy."

"Seems so, young man," said Bessie. "I jus' can't believe it. Why you never tell me, Ben?"

"I knows how you love 'em, Bess. So I say nuthin'."

"If that isn't love," said Troyan, "what is? I hope I can live up to you, Ben."

"What else am I not woke to, Poppa?"

"I didn't say, honey girl."

"Well, say."

Ben shook his head. Instead he turned to Brian.

"That was a beautiful meal you made us, Brian. I knows it was for Shakira …"

"… no, for all of you, I promise."

"Well, thank you most kindly."

"It was my pleasure. But I can feel Troyan has something up his sleeve. From the look on his face, it may even be more surprising than hating quarter pounders for a quarter of a century!"

"Actually, I do …"

"Oh no, Troy," said Shakira. "Don' tell me an alien bambino is gonna burst outta yer belly?"

"How could you know that, Shak? (He jerked to simulate the belly burst; Shakira did her diaphragm bend.) No, something a lot less painful. I thought this would be a good time to tell ya that I got you a family membership at Delhaven. You've spent your life there, Ben, and you're probably going-a, Shak – 'cause I know how you love it – all that time there, but not as members. Now, you are … members for life."

"Now I know I'm gettin' pulled 'cause workers can't be members."

"They can if I own the club!"

Why a neighbour didn't call the police when a high-pitched scream was heard on a nearby rooftop will remain a mystery. It took Shakira a good half hour to calm herself, with Ben shaking his head incredulously and Bessie chuckling throughout, interspersed with moments of serious reflection. Troyan invited them to have lunch at the club the next day to make it official.

Before noon, the Buckinghams strode into the clubhouse at Delhaven Golf Course as if they owned it. Several staff tried to disavow them of that notion until Troyan met them and escorted them into the dining room with great fanfare. On their way to the owner's alcove, Troyan called over the manager who was seated at another table.

"Jack, a word, please."

John Nicholas came over with a bustling deference, nodding to Ben and Shakira with a smile.

"Ben, Shakira, Mrs Buckingham. Yes, sir, what can I do?"

"Help me seat our honoured guests first, you the ladies, I'll look after Mr Buckingham."

When everyone was settled, Troyan made sure menus were handed around.

"Jack, I want all the staff to know that the Buckinghams are now life members and must be treated like all other long-term members plus they have preference for this table and the owner's cabin on the 18th hole. Please be sure everyone knows by the end of the day."

"Yes, sir, I'll see it's done. And welcome to all of you as new members."

Shakira and Ben felt distinctly uncomfortable in the main dining room for the first time. Bessie rode the wave with a *que será* serenity. In fact, Ben was nervous enough to order the cheapest entrée, the hamburger plate. It brought a surprise gasp and protest from Shakira. Troyan laughed and said he could arrange to have the hamburger made with ground steak if that helped. Ben just ordered the steak. Shakira nodded, muttering. Bessie chuckled.

Before lunch came, a staffer came over with corsages for the two women. Shakira pinned one on her mother, then Troyan on his fiancée. A second tip that Brian had given Troyan was to pay special attention to Bessie, endearing both women. But it was his own idea to ask Ben at that lunch to be his personal guide in a golf cart to learn the course as the owner rather than a casual player. Then, something for Shakira:

"Would you like to get married here at Delhaven, Shakira? If you do, I'll start to make the arrangements."

Shakira wanted to shriek again but caught herself. Then she wasn't sure about it. She looked to her parents. Ben thought it was a great idea; Bessie shook her head.

"Why, Momma?"

"You work here, Shakira. You wan' to get away. And I was countin' on you gettin' wed at the church."

"You work *there*, Momma."

"Yeah, but I'se not gettin' married."

"Scabrous! Church it is, Troy. Just as we planned."

"Done," said Troyan. "We'll have the reception here. And if you agree, Shak, I'm gonna ask all the members of the club to come. (She nods.) Good. And why not? They're hardly strangers. I'll make sure it's an invitation they can't refuse."

"How you do that, Troy?" asked Shakira.

"Because I'm gonna tell them that Delhaven's my wedding present to you."

This time, Ben let out a yell. "Oooeeee, that'll sure do it. Every man child and his momma will be here or else!"

"I could only buy a quarter share of the club. But I'll add to it every anniversary."

Shakira's shock gave way to tears that she buried in her napkin.

Back in Jail

Brian sat on the same hard wooden chair before the same metal table hearing the same metal door open and the same jingle of shackles preface the appearance of his hollow-hearted love. He had the same emotional tension as before too, but this time because he was braced for a truly grisly afternoon.

"Marla."

"Brian."

Marla looked the same; she made no effort to gussy herself up. It didn't matter to Brian; he was happy to see her. There was a pause, neither knowing who should start. He did.

"Had a nice time with Shakira and her family the other night. They all came to dinner on the patio. She told me they went to lunch at Delhaven the next day. And get this: Troyan blew her away by telling her he was giving her the golf course as a wedding present. How about that?"

"That makes Shakira suddenly worth knowing."

"I thought you two liked each other."

"No, she likes me. Haven't a clue why. I never did anything special for her. I'd remember because I never do. Except for you. I took you to bed."

"Surprise – I haven't forgotten."

"Why are they letting me see you alone? Again. Something's not right. Check the walls for microphones."

They got up and surveyed the entire room, including under the table and chairs.

Marla continued talking. "They watch me with an armed guard whenever I'm around anyone else. Why not with you? They gotta know you wouldn't be safe even with these chains."

"I'm not completely helpless, Marla. Your restraints give me the edge. I don't think I could hit you, but I could use the chair to keep you away from me like a lion tamer." (He laughs.)

She smirked. He shook his head at her, nothing found. She nodded. Then she went up to him and put her hands awkwardly on his chest. She nodded again. They sat.

"Even if they're not spying, my lawyer told me not to say anything to anyone, even you."

"It's all right with me. And it's why they left us alone," said Brian. "I told them we were lovers. I said you'd behave."

She smiled. "You're pretty sure of yourself. I like that Brian. I have to say you *are* different from other men I've met."

"How?"

"You're not an angry, needy, selfish asswipe."

"Like Zacharias?"

Her eyes fixed coldly on him, a viper's stare.

"Like Zacharias."

"How did you end up in that bastard's evil clutches anyway?"

"So, you're ready to hear my shit story, are you? Okay. But do you promise never to repeat what I say? Ever?"

"I do."

"I told you once if there was ever a man I could trust it would be you. So for the first time in my life, I'm going to. Don't betray me. I once had a dream of someone betraying me. It was an amazing dream: I killed him by the inch."

Her dark pools for eyes submerged him. He nodded with a slight smile and silent gulp.

Carnage Incarnate

"Here it is. My parents died in a car crash when I was 12. I was in the back seat and was banged up pretty bad but came through it in one piece. Then I was sent off to live with relatives – the only ones that would take me. He was an uncle on my father's side from the other side of the tracks, like we used to say. Zach's wife, Gladys, was alive then and as dumb and cruel as they come. From the time I got to their farm, he started to have sex with me; Gladys knew and shrugged it off. It never occurred to her when he was screwing me, he was also screwing me up. They fed off each other's crap. And I was the whipping girl. I was worked to death; put down about everything and beaten constantly. They looked for reasons to beat me, except … except when he was sticking it to me. Even Bull, the damned dog, just a pup then, took nips out of me. The day Gladys died, I danced on her grave. I was 17 by then, big and brawny from all the heavy work Zach stuck me with …"

"God, Marla, didn't you have anyone in your corner, no one to show you a little love?"

"Love? Ha. Who? Boys would be buzzing around the place, but they only wanted one thing. And Zach wasn't going to have his prize heifer violated by anyone else. The moment came when I had enough. It was leave or fight back. He tried to stop me at first. But even he knew he couldn't hold me, not legally. So, he drove me to the bus in town, gave me enough for the ticket – no more – and told me never to return. He called me 'an ungrateful cow' and drove off in a cloud of dust."

"That's a shit story all right. I'm surprised you didn't try and run away."

"I did at first, lots of times. But I was underage and the cops always picked me up and took me back. Then punishment was very bad because I had embarrassed them with outsiders. When I finally got out of that hell, freedom was crazy wonderful. This prison is nothin' compared to the slave camp I came from."

"But you did go back, didn't you?"

"Yup, once."

"Why? Unfinished business?"

"I needed – what'd you call it?"

"Closure?"

"Closure. And I was curious to see how far he sunk. Zach taught me how to farm so I could do it *all* for him. With me gone, maybe eight years, I figured he'd let it slide away. And he did. The first thing he said was:

"You! What are *you* doin' here? Come back to catch up the years o' work you didn' do?"

"Nope. Just curious to see if you could hold on to the farm without your little slave."

I planted a bottle of single malt down in front of him. His eyebrows went up – this was nectar to the gods for a man weaned on the rot gut from his illegal still out back. Without a word, he opened the bottle and took a giant swig.

"I'm still here, ain't I?"

"I don't know. Are you? You look like shit."

"Watch yer mouth. Yer still good for a smack."

"If it's courtesy you want, how about offering to share a drink if you can find a clean glass?"

"Zach washed a glass and wiped it with a dirty tea towel. The bottle was gone in the time he tol' me of his downward spiral. His cattle came down with BRSV – that's a respiratory virus. It took most of the herd because the vet wasn't getting paid and stopped coming. That's also why old Bull lay sick and untreated in the corner. Zach had a lot wrong with him as well – chronic lung disease, bad hearing, bad eyesight, arthritis in his hands. Then he confessed the farm was in foreclosure. This was music to my ears, of course, but I pacified him with a phony show of sympathy. I put a second bottle on the table.

"It wouldn't have taken much to get Zach where I wanted him, but liquor was quicker. A third into the second bottle, he was pleading for a little sexual tenderness. I let 'for old time's sake' and 'the only one I truly loved' spill off as easily as any emotion I never felt. Then, I suddenly stood up, stripped off my clothes and went giggling to my old bedroom with Zach hot on my tail, forgetting his aches and pains. I pulled the dust cover off my bed; years of dust flew in the air. When both of us were naked in bed, I squirmed with low moans to help him tool up. He worked hard at it. I felt under my pillow. It was still there. I drew out my old Bowie knife I kept close for years in case things got too bad. With one hand on his neck, I extended my arm full out, pushing him away; with the other hand on the knife, I put a great puncture in his chest, avoiding his heart for best. He screamed and tried to fight back. But after three more good leaks in him, the fight went out of him. He fell on the floor, groaning in agony.

"Bull ran in, saw his master rolling in pain and attacked me. I put the pillow up to take his bite, then plunged the knife deep into his side. He howled and yelped away dragging his wound on the ground. I grabbed Zach, tossed him up on my shoulders, and headed for the barn. He knew what was comin'. He pleaded in gasping sobs to stop. I strung that bastard up in chains, arms out tight, and started to carve away."

"What, you mean you *butchered* him?" asked Brian, horrified.

"Yup. just like dressing a steer," she said motioning as much as her chains allowed. "It seemed right. He taught me how to do it. I kept asking him, 'How am I doin', Zach? Am I doin' it the way you like it?'"

"Jesus, Marla. That's as bad as it gets. Was he conscious?"

"He was there for some of it, but he didn't have a lot of conversation, mostly pleading and screaming."

"I hate myself for thinking this, but I *am* a guy. He raped you for years, so did you look after that ... part ..."

She laughed. "You got it, sweetheart. I sliced it off, spiked it like one of our rats and sent it deep up his ass."

"Why his ass?"

"For all the times he back-ended me."

Brian felt it coming up. He wasn't going to be sick, he told himself. He had to see it through.

"I, I get it. This was justice for you."

She nodded, appraising him. "I know you think I'm a monster. But the fact is, if they treated me okay and not made my life a hellhole of torture all that time, I wouldn't have touched him. I'd have gone back every Christmas and brought them something they needed for the farm. Instead, he finally got what was comin' to him and, as a favour from me, he got it all at once."

"And if Gladys hadn't died ..."

"I'd have chained her in the next stall. Routine job, mostly trimming fat."

Brian breathed in deeply and rubbed his eyes.

"Okay, I asked for this. Finish the story. I suppose you left his heart for last?"

"Right again. You got the killer's finesse, Bry. He was played out by then. I tore his black heart out of his chest and threw it on the ground in front of him. Oh yeah, there were three mangy head of cattle left in the barn; all that screamin', they were jumpy as hell; they always know when death is close. For me, it was like old home week at the slaughterhouse. I didn't know how much I missed it. Never done it naked though – sort of got off on that. Shoulda seen me – covered in blood, top to toe.

"I hauled Zach back to the house and pitched him on the kitchen floor, mostly just skin and bones left. Bull was whimpering away in his corner, lapping up his blood. I took a good swig of the whisky and had a shower. Then, I put my clothes back on, got Zach's favourite shotgun and put both barrels to that cur's miserable head …"

"The dog's …?"

"Yeah, Bull. Then I emptied the bottle – and a third one I'd brought along – all over the floor of the farmhouse and set it on fire. I went back to the barn. I lit some old kerosene lamps Zach kept for power failures and threw 'em on a pile of stacked bales before I drove off. As I turned the corner outa the property, I looked back and saw both buildings eaten up by flames. Then I thought, *Oh shit, I just did that sonofabitch a big favour.* He let the farm run down and was gonna get tossed out. I made the end easy for him. (She laughed.) Sort of. But I was glad to give him the send-off he had coming."

Brian nodded at her. He was so conflicted he couldn't even speak for a time. She looked at him with no clue what he was feeling but waited with the patience all killers must acquire.

"This is my last visit, Marla. They won't let me come again. And despite all the horror you just told me – and it's goddam horrible – I'm going to miss not seeing you. I'm amazed I'm even saying this, but it's true. I'm going to miss you."

"Yup. Okay. We talk. It's good."

"What I think about you now is very different, but I can't suddenly change how I feel about you. I'm in love with you, Marla. STILL. Even though I know you're a heartless, cold-blooded killer! How crazy is that?"

"You're not crazy, Brian. Maybe a bit like Kelly. She picks 'em seamy. You pick 'em lethal."

"It's more complicated than that."

"I sure wish we coulda' met when I needed you back then. Maybe a little TLC woulda changed how things worked out. I don' know. Maybe I wouldn't have seen it for what it was, if I met you back then. But you sure made it nice in the Hall. You made it easy for me to hide there."

Just then, the guards came in to get her. The police obviously had all they needed.

"Goodbye, Marla. I'll be at the trial. Oh, almost forgot, the butchers at Duguid's were asking about you."

"Asking what?"

They took her away. When he went to the warden's, he asked to use his bathroom where he yorked his guts out. He'd held in the revulsion as long as he could. The trip home in the police car was silent. They said nothing; he asked nothing. He was shaking involuntarily. He got out without a parting word. He wondered now if he wanted to tell the Girls Marla's story. What was the sense of putting them through it? Maybe he could give them a toned-down version. How d'you tone down that horror show? Maybe he could just tell Joanna the story. He'll tell her and she could pass it on to the rest of them. No, that's not how it works in the Hall. It's all for one. R-ight. Not that there are any Girls in the Hall anymore. They've gone their separate ways … mostly. No, there'll always be the GITH whenever they get together. He had promised he'd tell them. He would.

Back with His Girls

"We love the new house, Brian," said Melissa brightly. "It's perfect. And we just about have it furnished. Housewarming soon, Girls."

"I know you'll be happy there," said Brian. "Nice neighbourhood, four bedrooms for a family, backs on a ravine for a permanent vista. What about you, Shakira, did you tell the Girls what Troyan did to *you*? A real shocker."

Shakira did her tummy bend. The GITH hadn't heard; they perked up and asked, "What? What?" fearing the worst.

"No, it's Gucci, Girls. That ornamental man-o-mine just went and dropped a golf course on me."

"A wedding present. How about that?" added Brian.

"Yeah, Delhaven. Troy'll have to run it. But as my husband, I'll hire his sweet ass for a dollar a year."

"Shit. When do the bells ring for me?" asked Kelly. "Mel gets a house; Shak gets a friggin' golf course! I get Vito."

"How're you doing with Virile Vito, Kel?" asked Joanna. "We're all curious …"

"… if I picked another dud? Yeah, he's a piece of crap. I could tell by the way you looked at him, you knew. But here's the good news: I dropped him. It's a positive step for me, Girls. I don't hang on to 'em anymore. Gotta stay loose for a real guy … in my dreams."

"My reception's at Delhaven, Girls. You're all comin'. Everybody's comin'. So, you'll find a hot guy there, Kel, or there ain't one."

"There ain't one, Shak. But I'll be there. You Girls outa help: spread the story about how hot I am, then start shovelling 'em my way."

"Or you might find one at my wedding, Kel," said Joanna. "I'm up next. Get your bridesmaid dresses out of mothballs, Girls, recycle and reuse. You don't mind, do you, Mel?"

"Oh no, great idea. I'll get one made. Hey, it's in less than a month now, Jo. Wow. All of us are getting marr … Oh! Sorry, Kel, sorry, Bry."

"Start shovelling, Girls," said Kelly. "Or I'll end up hitched to Brian."

They all groaned in protest. At some point, they all thought him a catch.

"Brian's no pussy, Kel," said Joanna. "He's the only one to sleep with a mass murderer and live to tell about it."

"How d'you know that?"

"We all know, Bry," said Kelly. "You can't live in the Hall and keep *that* secret."

"The reason we're here, Girls," said Joanna, "is to hear how he got a confession out of Marla. It couldn't be easy. We all know how he's hopelessly in love with her."

"I didn't know you *all* knew that!"

"We know it all, Bry," said Kelly. "We're the GITH you keep boasting about. You're just a guy. And guys are not alive 'til they're 45."

"Jeez, what else d'you know?"

"We jus' love, love, love yer silk undies, Bro," said Shakira. "Smexy!"

Brian's eyes grew wide, then he threw his head back and laughed. They laughed too, except Melissa, ("Oh, Girls!") who was embarrassed their secret was out.

"Okay, here it comes. You've got to keep all this hush-hush, Girls. I'm breaking a promise I made to her and the cops to say nothing. But if anyone deserves to know, it's you."

Brian then launched into the details of what transpired with Marla. He covered Keith and Thane first, to introduce the horrors, especially of Zacharias, gradually. Kelly was frozen by the first testimony about her boyfriends. Brian had left her a full bottle of white wine of which she made emptying use. When he had finished the gory account about Zacharias, they went through shock, disgust and tears in rapid order. He waited for them to recover, filling their glasses, half-hugging them as they sat in a stunned silence. He kissed Melissa on the cheek, because she seemed most distraught.

She looked up at him. "What's the point if it could be over any minute?"

No one answered the unanswerable.

"Okay, Brian, tell me this," said Kelly, now slurring her words and slightly defiant. "How come she kills all my boyfriends and 10 or shit, maybe 20, 30 more guys, but has a fuck-fest with you and doesn't slit *your* throat?"

"She gave me a clue. I was useful in making the Hall a great place for her to hide."

"I'm woke to us all doin' that," said Shakira. "An' maybe that saved all our tooshes. But roastin' chicken with a serial killer is pretty skitchy, Bry. One wrong word and she'd bounce you to the next world."

"R-ight. And if you knew she was a killer while you were 'roasting', you'd say something wrong for sure. I'll tell you this though – Marla was like no one else I've been with."

Joanna looked quizzical. "Should we ask *how*, Girls?"

"No, Jo," cut in Melissa, "we should not."

"I'll tell you. She had to work at being gentle because she's he-man strong. It felt a bit weird like being in bed with a guy, I suppose, except she had these great breasts and no … ding-dong."

"I know what that's like," sloshed Kelly.

"Whadyamean?" asked Melissa.

"Keith. He had these huge pecs, tiny …"

She threw her finger up and whistled. Everyone laughed. Kelly's cryptic humour had its uses for, in this case, it saved them from a deep wallow in despair and disgust from the horror of Marla's butchery.

"Marla can never get out," said Joanna. "When she learns you wore a wire …"

"I didn't have much choice …"

"That won't matter to her. If she ever gets out, she'll take a long time killing you."

"Stop being such a scaremonger, Jo." said Kelly. "She'll never get out. She's killed damn near every varmit that crossed her evil path."

"Then she moved up to men."

"That's not moving up, Mel."

"No worries, Girls, Marla won't find me," said Brian. "I've decided to sell the Hall and move on."

"Sell? Sell?"

Moving Out *10*

Kelly liked to sleep in and was usually able to with her schedule. But she was up bright and early the next morning to talk to Brian about the bombshell he'd dropped on them the night before.

"Morning, Kelly. Come on in. Have some breakfast. French toast today."

"Thanks. I will. Coffee?"

"Sure. Help yourself."

"That was some surprise about owning the Hall, Bry. But it's your business, I guess."

"Right. I didn't want it to get in the way of making it happen for us. I know I probably should've told you first about selling, but I just made the decision yesterday and it sort of slipped out."

"Yeah, you shoulda told me. I need to give you notice. You gotta do the same."

"You're right. I apologise. But we can find you a place you'll like and fast."

"How?"

"Telvan manages different properties. We'll work at getting you a good place at a great rent. You may want to go in with someone. Otherwise it'll be a big change after being with all the Girls. Tell you what: I'll get the agency to check it out this morning and we can talk tonight."

"Okay. I'd like to stay in the neighbourhood."

"Good. I'm going-a look for a place around here too. Oh, one other thing."

"What?"

"Can you take Oprah? She likes you best. She'll be happiest with you. I work all the time. It wouldn't be fair."

"What about my buying trips? I'm away for a week or two at a time."

"That's okay. If you're not rooming with someone, you can give her to me when you're away. That'll be a way we keep in touch."

"Deal. I love Oprah. I've always loved cats. They treat me better than men."

"That's easy."

Court

Brian had waited impatiently to hear if the wire tape confession with Marla would be admissible in court. He knew the police would be working hard to make it so. But a court, more properly a judge, would have had to make that decision based on all the evidence. Because of the public profile of the case, and the rather persuasive prompt of no fresh killings since Marla's incarceration, the wiretap was allowed. And the trial was moved up the docket, as predicted.

For every day of the trial, the Girls made sure that one of them was with Brian. In the event that couldn't happen, they'd throw in one of their men to sit with him. On no account would they let him be alone. They felt it was the least they could do for their beloved Brian who was going to see the woman he loved put away forever and largely due to his efforts.

The defence was able to make a strong argument regarding the physical evidence – Marla's knickknacks – as circumstantial and to assign 'reasonable doubt' to all the coincidences that arose; obvious here were the many items identified, but also two of the killings being boyfriends of a fellow tenant and the cessation of killings during the time they were in Africa or Marla's time in jail.

There was also no supporting evidence. The killer was impeccable about leaving no clues. Even in the Keith murder, no blood anywhere; the locker room was swabbed clean of footprints even. Another suspected victim was emasculated and left to bleed out in his car; there were no keys, doors locked, and not a fingerprint inside the entire vehicle except his. At Zacharias's farm, the only forensic evidence was charred human and animal bones from the fires that destroyed house and barn. Nowhere on any of the serial killer's corpses with slit throats and beheadings was anything traceable: no foot or finger prints, hair, skin under the nails, a rag of clothing, no DNA. *Nothing*. Her defence ended there. Then the wiretap evidence was presented. It was the pivot on which the case was to turn, and it turned dead against Marla.

When that evidence was broached, Marla's head snapped back, and the atmosphere in the court went electric. She moved her head menacingly toward Brian with a face that broke every commandment. It was a ravening stare and it held Brian frozen in place. It was clear to him, if she could get to him right then, she'd tear his heart out of his body without the use of an implement.

She didn't look at him again for the rest of the trial that put her away for life without parole. The GITH were all with him for the sentencing and they all had their hands on him when it was read. He was overwrought as much from guilt perhaps as loss. The Girls wept. Marla waived having anything final to say and was whisked out of the courtroom.

Afterwards, Melissa took the wheel and they all crowded in to take him back to the Hall. He apologised when they got to his apartment; he was whipped and needed to go to bed. So, they put him to bed – one took off his shoes, another threw a cover over him. Not down to the silk this time. Each gave him a kiss with a word of comfort:

"You're iconic, Bry. That will nev-a change for us, ev-a!"

"She's gone. You can move on now and leave her behind."

"You're our boy."

"You love her, we love you. How fair is that?"

He smiled at each solicitude and drifted off. They went to sit in the living room, all talking at once to get their nerves to settle. Kelly went into the kitchen to get some ice for their drinks when she noticed.

"Oh, shitbags!" she broke. "You wily, wonderful boy scout. Look, Girls. Look."

Their loaves sat on the counter. They were so pre-occupied with Brian and letting the anxiety run out of them, they hadn't seen the tidy rows sitting there. This time, the labels had their names first and below in bold letters, **Of the Hall.** Notably missing was Marla's loaf.

"He knew," said Joanna. "That's really special."

"He knew we'd bring him back," said Melissa. "All of us. That's darling."

"No Marla this time," said Kelly, tearing a little. "How can he do this to us? Shit, he's only a guy."

"He's only a guy, Kel, but he's GOAT!"

They took their loaves and hugged them the whole time they had a drink together, toasting Brian and the end of Marla. Joanna reminded them that her dinner would be the last time they'd all be together in the Hall. Brian had promised to have it soon after the trial. Now that trial was over. As they left, they all looked in on him with their loaves still squeezed close. They all kissed Kelly, then walked down the Hall and viewed their empty rooms in passing, remembering …

When Melissa had driven Shakira and Joanna to the Hall to collect Brian and Kelly for the court sentencing, they saw the 'For Sale' sign on the front lawn. It gave them a choking kind of sadness. On their way out of the building, the Girls now felt more of a gripping nostalgia for their time there.

Kelly sat alone in Brian's apartment. Where was Oprah? She looked in his bedroom. Oprah was at his ear, purring away. She petted her, moving her aside to get in beside Brian. He stirred slightly. She snuggled carefully not to wake him and joined him in a sound, comforting sleep.

Last Call

Coming in for the last drinks party for Joanna's dinner a week or so later, the Boys of the Hall saw the SOLD sign on the front lawn and had a different reaction. They saw Brian in a new light, especially Troyan, not just as a nice guy but a savvy real estate investor.

Once they were all up on the roof with a drink in their hands, Kelly was bursting to tell them she had found a great apartment with Brian's help and, safely, with a female roommate. The move'd be in a couple of weeks.

"Tell us what day and we'll move you," said Troyan.

"Really?"

"Of course," said Jeffrey. "You're a paid-up member of the GITH, with all the privileges pertaining thereto."

"I worked for a moving company when I first came to this country," said Ma. "We can make it work pretty good for you at a price you'll like."

The Girls chimed in they'd help too and have a bash in her new digs after.

They never knew when Brian would spring a surprise. And on their last night on the patio together, he wasn't to disappoint. He handed each of them a present, wrapped in gold paper, all identical and without cards.

It was a framed photograph of the six of them standing together on the renovated patio; it was the only snapshot of them together. They were naturally touched by it, though seeing Marla there gave them a start. To have her brushed out was not something Brian would do. She was part of the GITH's history, probably the happiest times of their pre-married lives. She belonged there. And he particularly needed a reminder of her.

The Girls had never met Joanna's parents. They could have guessed from knowing Joanna that her people would be scarily bright. Charles was her father, a fusion scientist working with an international team to refine the technology to make fusion energy the future promise for cheap power. Her mother used Adrienne for her western name and was a professor of Chinese studies. Their natural curiosity put the Girls at ease (and embarrassed Joanna) because they wanted to know everything about the 'wonderful people' their daughter had spoken about. If the discourse felt a bit like an interview, the Girls didn't seem to mind divulging whatever it was about themselves that would satisfy their curiosity.

But most of the time was spent talking about the logistics of the wedding which was a week away. The service was to be at a Buddhist temple her parents had been going to from the time they were new to the country. Ma was a non-practicing Buddhist but had been prevailed upon to take an interest in being wed in a temple ceremony. Bridesmaids are not usually a part of it, but they would be brought in to witness the ritual in a way similar to a western-style wedding.

The animated conversation also embraced Shakira's wedding, delayed because Delhaven had to find a spot in its schedule and make all the detailed arrangements Troyan laid down for the reception. In the ensuing days, the Girls would get together to discuss the preparations for both weddings at respective bridal showers in their boyfriends' houses, not the Hall – a clear sign that their old haunt was fading as a part of their lives.

The gong sounded signalling the end of the cocktail hour and for dinner with the family to start. The other couples decided to have dinner together downtown and asked Kelly to join them. As they filed out, Brian was busy getting dinner on but the Girls hugged him and thanked him for their pictures. He could tell it meant a lot and would anchor the memories of the Hall forever in their minds. For the last, sad time, they took their loaves, each one of them soon hugged out of shape.

The dinner started with Brian offering a small aperitif. He lifted his glass to the betrothed.

"All the best for the future, Joanna, Ma."

Everyone drank a sip of the liquor. Her parents both let out a laugh and looked at Brian with surprised delight.

"Osmanthus!" Charles nearly shouted. "It's Osmanthus."

Joanna was intrigued. Then she laughed.

"Oh, Brian, you keep doing it. What the hell's Omsamthus?"

"No, Jo," said Adrienne, "Os-man-thus. It's a wine from Guilin. Made from the Osmanthus flower. The ancients used it as a favoured medicine. A nice surprise, Brian."

"I haven't had Osmanthus since we left China. You did surprise."

"I know it's a wine for dinner or after dinner, but I like it as an aperitif. And it's always a thrill to get one up on Joanna."

"You got me, Bry. What scares me is what happens next. No live monkey brain please."

"I promise, sweetie. That's a great looking ring. Jade, right?"

"Yuh, it's my engagement ring from Yongxin."

"It's the pick of our collection. Jo always admired it when we sold our Jade line together on the network."

"Great. Please sit everyone. First course, soup."

"Can I help?"

"No, Joanna. You're my guest of honour. Maybe Ma could lend a hand."

"Sure, let's go."

Brian kept surprising Joanna and her parents. The imitation Shark Fin soup with bean noodles was close enough to the real thing to fool and shock them. He had to assure them 'no shark was killed in the production of this dish'. Then on to Moo Goo Gai Pan, a western version of a Cantonese chicken stir fry, and finishing with Red Bean Buns and warmed Egg Tarts with another slurp of Osmanthus.

Through the courses, Brian was brought up to date on what they were doing. It happened that Ma had already put a down payment on a house and wouldn't let her parents help. So, they decided to give them a honeymoon and look after Joanna's expenses for graduate school. It was preordained she'd get her doctorate, but now she would specialise in disorders like psychopathy, an unintended legacy from her relationship with Marla. Brian was perversely pleased to hear that.

"Joanna was the one who uncovered the 'killer among the doves' here – that's Kelly's descriptive phrase. So, it makes sense she wants to understand more about people like Marla."

"She's always talked about going back to school," said Ma. "That life's in their blood."

"Jo's told us the story of Marla and your part in it," said Adrienne. "She has great respect for your bravery."

"Yes, it is impossible to imagine putting the one you love in jail for her lifetime."

"It was terrible, sir. Joanna will tell you I could never have a normal relationship with Marla. But I felt rotten and very guilty to be the one to do it."

"You'd never know she was this killer," added Ma. "She fit in so well, except she was this stunning beauty and very sexy."

"I wouldn't continue talking that way, if I were you," said Joanna.

They all laughed.

"Actually, all the Girls in the Hall are unique," smiled Brian, looking into the distance. "Kelly is a salty cynic but really quite funny. Melissa is your sweet, blonde girl next door and very authentic. Shakira is a sparky, sporty gal who sees life as it is with a full heart. Joanna ..."

"Yes, Joanna?" imposed Joanna.

"No comment ..."

"Hey!"

"Joanna is the brilliant one in the group, but still very warm and caring."

"Better."

"And Marla. Marla is a disconnected, conniving, cold-blooded serial killer, a psychopath from Hell and my one true love."

Brian's description, said with heartfelt not hostile emotion, riveted his company. Joanna put her hand on his forearm, a tear falling down her cheek. Ma put his arm around her. Joanna then took out her framed picture and showed it to her parents.

"She's that one. Yongxin's right about her. She naturally attracts men. She must have a particular blend of hormones, maybe high levels of androstenol or copulin, that makes her a guy magnet. Though sex studies into pheromones are inconclusive so far."

"I don't know about her chemicals," Ma stated. "But one thing is sure: she's beautiful and deadly."

Charles and Adrienne looked with a curious stare but made no comment. Brian wanted to change the subject and asked Charles about fusion power. Joanne looked dubiously at him and if to say 'don't get him on his subject, you'll never get him off'. So the rest of the evening was a complex description of the various trials to put a powerful magnet under immense temperatures to generate clean and abundant electricity.

As they were leaving, Ma suggested he'd stay back to help with the dishes. Brian demurred.

"Thanks, Ma, but no need. Fusion Freddy over there can convert electricity into immense temperatures to produce clean dishes."

Charles placed his hand lightly on Brian's shoulder with a laugh.

"D'mean the dishwasher?" asked Ma.

Joanna sucked her teeth. "Of course, the dishwasher. That's pretty good, Bry."

"I must tell my colleagues about Fusion Freddy," said Charles, still chuckling.

"Good night, Brian," said Adrienne. "I can see why Jo likes you. You're a nice man."

"That's my mother talking. Me talking is: I love you Brian and you're a *wonderful* man." (Joanna threw his arms around Brian.)

"I wouldn't continue talking that way, if I were you," said Ma.

That echo comment brought a laugh, especially from Joanna; she wanted him to be clever.

Brian saw Joanna and her parents out, pointing where the Girls lived in the Hall, ending at Marla's. They peered more keenly into her apartment expecting it still to hold some sinister presence.

The Final Moves

At the appointed hour, the GITH and their trophy men arrived to shift Kelly into a new life. Troyan rolled up with the truck, Yongxin the dollies and Jeffrey padded blankets and towels. The Girls brought flowers, plants and food for a night in her new place and went on ahead with Kelly to prepare. Brian purveyed wine and champagne and helped the boys with the haulage.

The furniture was moved in and the essential and heavy pieces were all in place by late afternoon. Then it was time for their impromptu housewarming until the early hours. Everyone got to meet Kelly's new roommate, Sandy. Kelly herself responded throughout with a sad-sweetness they had never encountered. Oprah sat fatly as the centre of attention and was officially dubbed the Feline in the Hall (the FITH), a figurehead with acceptably few titular duties. They even put a crown on her head, which she quickly tore off and batted around the room until it disappeared.

After the party, Brian went home to the Hall. A little squiffy to be sure, he walked glumly down the corridor. His footsteps seemed to echo. The emptiness of the place. where there had been such life, such happy life, tore at him. What he needed was for Marla to be waiting in his bed for him.

"Not damned likely," he said aloud, "with any luck."

The next morning, he arose and was drinking his first cup of coffee when the movers came to take his furnishings to his new house just three blocks away. Telvan had arranged the move as part of preparing the place for sale, so nearly everything but his kitchen was packed and out it went. His gear from the kitchen was always something he handled himself.

He wanted to take his own picture of the building with the SOLD sign out front. On the market for 10 days, 255 Covington Place went to a developer, as he predicted, and brought a third more than he paid for it. He snapped the picture. It would be his personal record of the building and would mean more than the promotional photos taken for the sale. He knew full well the Hall would soon go under the wrecker's ball for a fashionable row of townhouses those young moderns sought in pursuit of their Ikea lifestyle.

He couldn't leave without a picture of the roof garden, home to so much of their time together over the past year. That short? Yes, as he looked back, it seemed little more than a few happy months in the sun. Brian stopped at Marla's empty apartment realising you could be sentimental about the Hall itself, but it was only the scenery for all that really mattered – the GITH.

He climbed the stairs to the patio. Easy to remember what a thrill it was to have that roof renovated, the first big project. He took some pictures. A trap sounded. A rat was caught. He knew the ratter blade would be with the barbeque that was later to go to his new house with the pergola for possible GITH gatherings. In the distance, a siren blared. He mused if anyone could ever tell the difference among various emergency sirens. Whichever, they all seemed to get louder and louder until they literally flew by your house.

He went over and brought the blade down hard. The rat made a noise, wriggled briefly and then lay still.

"A clean kill," said a voice behind him.

He wheeled around.

"Marla!"

About the Author

Tony Andras has spent his entire life getting to this point as a novelist. He's been a journalist for the story, a speechwriter for the dialogue and a public relations executive for what works on paper. Tony lives contentedly in Toronto with his wife and two cats.